HIS LOVED LYCAN LUNA

LYCAN LUNA SERIES

BOOK THREE

JESSICA HALL

CHAPTER

ONE

IVY

I have no idea how long it had been since I shifted. The memories are hazy, but I can recall I spent most of my time while shifted on the phone with Abbie after Kyson called her for me. She remained on the phone until I could no longer keep my eyes open, and with the help of Kyson's calling, eventually, I was lulled into oblivion. However, I do recall Abbie was just as shocked as I was about me being Lycan but also found it quite hilarious that I could lick my own eyeball, which I discovered accidentally. Who would have thought Lycans had such long tongues?

The feeling of my bones breaking and dislocating wakes me out of my deep slumber, though the transition back is nothing compared to the initial shift. But it still makes me whimper when I feel the expanding of my spine, sending a shudder through my body.

Kyson's massive hand on my back caresses me softly, and I blink, trying to wake up from where I lay. A rumbling caress resonates from deep within his chest. Even asleep, he still purrs, using the calling as a sedative. Tired, I blink rapidly, yawn, and rub my eyes. Still, I would rather not move from off his chest, content with just lying here

1

wrapped in his warmth. His fur tickles my nose, his clawed fingers tracing the ridges of my spine gently as I feel the transition coming to an end.

His purr grows louder, and I melt against him, relishing the sound and the beat of his heart. My heart falls in time to the sound when he pulls me higher, his tongue running over my mark, lapping at it. Arousal washes through me, making my toes curl, but I am still angry with him. As much as I enjoy his touch, I am still angered by everything.

Kyson rolls over, shifting as he does so. The cracking of his bones makes me grind my teeth as fur becomes hot skin and he rolls me on my back, his body pressing between my legs. His thick, muscled arms rest on either side of my head. I watch as he shudders before turning his head, cracking his neck, and his eyes go back to their dazzling silver color. He smiles down at me before pressing his lips to mine gently. His tongue traces the seam of my lips before forcing it between them. I sigh, kissing him as he rocks his hips against me.

His hand moves to my neck, and his fingertips graze my scalp as they slide through my thick hair, pulling me impossibly close as he deepens the kiss. His tongue demands and dominates my mouth, tasting every inch and stealing the air from my lungs. He pulls away and chuckles softly, dropping his head onto my shoulder.

"What?" I ask, wondering what he thought was funny.

"Nothing," he chuckles, purring louder. My eyes widen, realizing I, too, am also purring and hadn't realized it, mistaking the vibration as coming from him. My face heats, and he nibbles my lip, yet I can't seem to stop the noise even if I'd like to.I have no control over it.

Kyson lifts his head, his hand moving to my face, his thumb strokes over my cheek gently; my skin flushes with my embarrassment as I continue to purr like a damn cat getting its back scratched.

"Don't be embarrassed. It's normal Love. It's your body reacting after it shifts; it recognizes our bond and wants to mate," he purrs, and I shake my head. I don't want to mate, my body just went through hell. Yet, the moment he says the words, I become instantly aware of the throb between my legs, the slickness coating my thighs.

Kyson thrusts his hips against mine. His hardened length slips between my wet folds, coating him with my arousal. He brings his face closer, his lips gently brushing against mine. He sucks the bottom one in his mouth and nibbles on it. A moan escapes my lips as he sucks on it. His cock glides between my wet folds and hits my clit, making me gasp as my eyes fall shut at the sensation. My hips rock to his rhythm, chasing the feeling, wanting to ease the pulsating as my pussy aches, throbbing to its own beat and causing me discomfort. Kyson growls softly, and my eyes fly open at the sound, only for him to kiss me again. His tongue gives me no rest as it invades my mouth once again.

"I don't want to mate, Kyson. You should stop," I mumble around his lips. His plump, full lips leave mine, letting me catch my breath.

"You're lying to yourself," Kyson tells me in a low whisper, and I shake my head.

Kyson pulls back, looking down at me, watching my face when he rocks his hips against mine. A needy moan escapes me, and my face heats. "No?" he purrs, yet I see the desire swirling in his gaze.

"Deny me all you want, but don't deny yourself. I'm here. Let me help the ache stop," he purrs, nipping at my lips.

"I don't want to sleep with you," I blurt as his lips travel along my jaw and down my neck, nipping, sucking, teasing my flesh.

Kyson ignores me. Instead, his lips travel lower to his mark, which now lies etched into my skin. He growls, nipping at it, making my toes curl, and my walls clench, the pulsating becoming worse and driving me near insane.

"Then I won't mate you," he growls, nipping at my skin while his teeth, lips, and tongue moves lower, tracing a path to my breasts, my nipples so hard they are nearing pain. My back arches at the feel of his tongue tracing over the hardened peak. Sparks rush over my skin, heating it, and my breathing becomes ragged as he sucks on, swirling his tongue around my areola. My muscles tense at the pleasurable feeling building lower within my stomach.

The purr that emanates out of me resounds around the room before I whimper as he bites down on my tender skin. The pain, however, is only fleeting as he sucks on it harder, chasing the pain away, then turning his attention to the other, his hot mouth moving slowly, teasing my flesh and enticing more moans and whimpers.

His mouth continues its descent lower, teeth grazing my ribs and across my hip bone. I growl when he doesn't move faster, my entire body craving his touch as he bites into my hip. His hand pushes my legs wider as he settles between, sucking on the inside of my thigh, making my hips buck the closer he becomes to the apex of my thighs.

"Kyson!" I growl, annoyed when I feel his breath sweep over my slit.

"Patience Love, I will give you what you want," he purrs as his hands grip the backs of my thighs, and he yanks me down to the end of the thick mattress. He moves off it to sit on the floor. Growling, his hand slides to the backs of my knees, forcing them to bend. Kyson shoves my legs higher, my knees resting along my ribs, exposing me further to him. I have no time to feel embarrassed about the position he has put me in, everything on display makes me want to close my legs, but his grip won't allow it when he sweeps his tongue flat across my folds before his entire mouth covers my pussy, sucking on my swollen flesh.

I mewl, melting against the mattress as his mouth continues its relentless assault. His tongue parts my lower lips as he licks a line straight to my clit. He sucks hard on it, making me writhe and move my hips. His grip on my legs grows tighter, his fingers digging into my skin, bruising me to hold me still while his mouth devours every piece of me, making me cry out as my legs tremble. My pulse pounds uncontrollably. Tension coils in my lower belly as I squirm and pant. My inner walls clench, and his tongue glides lower, lapping at my entrance before it plunges inside me. My inner walls squeeze at the feel of his tongue inside me before his mouth moves lower.

HIS LOVED LYCAN LUNA

A squeak leaves me when I feel his tongue lick around the tight muscles of my ass, and I hear him chuckle, amused, while I feel mortified. His mouth goes back to my clit, sucking on it hard and making me forget the earlier embarrassment seconds ago. He moves slightly, taking his hand off my thigh before sitting up slightly, his arm crossing over the back of my thighs, holding them in place. His other hand traces down my thigh to my ass, squeezing it as he sits up. My legs are now pinned in the same position held by his arm placed over them.

I try to drop my legs, not liking the position I am in with him gawking between my legs. His hand palms and kneads my ass before I feel his thumb part my lips before he dips his face between my legs, lapping at my clit when he shoves his index finger inside me. My inner walls squeeze around it, and my hips buck at the sudden intrusion, his mouth sucking my clit as he drags his finger out, scraping my walls before sliding it back in slowly.

My purr grows louder, and my nerves scream at the building friction. He glides his finger out before adding his middle finger, making my legs shake as he stretches me further. My inner walls clench around his finger, and he sits up, watching his fingers slip in and out of my tight channel, drenched with my slick.

Kyson growls, his eyes hungry, watching his fingers delve inside of me. He curls them, making me cry out, and as he hits that sweet spot, eliciting endless moans. My eyes close, the sensation growing intense, hotter, as he continues dragging them in and out, curling them as he plunges them deeper each time.

I feel his fingers curl once again inside me, and his ring finger presses against my ass. My eyes open to find him watching me, pitch black as the beast that resides within him surfaces. His fingers offer no reprieve as he plunges them in harder, dropping his mouth back to my pussy before I feel him slide his ring finger inside me. I squirm, the feeling unnatural, as he breaches the barrier of the tight muscles of my ass. Despite the discomfort, my pleasure grows in a sinful sort of way, his fingers moving simultaneously while he sucks on my clit.

5

My skin heats, my pussy throbs and my inner walls clench, my stomach tightens. Tingles slice and weave up my spin, and my toes curl as I reach the precipice.

A gasping breath leaves me as I shatter. My moans resound around the room as waves of pleasure ripple through me, my pussy clenching his fingers, which slow, allowing me to ride out the sensations as I pant and writhe. My entire body is shaking with the intensity of my release, rendering me limp and boneless as the last wave ripples through me.

Kyson slowly withdraws his fingers, lapping at my juices, his tongue causing aftershocks to course through me, my skin now very sensitive to the touch. He moves his arm, and my legs fall limply on the bed while I try to catch my breath. Kyson crawls between my legs, hovering above me, his erection digging into my lower stomach as he leans down and kisses me.

He forces his tongue into my mouth, but I am too exhausted to care as he makes me taste myself on his tongue. He growls, nipping at my lips.

"I'll run you a bath," he whispers against my lips. All I can do is nod. My brain liquefied. He laughs softly, climbing off me and wandering off toward the bathroom.

CHAPTER
TWO

GANNON

    The aging door creaks open, its old hinges emitting a loud groan that reverberates through the room. As the light streams in, filtered and subdued by the curtains, I see the space is enveloped in a dim, ethereal glow. Liam, a tall and imposing figure with broad shoulders and a chiseled jawline, strides into my sanctuary. His dirty blonde hair tumbles messily into his eyes, adding an air of ruggedness to his already formidable presence.

Despite his commanding demeanor, there is a certain enigma that shrouds his face, concealing the savage nature that lies within. Frustration etches his stance as he saunters towards me, dressed only in a tank top and jeans. The sinewy muscles of his bulging arms are on full display, adorned with thick, corded veins that seem to pulsate with every step.

"Get up!" he demands, his voice laced with an undeniable authority. I groan in protest, reluctant to be torn from the peaceful embrace of slumber, but Liam's relentless determination leaves me no choice.

Standing at the foot of my bed, Liam begins clapping with a

resounding intensity. "Up! Get out of bed," he insists, his words punctuated by the forceful removal of my blanket. A mischievous glint dances in his eyes as he exclaims, "Oh la la, what have we here? Sleeping in the buff, I see. Me likey."

Before I can react, his hand connects with my exposed skin in a swift slap that leaves a searing imprint on my ass. The sting radiates through my body as if every finger has been branded onto my backside.

I snarl in defiance, rolling over onto my back and fixing him with a glare that could ignite the room. "Liam, you fucking Twat!" I hiss through gritted teeth, my hand instinctively rubbing the welted flesh. "Get out of my room."

But Liam remains undeterred, his resolve unyielding. "No, can do. I have a job to do, and you are coming with me," he declares with unwavering determination. I groan in resignation, reaching for my blanket and attempting to reclaim the warmth that has been so abruptly snatched away. However, Liam's grip is firm as he snatches it again, tearing it completely off the bed.

"Up, or I will make use of that ass by turning it into my personal cum dumpster," Liam snaps, his words laced with a dangerous edge. Anger courses through my veins as I begrudgingly sit up, tossing my legs over the side of the bed. As I do so, Liam nonchalantly strolls towards my drawers, rummaging through them and flinging clothes in my direction.

With a mixture of annoyance and resignation, I snatch the garments and begin dressing myself. "And where are we going?" I inquire, a tinge of curiosity seeping into my voice.

"Anywhere but this room. I am sick of watching you sulk," Liam retorts, his exasperation palpable.

Great, I think to myself, *the psycho woke me for no damn reason.* Pulling my shirt over my head with an air of defiance, I fix him with my meanest glare.

"Has Abbie called you?" I ask him as I slip on my sneakers, stealing a glance in his direction. He shakes his head in response.

"When was the last time you spoke to her?" he queries, tilting his head slightly to the side.

"Days ago, a week maybe more," I shrug nonchalantly, an air of uncertainty clouding my mind. The days have blurred together since she left, merging into a haze of indistinguishable moments.

"She'll come around, Gannon. She will realize what sort of man he is," Liam assures me, his voice carrying a hint of optimism. Grabbing my belt from the bedside table, I deftly thread it through the loops before securing the buckle, following him out of the room.

"Maybe ask Kyson for permission to visit her," Liam suggests as we make our way through the corridors. Unsure of our destination, I continue to trail behind him, my mind preoccupied with thoughts of Abbie. We eventually find ourselves in the labyrinthine depths of the castle's basement, specifically the kitchens. Descending deeper into the bowels of the building, we finally come to a halt in a dimly lit chamber.

"Kyson wants me to find all the archives on the Azalea Landeena," Liam informs me, his voice carrying a note of urgency. We had long suspected that Ivy may be the missing Landeena princess, the rightful heir to the Landeena Kingdom. The implications of this revelation are staggering, as it meant Kyson's treatment of her had been misplaced. He had believed her to be the daughter of the infamous serial killer Marissa Talbot, but now doubts began to creep in. Too many pieces of the puzzle failed to align.

Having voiced my concerns to Damian on numerous occasions, I had become increasingly convinced that something was awry with Ivy's behavior. Her instincts seemed more akin to those of a Lycan rather than a werewolf. However, Kyson remained steadfast in his refusal to listen to our doubts. Until now.

Navigating through the cluttered expanse of the storage area, we begin dragging boxes out and sifting through them in search of any information pertaining to the Landeena family and their missing daughter, who would be roughly Ivy's age. Our efforts yield a few scattered files, which we quickly scan before deciding to consult

Damian for further insight. Unfortunately, it becomes apparent that we have barely scratched the surface of this vast labyrinth. The cell is almost inaccessible, with towering stacks of boxes reaching all the way to the ceiling. And there are six more cells just like it.

When our search finally draws to a close, Liam leads me to a training session with the castle's men and what remains of the Landeena guards. The day stretches on, filled with physical exertion and the relentless pursuit of honing our skills. Amidst it all, I attempt to call Abbie, my longing for her presence gnawing at my heart. Liam, ever vigilant, seems determined to keep me distracted. I wish he would stop babysitting me.

As the shift comes to a close, we make our way back to my room within the castle's confines. Stepping through the threshold, I groan in frustration as Liam follows closely behind.

"Come on, Liam, leave me be," I growl, my frustration seeping into my voice as I stalk towards the bathroom in need of a quick shower. The hot water cascades over me, washing away the grime and tension of the day. However, when I step out, I find Liam still lingering in my room, his eyes fixated on my personal belongings. Snatching the photos of Sia and Abbie from his hands, I confront him with a mixture of annoyance and anger.

"Liam!" I snarl through gritted teeth, my voice laced with frustration. He exhales heavily before moving towards my bed and taking a seat.

"By the way, Kyson granted you leave to visit Abbie," Liam states matter-of-factly, his words hanging in the air. I sigh in acknowledgment, realizing that he must have convinced Kyson or perhaps enlisted Damian's help in persuading the King.

"You didn't have to get involved," I mutter, placing the photos back in their folder with a sense of careful reverence.

"When you get her back, are you going to tell her about killing her aunt?" Liam's question hangs heavy in the air, causing me to swallow hard as my gaze averts to his penetrating stare.

"More importantly, are you going to tell the King about who Sia truly was?" he presses further, his voice filled with a mix of concern and curiosity.

"It changes nothing. We dealt with Sia in the end, and she never had the chance to carry out her nefarious plans. What good would come from dredging up the past? Nothing but turmoil," I respond, my voice tinged with resignation.

"The King wouldn't be angered by your actions against Sia and her mother," Liam asserts, his gaze unwavering as he locks eyes with me.

"Are you speaking solely about my involvement or considering everything?" I counter, my tone laced with a hint of skepticism.

"If Kyson were to discover the truth, he might hold Abbie accountable. Assuming guilt by association. Look at what he has done to Ivy. I won't risk it with Abbie," I explain, my words laden with a sense of protectiveness towards the woman I love. Liam takes a seat at the edge of the bed, his posture reflective of deep thought.

"And what about Abbie?" he probes further. "You have to tell her about us. She will find out, Gannon. Secrets like this don't remain hidden forever."

"Tell her what exactly? That my mate chose you over me? Or how I felt the bond breaking every time she fucked my best friend? Or perhaps I should inform her about how we tore her beloved Aunt apart when we discovered the truth about each other?" The bitterness in my voice is palpable as I unleash my pent-up frustration.

Liam sighs, his expression filled with a mixture of sympathy and understanding. "Abbie would understand. I just don't want this one secret to tear you apart again once you have her back. If she were to uncover it on her own, the consequences could be dire."

"The only person who knows about this, Liam, is you. Unless you plan on revealing it to her, there is no way for her to find out," I retort sharply. Liam shakes his head, his expression a mix of resignation and concern.

"Just think about it, Gannon. I will support you, no matter what you decide. But I believe Abbie deserves to know the truth about her parents and the circumstances they were running from."

"We can't say for certain. We only recently discovered that Sia had a twin sister. There could be numerous reasons why Abbie's parents went rogue," I argue, desperately clinging to the shreds of doubt that remain.

"But it does make sense, doesn't it? Why would Abbie's parents willingly become rogues? They were fleeing from someone. We might not have known about it until Abbie entered the picture, and you stumbled upon those files, but now it's clear who they were running from. Abbie has a right to know, at the very least, that her Aunt was your true mate," Liam concludes before turning towards the door.

"Get some sleep, brother. I'll make sure your car is ready for your departure first thing in the morning to see Abbie. Hopefully, you can bring her home," he says, his voice filled with a sense of hope and determination. With that, he shuts the door, leaving me with a whirlwind of thoughts and emotions.

I exhale deeply, retrieving my clothes and slipping into bed. Tomorrow holds the promise of reuniting with Abbie, and I can only hope that my words and presence will be enough to convince her to return with me. If not, I am left uncertain of what other avenues remain open to me. However, I know that if I were to ask Liam for assistance, he would willingly aid me in exacting vengeance upon Kade and sweeping the consequences under the rug. Unfortunately, such an act would require the annihilation of his entire pack.

As sleep begins to claim me, I am left with lingering questions and a sense of trepidation. The truth weighs heavily on my heart, threatening to unravel everything we have fought so hard to build. But in the depths of my soul, I know that secrets can only remain buried for so long.

CHAPTER THREE

GANNON

Last night, the King granted me special leave while Ivy was transitioning. I have been in the car ever since.

Desperate to reach Abbie, I repeatedly dial her number, hoping to persuade her to see reason. Yet, my calls go unanswered, just as they have in our previous attempts. Abbie has been purposely avoiding me, shutting me out of her life.

My mission is to report any issues. It angers me that Kyson won't allow me to forcefully remove her from her mate. Such an act would certainly create tensions as well as be deemed unlawful, especially if she wished to remain by his side. As his mate, she belongs to him. However, the temptation to break that law gnaws at me relentlessly. Love makes you do weird things. I am prepared to face any consequences, be it imprisonment or lashings. I just don't want Kyson's already fragile political situation as collateral damage. If it meant freeing Abbie from her undeserving mate, I would do it

I knew Kyson would hesitate to pass such a sentence, especially under pressure from the packs he governed. It wouldn't bode well for a King to defy the very laws he helped establish – laws put in place to halt Alphas from forcibly marking multiple women and tearing them away from their true mates. That was precisely why Kade refrained from marking any of his wives; technically, they were free if they found their destined mates.

However, Abbie was an exception. He had marked her, fully aware that having a mate made him stronger. Despite the futility of my efforts thus far, I had no choice but to persist. Going against a mate bond was nearly impossible for she-wolves, and my attempts to expose Kade's infidelity had fallen flat.

So, for now, my only option was to convince Abbie to willingly leave him. He didn't deserve her. Neither did I, but I would spend the rest of my life trying to prove my worth to her if she would have me. As stupid as it might be to try, I had to.

We rarely came this far out into the pack. Even when invited to stay, as we passed through it sometimes, we always sought accommodation elsewhere. We felt uncomfortable within packs, never fully certain of their allegiance or potential ties to the hunters. Caution dictated our actions. Nonetheless, Alpha Kade had shown us kindness, always extending his help unquestionably whenever we needed him to send his men to scout for hunters in his area. He was still a disgusting werewolf, treating women as if they were nothing more than trophies or possessions.

My phone jolts me from my thoughts, and I pull over to answer it, knowing I will soon need to input the address. Damian's name illuminates the screen, and I swiftly connect the call, placing the phone against my ear.

"Have you obtained the address?" I inquire, rummaging through the glove compartment searching for a pen and paper.

"Yes, I have it right here. Remember, Gannon, remain unseen. If you are caught lurking without formal notice, suspicions will be raised," Damian advises, caution evident in his voice.

"What did you tell him?" I query sharply.

"I informed him that Ivy wanted to send a care package," he responds.

"Very well. I'll stop along the way and purchase some items; I can play the role of a delivery boy," I retort with a hint of annoyance.

"Good idea. But please, Gannon, refrain from causing harm. We cannot afford any bloodshed," Damian pleads.

"I am solely here to retrieve Abbie," I state firmly.

"You mustn't force her; you know the consequences if you do," Damian reminds me sternly.

"Perhaps I am willing to accept those consequences," I confess defiantly.

"And what becomes of Abbie if she chooses to return to him? You would be banned from entering his pack, leaving her trapped there. The King would have no choice but to administer one thousand lashings and imprison you, as per the law. Don't make him do that. You witnessed what happened last time; it nearly destroyed one of our own," Damian counters.

"But that imbecile forcefully claimed the girl. I am not seeking to claim her; I only wish to take her away," I argue.

"Semantics matter little, Gannon. Don't force my hand in ordering you to retreat," Damian warns firmly.

"This is Abbie we're discussing, Damian," I breathe, desperation tinging my voice.

"I am well aware, but our hands are tied. Kade is the only Alpha with whom we have a genuine alliance," Damian explains, his tone laced with resignation. I glare out at the forest beyond the windshield, frustration coursing through my veins.

"So, what's your decision? Shall I command you to return, or can you restrain yourself?" I snarl.

"Fine, I won't force her. But if he has harmed her in any way, I swear I will kill him," I vow vehemently.

"The King mentioned that he saw Abbie, and she appeared to be in good health, aside from Kade's infidelity," Damian interjects.

"And that is still hurting her," I counter sharply. "There's no way it can't."

"Gannon!" Damian's voice rises, reprimanding me.

"Fine, I will keep my hands to myself. Just give me the address," I concede, fearing that he would order me back home after driving all this way. As a mere Gamma, alongside Dustin and Liam, I held little power compared to Damian, who holds the rank of Beta. If he commanded my return, I would be powerless to resist. With haste, I jot down the address before ending the call and inputting it into the GPS. The destination was indeed located outside of town, miles away. I had expected Abbie to be at the packhouse, for that was where an Alpha's mate should reside – not hidden away in some secluded cabin. Kade had isolated her from everyone and everything, including the town itself.

A growl escapes my lips as I realize that she is out there alone, especially with Hunters on the prowl. Starting the car, I drive to the nearest town before stopping at a general store to fill a basket with items. I carefully selected all her favorite fruits and candies, products I had persistently encouraged her to try since she was initially hesitant to accept anything from me back at the castle. Towards the end, however, she had let her guard down, and I had managed to convince her to be with me, only for that wretched Kade to intervene and shatter our fragile connection.

Surveying the store for additional gifts, I find that even flowers are absent from this meager establishment. Perhaps Abbie would appreciate a book, I muse momentarily before remembering her inability to read. A comic book might suffice; maybe she could interpret the story through the illustrations. If she were to return with me and reject her mate, I could take it upon myself to teach her how to read.

Thirty minutes later, I arrive at the outskirts of Kade's territory. Abbie's dwelling is barely on the border, and I navigate down a long, winding dirt driveway. The place before me hardly deserves the title of a house; it resembles more of a shack – a structure that seems poised to crumble with a mere gust of wind.

I catch sight of Abbie at the clothesline, her gaze shifting towards my approaching car. Shielding her eyes from the sun's glare, she squints to discern my identity. Swiftly parking the car, I send a text message to Damian as per his request. Abbie gazes apprehensively at the vehicle, her worry evident. I wonder why a random car would cause her concern. Nevertheless, she appears unchanged – save for a slight tan, as if she has spent ample time outdoors. Her cheeks bear hollowed contours, more pronounced than when she departed, and her skin wears a wearied pallor. Despite these signs of fatigue, she seems to be holding up well, or so I hope.

"Oh, it's you," Abbie states, her tone laced with nervousness as she approaches. "Why are you here?" she asks, her lips caught between her teeth.

"What? Is that all you have to say?" I inquire, raising an eyebrow in surprise. A small smile tugs at the corner of her lips before she rushes towards me, and I swiftly enclose her in my embrace.

"God, how I've missed you," I confess with sincerity. Abbie nods, her thin arms wrapping around my neck. She lets out a relieved breath, and I can't help but wonder why she was anxious about an unfamiliar vehicle. But for now, she is safe – and that is all that matters.

"Why are you here?" she murmurs.

CHAPTER
FOUR

GANNON

My face nestles in the curve of her neck, seeking solace in the delicate intermingling of scents. The familiar fragrance of her skin, a sweet blend of vanilla and lavender, wraps around me like a comforting embrace. Her question hangs in the air, dripping with skepticism and a hint of longing.

"Why are you here?" she repeats, her voice wavering with a mix of curiosity and apprehension.

"To see you," I reply, my words laced with an undercurrent of urgency, trying to hide my disappointment that she isn't more excited to see me. "Why else? You haven't been answering my calls." Gently, I guide her back onto her feet, my gaze fixed upon her. It's impossible not to notice the weight she has lost, a feat that defies logic given her already slender frame. Her pants, rolled at the hips to keep them from slipping off, appear several sizes too big. Even her white shirt, a piece borrowed from Kade's wardrobe, hangs loosely on her fragile form. And as I observe her, I can't help but notice the nervous glances she steals down the driveway. Instinctively, I turn my head to follow her gaze.

"Expecting someone?" I inquire, a note of caution creeping into my voice.

"Kade hasn't been by for a couple of days," she confesses, her voice tinged with uncertainty. "He said he was out of town, but..." She trails off, leaving the unspoken words to hang between us.

"But what?" I press, my curiosity piqued.

"Nothing," she dismisses with a forced laugh. "Probably just me being paranoid." She gestures towards the kitchen. "Coffee?"

I nod in response and make my way back to my car, retrieving the bags before joining her inside. The worn porch creaks beneath my weight as I step gingerly across its aging planks. As she opens the door, it swings with a slight tilt, its hinges worn and weary. Stepping into the dwelling, I can't help but be struck by its tiny size. The kitchen, bedroom, and living room mold together as one in this cramped space.

"Where is the bathroom?" I ask, my curiosity leading me to seek out the necessities.

"There's an outhouse out back," she nonchalantly replies, her attention focused on turning on the stove and filling a camping kettle. I scan the surroundings in disbelief, my mind struggling to reconcile this meager existence with the knowledge that Kade, the leader of one of the wealthiest packs, is her mate. There is no bed, only a fold-out couch neatly made and calling to mind images of discomfort. I perch on its edge, feeling the groan of weary springs and the unyielding bar that digs into my backside.

"You should come back with me," I implore her, my voice tinged with a mix of concern and frustration.

"Not this again, Gannon, please," Abbie whines, her plea echoing with weariness. A growl forms deep within me before I remember the bags clutched tightly in my hands. I extend them towards her, watching as her brows furrow confused.

"Take it," I insist, a hint of urgency lacing my words. She sighs heavily, her steps carrying her towards me as she accepts the bags. Placing them on the table, she peers inside, her eyes lighting up with delight as she pulls out a bag of sugar clouds. It's a small pleasure that I've noticed she treasures; whenever we ventured into town together to gather supplies for Clarice, I couldn't help but notice her longing gaze fixed on these sugary treats. And so, I made sure to keep a constant supply on hand whenever our paths crossed.

She pops another sugar cloud into her mouth, which stains her lips crimson and coats them with a fine dusting of sugar. A chuckle escapes my lips as I watch her struggle to pull her loose pants up, the candy acting as both a delightful distraction and an inconvenience. Her pants continue their descent down her hips, and she absent-mindedly rolls them up once more. Observing her movements, I can't help but notice the emptiness of the tiny fridge, save for half a bottle of milk and a solitary block of cheese. Rising from the couch, I swing open the cupboards to find them nearly bare.

"Why is there no food here?" I growl, my frustration simmering beneath the surface. *What is going on here?* Something isn't right.

"Kade said he would come out soon to bring more," she shrugs, her voice carrying a hint of resignation as she retrieves coffee and tea bags.

"What have you been eating then?" My words escape with a sharp edge, directed more out of concern than anger.

She nervously chews on her lower lip, her gaze drifting towards the forest visible through the window.

"Have you been hunting for your own food?" I inquire, my tone softening as I try to understand her circumstances.

"No, I promise. I didn't kill anything," she stammers, her words stumbling over each other in a rush to explain. "I just took some bird eggs." Her gasp betrays her fear that my anger is directed towards her for resorting to hunting.

"Bird eggs?" I scoff, my disbelief evident.

"I tried to catch a rabbit once, but I couldn't do it. I swear," she stutters, her voice tinged with guilt.

"I don't care about you hunting, Abbie," I assure her, wanting to alleviate any sense of blame she may feel. "My point is that you shouldn't have to. You are an Alpha's mate, not some slave or a hidden secret." My voice bristles with indignation.

"I'm not... He's introducing me to the pack soon. It's just not safe right now. He's having issues with a neighboring pack," she stammers, her eyes darting back to the kettle that has started to whistle.

"Do you realize how absurd that sounds? You're his Luna, and yet he has you living out here in these conditions," I argue, exasperation tingeing my words.

"It's not safe," she defends him, her voice laced with a mix of loyalty and fear.

"The safest place for you would be by his side, don't you think? Not out here along the border where anyone could get to you," I reason, my frustration mounting as she continues to offer excuses, lies that he has fed her.

It's like arguing with a brick wall. I despise this mate bond nonsense with every fiber of my being. It blinds she-wolves to their mate's faults, making them gullible and vulnerable. And all it takes is the smallest flicker of what they perceive as kindness, something she has been deprived of for so long, to make her believe that she should trust him blindly simply because he is her mate.

"No, you're coming back with me," I declare, my grip tightening on her arm.

"What? No! I have a mate. I can't just leave. He'll worry," she protests, her voice trembling with a mixture of fear and uncertainty.

"Worry? Then where the hell is he, Abbie?" My frustration boils over as I try to drag her towards the door.

"No!" she screams, thrashing against my grip. "Gannon, stop!" Her voice cracks under the weight of her emotions, tears streaming down her face. "He loves me. He said he loves me. He'll be back," she sobs.

"I fucking love you. He doesn't," I scream at her, my words dripping with desperation.

Abbie whimpers, and I suddenly become aware that my claws have slipped out, grazing her delicate skin. Thankfully, the wounds are shallow, and I release my hold on her, watching as they swiftly heal.

"You have a mate out there somewhere. How can you say that?" she demands, her tear-filled eyes searching mine for answers.

"No, I don't. I want you. Can't you see that?" My voice cracks with a mixture of longing and frustration.

"But I am not yours. I am Kade's mate. He loves me, and I love him," she insists, her voice wavering with a mix of conviction and doubt.

"If you think this is love, you are mistaken. Love doesn't hide someone away. Love doesn't force them to live like this," I snap, my words tinged with both sadness and anger. Her brows furrow, tears pooling in her mesmerizing hazel eyes. She shakes her head before sniffling and wiping her hands on the front of her shirt.

"You should go," she whispers, unable to meet my gaze.

I swallow hard, my heart heavy with unspoken words. She wraps her arms around herself, seeking solace in the comforting pressure of her own embrace as she turns back towards the kitchen.

"Abbie?" I call out to her softly, my voice filled with a mix of longing and resignation.

"Gannon, please... just don't," she breathes, her words barely audible.

"Tell me... Tell me you're happy here," I implore her, my voice a mere whisper in the air. "Tell me something because this... this isn't right. I would take care of you."

"I'm not yours," she says slowly, emphasizing each word with a quiet determination.

"But you could be," I murmur earnestly. "You just need to see beyond the bond, Abbie. See through his lies." My voice trails off, uncertain if there is another way to convince her, to break through the walls that surround her heart.

"You were willing to be mine before Abbie," I tell her.

"That was before I discovered my mate, and you're a Lycan it would never work."

"I would change you, make you a Lycan, but you need to reject Kade and come home with me."

"I can't, he...he... He loves me," she says, looking at the ground.

"But do you love him? Think about Abbie. If he wasn't your mate, and you are locked up here, would you stay or come back with me?"

"That's not fair," she says.

"Answer me," I demand.

"That would be different," she says, looking around at the place.

"You live in a castle. Who would choose this place over that?" she finally says.

"Fine, then if he wasn't your mate, who would you choose, him or me?"

"But he is my mate!"

"Exactly, the mate bond tells you to love him, to stay with him, it is not a damn choice! But if you had one?"

She bites her lip. "I don't know! I... please you must leave, you're confusing me, stop. It all needs to stop."

"Come back with me, even for a little while, just come back, come see Ivy, you wanted to see Ivy, right?" I beg.

"It's unsafe; I have to stay here; Kade will take me to see her. He promised he would."

"I'm fucking Lycan. What safer place is there to be than by my side?" I curse while shaking my head and pinching the bridge of my nose in frustration.

"He's my mate," she says, even though she looks confused about what she wants. And that stupid marking on her neck I wish I could remove so she could think clearly.

I move toward her, and she backs up, her bum hitting the kitchen sink. "Come back with me."

"I can't, Gannon."

"But you want to, don't you?" I ask her, and she looks away.

"I can't leave my mate. It would hurt him if I did."

"What about the pain he causes you?"

23

"Ah, not this again, he wouldn't do that; I'm his mate," she says, trying to push past me.

"He has multiple wives, Abbie. Why do you think he keeps you out here?"

"You're lying, I already asked him, and he said you are just jealous."

"Of course, I am jealous, but I wouldn't fucking lie to you," I tell her.

"You need to leave," she says, but I grab her, pushing myself against her and gripping her neck. My lips crash against her plump ones, and she tries to shove me away when my tongue forces its way between her lips.

Abbie moans as my tongue invades her mouth. Her attempts to shove me off stop and her hands run up my chest, and she kisses me back hungrily. I grip her thighs, placing her on the edge of the sink and pressing between her legs when she gasps, pulling away from me.

"Why would you do that?" she growls.

"Still think a mate can't cheat on a mate?" I ask her.

She shakes her head. "No, it's because you're Lycan, you did something!"

"I didn't make you kiss me back, Abbie."

"She-wolves are attracted to men of dominance, it's...it's... it's in our DNA! You need to leave," she says, shoving me away feebly. But he is much too weak to move me.

"Abbie, he is no good for you."

"He is my mate; he is who I am destined to be with him," she sobs before pointing at me. "You made me; I wouldn't have if you..." she shakes her head.

"It's okay to love someone else, Abbie."

"I don't; I love my mate, I..." she says and looks around frantically, her body trembling.

"Really, because back home, you seemed to like me too."

"Yes, before I found my mate."

"You still do!" I tell her.

"Of course, I do, Gannon; you're Lycan I'm a werewolf. It makes me submissive to your kind."

"Doesn't make you love someone," I tell her.

Seek us out, yes, but I can't make her love me. It was in their DNA that she-wolves sought out dominant males for safety, but that didn't mean they loved them. I know she loves me too, or she wouldn't have always sought me out or let me follow her around like a damn lost puppy. Damian even offered to tell me to back off. Still, she refused, saying she liked me being around her, and she never reacted to Damian like this, and he was of higher rank than me, she even asked to be put in my quarters, and we all agreed before Kade came into the picture.

"You need to leave; I want you to leave, please."

"Come back with me."

"No! Just go. You can't force me. It's against the law. I may be stupid, but I know that much," she says, looking away.

"You are not stupid, misguided, yes, but not stupid, Abbie, don't say that," I tell her.

"Leave; I have asked you to, so please, Gannon, don't make this harder than it has to be," she says, and I sigh. I pull my phone from my pocket and glance at the time. I was only granted an hour here, and I was already 15 minutes over.

"When you change your mind, you ring me; I don't care what time it is; I will come for you. Do you still know my number?" She nods. "My number Abbie." She sighs and rattles it off, knowing it by heart. I kiss her forehead before nodding. "Answer my calls."

"I will okay, just leave," she says, and I chew my lip before turning and walking out the door. When I get in the car, I start the engine and look up to find her standing on the porch watching me. She waves before looking away, and I turn the car around. When I drive over the boundary, Damian rings.

"What?"

"Are you on your way back with her?"

"She wouldn't come. There is no food in that place. It is a shithole"

"She has to come willingly. You can't take her."

"It's fucking bullshit; I should command her," I tell him, and I should and take whatever punishment Kyson delivers, she would have no choice, I am Lycan she would do as I commanded.

"You do, and she will always question whether she made the right choice," Damian tries to reason. I growl, and eventually, he hangs up when I come to the town, I stop in. I nearly drive through before I curse and pull into the grocery store. I fill a trolley with different foods before driving back, unable to get the thought of her eating bird eggs and whatever she could find in the forest out of my head.

Returning to her place, I swiftly unload the groceries, careful not to make any noise that might disturb her slumber. Through the cracked window, I catch a glimpse of her sleeping on the fold-out bed. I knock gently on the door before walking away, unable to trust myself not to break the rules and forcibly drag her away. As I drive off, my mind consumed with thoughts of her, I catch a fleeting glance of her through the rearview mirror. Her gaze lingers on the groceries before shifting back to my retreating vehicle.

I know I'll face severe consequences for going back and being late, but I couldn't bear the thought of her going hungry. Damian will lose his mind when he finds out, but perhaps Kyson would understand the importance of ensuring Ivy's safety? If she knew about Abbie's living conditions and Kade's deceit, she would surely be outraged. I'll find a way to tell her, even if it means facing the king's wrath.

I VY

    Strangely, despite spending so much time sleeping, I felt even more fatigued than usual. The exhaustion weighs heavily on me, making it a grueling task to keep my eyes open as I hastily throw on whatever clothes my hands can find. Unconcerned with my appearance, I glance at myself in the mirror, only to be met with a disheveled mess of hair resembling a haystack.

Who would have thought that shifting would be so draining? I can only hope that this level of exhaustion isn't a constant issue every time I shift. Grabbing Kyson's phone, I attempt to call Abbie, but there is no answer. *Where is she? She told me she'd call me all the time.* Frustrated, I hurl the phone onto the bed and hastily gather my hair into a messy bun, determined to find Kyson to see if he can get ahold of Kade to get Abbie to answer. It feels like there's a big hole in my life without her here. Stepping out of the room, my eyes land on Dustin waiting by the door.

"Morning," I greet him, though Dustin can't help but chuckle.

"You mean afternoon, my Queen," he replies teasingly. I blink at him, it's afternoon already?

"How long was I asleep?"

"Only a few hours. I heard you earlier with…" Dustin's voice trails off, and he clears his throat, his entire demeanor suddenly changing as he side eyes me awkwardly. It doesn't take long for my brain to register why he has grown uncomfortable.

"Wait, you were outside the entire…" I turn to look back at the door, my eyes widening in horror, just imagining the things he heard last night.

"I heard nothing, my Queen," Dustin quickly states.

"Well, clearly you heard something," I retort, noticing the blush creeping onto his cheeks. The embarrassment is palpable, engulfing both of us. Clearing my throat, I shift my gaze towards the end of the corridor. "Have you seen the King?" I ask, changing the subject.

"He is in his office, my Queen."

"Ah, enough with the formalities. I hate being called queen, But silly especially after what you overheard, don't you think?" Dustin chuckles.

"I heard nothing," he insists, lips curling up in the corners as he keeps his gaze fixed ahead, desperately trying to suppress his laughter. Shaking my head with a click of my tongue, I gesture towards the end of the long hallway.

"Come on then, let's find my King," I huff before striding off. Dustin hurriedly follows, then races ahead, opening doors along the way, which irks me. It becomes a silent competition to reach each door first, a reminder of how everyone is constantly doing things for me. Finally outpacing him, I swing open the next door, only to collide with Kyson's chest.

The impact expels the air from my lungs, leaving me stumbling backward. Dustin swiftly grabs hold of my arm to steady me as I clutch my head, feeling the dizziness overwhelm me. Eventually releasing his grip, Dustin discreetly places his hand behind his back and stands taller.

"And where are you rushing off to?" Kyson asks, amusement

evident in his voice as he surveys me. I rub my forehead where I had collided with my mate like a bulldozer.

"We were looking for you," I groan.

"Well, you found me," Kyson chuckles, though I can't resist slapping his chest without considering how much stronger and quicker I have become since shifting. The force causes pain to shoot through my hand and makes the King grunt, but I don't even move him. Kyson shakes his head, draping his arm over my shoulder and pulling me closer as we retrace our steps towards the stairs leading back to our quarters. As we cross the foyer, we spot Clarice coming down the steps.

"Ah, there you are, my Queen. I left your afternoon tea upstairs on the table for you," she informs me.

"Thank you, Clarice," I acknowledge, preparing to climb the steps when Beta Damian's voice rings out from down the corridor, causing us to pause. Kyson leans down, pressing his lips to my head, and I purse my lips in response.

"I'll be up soon," Kyson murmurs before striding off toward his Beta.

"What's happening?" I question Dustin, my gaze fixated on Kyson's retreating figure. Dustin remains silent, prompting me to glance in his direction.

"You're not allowed to tell me, are you?" I ask, already aware of the answer.

"The King has everything under control," Dustin replies, and I bite the inside of my lip as I contemplate whether to go after him to find out, by the look on Damian's face, it seems serious. My eyes wander towards Kyson's office, where he has vanished.

Curiosity piques within me, wondering if this has anything to do with the missing women. Against better judgment, I begin to make my way towards his office, only to be halted by the sound of arguing. Dustin grabs my hand, trying to steer me in the opposite direction, but my feet don't move, the arguing grows louder, and Dustin tightens his grip on my hand, attempting to steer me back toward the stairs, but I find myself transfixed by what was happening.

"The King doesn't want you in there right now, my Queen," Dustin advises. I try to pull away from Dustin, ignoring his words.

"Ivy!"

"I want to know what's going on," I tell him when I hear something smash in his office. Dustin attempts to grab me when I rip my arm out of his gentle grip. Escaping Dustin, I shove the door open to find the King has shifted, and he has Gannon pinned on the desk, who is also shifted. They appear to be fighting while Damian is picking himself up off the floor. His lip is bleeding, and I see the healing bruise on his chin, showing someone had hit him.

Gannon snarls and shoves the King before swinging at him, only for Kyson to punch him, and Gannon stumbles backward and hits the ground. The pungent aroma of alcohol in the room emanating from Gannon tells me he is drunk. He growls, trying to get up but stumbling, and Damian goes to get between them when Kyson glares at him, and Damian backs away with his hands up.

"Stand down. She will see sense soon and come back, stop this," the King orders Gannon.

"This is fucking bullshit, and you know it," Gannon snaps at him.

"My hands are tied, you know this," Kyson says, letting him go, and glaring down at Gannon.

I stand back, confused at the scene before me. Normally it's the King who throws alcohol-induced temper tantrums. I've never seen Gannon act this way before. What could get him so worked up? Unless he's talking about... Abbie.

"You're the fucking King. You can make him give her back," Gannon snarls when his eyes fall on me standing in the doorway.

"I wonder what Ivy would say to that. Would you offer her the same excuse?" Gannon sneers.

"If I knew what?" I interrupt, stepping further into the room, my presence now visible to all men.

"Nothing, Ivy. Go back to our room, love," Kyson orders. At his command, my shock quickly turns into rage, feeling its subtlety wash over me.

Gannon goes to say something, and the King turns, a furious growl tearing out of him, but the look on Gannon's face shows he doesn't care about the consequences, or maybe he is too intoxicated to realize the trouble he is about to get in for disobeying a direct order.

"Dustin, get her," Kyson snarls, and Dustin grabs my arm, trying to pull me from the room when Gannon speaks up.

"Kade is mistreating Abbie," Gannon says. I stop.

I had just spoken to her the night before, and she seemed fine. Turning to face him, Dustin tries to yank me out, but I shove him off. I turn to Kyson, wanting to know what he is talking about, when the king snarls, pivoting and punching Gannon so hard it knocks him out cold. I gasp, my hands covering my mouth as Gannon suddenly becomes sprawled on the floor.

"Out Ivy, now!" Kyson snaps angrily, but I glare at him.

"Where is Abbie, Kyson?" I demand, my voice filled with a mixture of fury and concern.

"She is with her mate, where she chooses to be," Kyson replies, his tone daring. Furrowing my brows, I shift my gaze towards Gannon, who lies sprawled on the floor.

"Then what is Gannon talking about?" I press.

"It doesn't matter. I will join you soon," Kyson once again evades my question.

"You're lying."

"Pardon me?"

"I said you're lying. Now, tell me what's happening with Abbie?" I snap, my mind racing as I desperately try to make sense of the situation, searching for signs in her tone and demeanor that something was off. Has something happened since we last spoke?

"Go back to the room. Do not force me to give you an order, Ivy," Kyson warns.

"Then answer the damn question!" I retort, frustration and fear intertwining within me. My eyes dart between Kyson and Gannon, Gannon still unconscious on the floor.

"Ivy..." Kyson grits his teeth, his eyes darting behind me to Dustin, and he glares at him in some silent message.

"Don't glare at him. I want to know what's going on and why you are all fighting," I demand to know.

"Dustin, get her out of here and keep her away!" Kyson snarls. Dustin grips my arm, attempting to pull me from the room, but I forcefully wrench myself free. Regrettably, Dustin collides with the wall this time, and I feel a pang of guilt as he groans from the impact. Turning my attention back to Kyson, I want answers.

"Tell me," I demand, causing Dustin to reach out once more in an attempt to remove me from the room.

"Leave, Ivy," he growls.

"What is happening with Abbie?" I repeat, my anger now consuming me.

"Go back to our room. Do not test my patience further," Kyson warns, stepping around his desk to stand directly in front of me. Folding his arms across his chest, he meets my defiant glare. I can feel my hands trembling uncontrollably, a fact not lost on him. But this is Abbie we are discussing, and she means everything to me. More than my own life. And that truth remains steadfast, even in the face of my mate's domineering presence.

"Then answer the fucking question?" I snap.

"Abbie is with her mate, you know this. You spoke with her last night," Kyson says, and my eyes dart to Gannon.

"If I find out you're lying to me, or something is wrong with her..." My words trail off.

"You'll what, Ivy?" Kyson takes a threatening step forward. "I would advise you not to finish that sentence, love," Kyson says.

"Do not forget, Kyson, that I have other options now, other places I can go," I retort, my voice filled with anger. His growl ripples through the room violently.

"Excuse me?" Kyson snarls, his eyes flashing dangerously as his hands clench into fists.

"You dare address the Queen of the Landeena Kingdom so casually, King Kyson," I growl back. It may have been petty, but if he wanted to assert his dominance, then I would do the same.

Despite my reluctance to embrace the role of Queen, the fact remains that I hold that title and possess a kingdom, even if it has a population of zero. It is still mine by birthright, and I won't back down, especially when it comes to Abbie. Even if it means risking my own life.

"Is that so, Ivy?" Kyson responds through gritted teeth.

"Queen Azalea," I clarify, catching him off guard. If I am going to make claims, then I will claim it all, including the name. Damian edges closer at my words, his eyes on Kyson like he is afraid Kyson will hurt me for challenging him. Dustin's fingertips brush my arm like he is preparing to rip me out of the way if needed. While Kyson and I stand locked in a battle of wills, neither of us is willing to yield to the other. The tension is palpable as the muscles in Kyson's jaw clenched.

Though I fear his ability to use his calling or issue orders to me, unsure of how to combat his aura, I can't forget that I possess the command and aura of an Alpha as a Lycan Queen by blood. With this realization fueling me, I wait for Kyson's next move.

KYSON

Ivy is furious, and I can feel Damian sneaking closer, worried that I will lose control. Honestly, I am on the verge of snapping and dragging her back to the room, and her following words nearly make me.

"Don't forget, Kyson, I have other places I can go now," Ivy snarls at me. Her words make me growl; how dare she think she can threaten me, threaten to leave me over something that is out of my control? I can't force Abbie back here.

"Excuse me, Ivy?" I growl, trying to keep my blistering, fiery rage under control.

"You dare address the Queen of the Landeena Kingdom so casually, King Kyson," she spits at me. The words that rolled off her tongue were pure venom. Her anger is nearly as hot as mine as she glares at me.

"Is that so, Ivy?" I ask her through clenched teeth. My entire body trembles and I am on the serious verge of shifting again. She only just learned of her title, and she is already using it against me when she doesn't get her way.

"Queen Azalea," she snaps at me, and I lunge at her, trying to grab her, as Dustin stands horrified behind her when he suddenly rips her back just as I shift, losing complete control.

She dares challenge an Alpha King, her King! My hand grips Dustin's shirt instead of her, and my nostrils flare as I pant, trying to regain some form of control, shocked at myself that I had lost it completely. Dustin remains utterly unmoving, and I feel Damian's hand fall on my shoulder when Gannon groans behind me, regaining consciousness.

"Let him go, Kyson; you hurt him, and I will walk out those fucking doors and out of your life faster than I stepped in it," Ivy snaps at me. Her hand grips my wrist. I can feel the tremble in it, making me look at her. Her eyes are blazing with fury. Looking at her now with her eyes burning with so much anger and fear, she honestly looks like her mother, Queen Tatiana, in this instance. How did I not see it before?

"We will speak in the room. Now go," I tell her.

"No, I want to know about Ab..."

"Room now!" I command, cutting her off, and I instantly feel terrible. Her anger blasts at me as it slivers through me, so cold and cutting like a knife's edge. Yet, she still can't fight the full weight of my Alpha aura, not yet at least. She growls before the command forces her to turn around and storm off back to our room. It isn't until Dustin sucks in a wheezing breath that I realize I am choking him with his uniform. I let him go, and he exhales, relieved.

"You know where you should be," I tell him, and he hurries off after Ivy. Turning back to my office, Damian takes a step back just as Gannon groans and gets to his feet. Moving around the desk, I grab him and shake him.

"Do you have any idea what you have just done?" I snarl.

"She had a right to know," Gannon growls back.

"You disobeyed a fucking order; I told you not to get her involved," I snap at him.

"And what about Abbie? Ivy may be the only one that can make Abbie see sense. Abbie trusts her," he says.

"That may be so, but now you have just caused me a giant fucking headache. I would rather not deal with this right now when she is so goddamn close to going into heat, and the bond has just fucking forged. I had to fucking command her, Gannon!"

"You didn't have to do anything, Kyson. You chose to command her because you don't like being challenged, so don't blame that on me," Gannon spits at me.

He stinks heavily of alcohol, and I know he isn't in the right headspace, but that doesn't mean he can get away with disobeying me and causing issues with my mate. I get he wants to vent his anger, but he did it the wrong way. We have laws even I must abide by, and until Abbie asks to come back, my hands are tied entirely unless I want a war with 80 nearby packs, and I already have enough enemies without adding them to that list.

"I know you are mad, but we can't afford this crap right now. You want something to do, go back to Silvershadow Pack," I snap at him. Gannon growls at me and tries to shake me off.

"I already got that bitch. She can't walk, for god's sake. What the fuck else can I possibly do to her?" I yank him closer.

"Not Daley, but make sure she is dead before you return home. I have another job for you while we wait for Abbie to come back." Gannon looks at me, something flickering in his gaze.

"No, Kyson, not while he is like this?" Damian says, and I smile. They both think this is over. Mrs. Daley's mistreatment, it is, but they still haven't heard the worst of it yet. I look back at Gannon.

"You want revenge, then take it out on the butcher. Daley will know who he is," I tell him.

"The butcher?" Damian asks, and I nod and look at him over my shoulder.

"Yes, he's Abbie's rapist," I growl, letting Gannon go. This would distract him until I find a way to legally bring Abbie home. At my words, Gannon roars, his skin ripping off. He shifts so quickly as the monster he can become steps forward. He stands and snarls, his chest pressing against mine.

"He did what to my Abbie?" Gannon snarls.

"I won't repeat it, it wasn't my place to say, but I was planning to tell you, anyway. Find Daley, and you will know where to find the butcher."

"I'm not bringing him in," Gannon warns, his eyes flickering and bleeding so hollow, I know the butcher will wish for death long before he receives it.

"He's all yours," I tell him, turning on my heel and walking out. I am halfway down the corridor when I hear the doors opening. I will have to answer to the council, but at the end of the day, I have immunity and so does my guard for killing anyone we deem fit for execution.

God have mercy on his soul because Gannon won't show him any; the man is a sadist at heart and is the one I always send when I need information. Just like my executioner, Liam, Gannon loves listening to their screams. He enjoys their pain, relishes in their blood. This man is about to learn who the real butcher is.

Walking back to my quarters, I growl at Dustin standing guard. The room is silent as I approach, and I should have been wary of that as I enter. Not seeing her until I shut the door, only to turn around, and her hand connects with my face. Her claws slash at me and I clutch at my face. Her claws have torn into my leathery Lycan skin like a hot knife through butter. Blood gushes from my face and sprays across the door behind me.

"You commanded me!" she snarls at me while I clutch my cheek and eye. My body ripples and my hands clench. "You bring Abbie back here, Kyson," she growls, and I pull my hand from my face to look at her. She takes a step back at the sight of what she did. My face isn't healing quickly either. It stings and burns horribly.

Her worry hits me like a tidal wave at what she has done and fear of how I will react. She looks at her fingertips, her claws still

37

extended, coated with so much of my blood it dripped from her fingertips.

"I didn't mean it, I..." she goes to apologize before her anger returns. "You should have told me about Abbie!" she says as I blink, trying to clear my vision and keep my cool. Ignoring her ranting, I walk to the bathroom and grab a washcloth, wetting it and dabbing the gashes that are bleeding everywhere.

I force myself to shift back, but it still doesn't heal. Fuck!

Ivy follows me in and gasps at the sight of my face. Her claws are still extended, and I know she doesn't know how to retract them. It's difficult when you're angry, and until she calms down, I doubt they will. Her body is foreign to her, and her lack of control over that form seems as bad as mine. Clearly, she inherited her father's temper. Garret also had a filthy temper.

"Get out!" I tell her, and she goes to say something.

"Azalea, go! Let me calm down. I don't want to hurt you, so please go back to the room," I tell her, gripping the bench.

She growls but walks back out and closes the door. I have a funny feeling Abbie is about to cause huge issues between us, but for now, we both just need to calm down before one of us does something we can't undo. I'm not about to risk the bond when I only just got it back.

CHAPTER
SEVEN

ABBIE

My mind reels with the fact that Gannon drove all the way here. I've missed him, but I know it's wrong to have feelings for someone else when you have a mate. It feels like a betrayal to the Moon Goddess to refuse the gift she has bestowed on me.

Honestly, I've never considered myself worthy of a mate, someone to love me unconditionally, until I met Kade. I miss him and wonder if being apart hurts him as much as it does me. Nevertheless, as I unpack the groceries that Gannon has brought and left on my doorstep, I am unable to refrain from thinking about him.

I can't wipe the goofy smile off my face as I chew on a strawberry cloud; he always gives me candy at the castle. Him remembering that these are my favorite has me smiling like an idiot, but then guilt sets in. I shouldn't be thinking about Gannon, I have a mate, and I scold myself for my reckless thoughts.

However, it feels strange seeing the cupboards with food in them. Kade brings a couple of bags every few days, but nothing like this. I'm always rationing everything, and even then, it still isn't enough to last before he returns. Days have passed since I last saw him, and I haven't eaten anything since the bird eggs two days ago.

It upsets me that Kade never stays long, only a few minutes before saying he has to get back to work. This place is quiet, sometimes too quiet for my troubled mind, and it makes me miss Ivy and Clarice more, the walls feel like they are closing in more each day. The nights feel colder and the longing to go home back to the castle grows worse each day.

After packing away the last of the groceries, I decide to go bring the washing in. I only have these pants and the shirt, plus the clothes I came here wearing. Hand-washing them every day in the sink is becoming tiresome. I have asked Kade for clothes, even fresh linens. He promises but never delivers.

Stepping outside, I shield my eyes from the sun that is slowly going down behind the trees. I've split some sticks to make my pegs, since none had been provided, and only half the clothesline still has wires. I can't wait to finally go to the packhouse. Kade has told me all about it and how beautiful it is. I just need to be patient, and soon I will be free to be with my mate and not be at threat of the pack war he is currently stuck in.

Checking the clothes, I see the hems are still wet, so I flip them on the clothesline and hang them up the other way. Another half an hour and they will surely be dry, and I can iron them for tomorrow. Walking back inside, I stop when I hear tires on gravel. My heart leaps with excitement, hoping it's Kade. But when I turn around, I see the mysterious black Mustang parked at the end of the driveway again. I stare at it, wondering why they come here every day but never introduce themselves or get out.

However, today is different when I see the car door swing open and a woman gets out of the car. She's gorgeous, with long curly blonde hair half pulled up. She wears sunglasses covering her eyes and everything about her screams luxury and money. The woman walks around to the front of the car, her knee-high black boots crunching on the gravel as she leans on the hood. She's wearing a white cami and blue jeans, her lips stained bright red from her lipstick.

The mystery sits on the hood of the car, and I wave to her, wondering if she's a pack member and if I should say hello. But Kade told me not to talk to anyone out here, so I stay where I am. She doesn't wave back, but instead only stares at me.

With one last glance over my shoulder, I rush inside, closing and locking the door. Not that it would do much; the door's hinges are loose, and the bottom of the door is waterlogged, making it challenging to shut and leaving a gap that the mosquitoes like to come in from at night.

I peer out the window at her, staying far enough back, hoping she can't see me. She sits there for a while, then eventually flicks her cigarette and leaves, making me wonder why she stops here. Once she finally leaves, I let out a breath of relief and return to what I am doing. My afternoon is like clockwork so it's not hard to get back on track.

I nap before bringing the clothes in, then hang them up along the window curtain on a coat hanger. I make my bed before grabbing the comic book Gannon got me. The pictures tell a story about a cat with stripes. If only I could read, the images might make more sense to me, but I am thankful nonetheless.

Feeling a bit hungry, I wander into the kitchen. The sun is down now, and the day has turned to night. The nights are the longest, so cold and empty, and that's usually also when the most pain comes. That horrible, heart-breaking pain that restricts my chest. My anxiety always peaks around this time, waiting for it to arrive. Next time I speak with Kade, I will ask him to take me to the pack doctor. Something must be wrong, or it wouldn't be so frequent.

CHAPTER

EIGHT

ABBIE

Walking into the kitchen, I grab a cup and fill it with milk, deciding on milk and cookies. I am too tired to cook, and the stove is temperamental, only working when it wants to. Dipping my biscuit in my milk, I bite into it. The sugary sweetness makes me giddy.

Sugar always has that effect on me. Kade says it's because I'm not used to having it. After I irritated him with my constant talking on the way here from the bag of clouds Gannon gave me before I left, he tossed them out the window and snapped at me to keep quiet because he had a headache. I haven't had anything sweet since, except for artificial sugar in my coffee that Kade brought the last time he came here. He said it was a treat for being good, but it didn't even taste like sugar and had a funny aftertaste.

Yet, just the reminder of him getting upset makes me tense. What if he comes and sees me with them? Maybe I shouldn't have anymore? I don't want to annoy my mate and make him leave when he rarely visits me as it is. I place the half-eaten biscuit back, planning to eat the other half tomorrow, just in case he comes to see me. Which I hope he will; the bond always relaxes the nights he does.

I put the open packet in the fridge and decide to quickly spring-clean to burn off some energy. Quickly rushing around, I fill the sink with water and start cleaning the kitchen. Nothing I do improves its state. The place is falling apart. After washing my cup, I place it on the sink upside down when I hear car tires again. My eyes widen with excitement, and I can't help the stupid smile that spreads across my face. Pulling my hands out of the water, I quickly dry them and race to the front door, tossing it wide open, unable to contain my excitement.

I squeal when I see Kade's car parked out front, and he hops out along with two of his pack enforcers whom I met back at the castle. Kade climbs out, looking gorgeous in his suit, and I rush down the steps, almost bouncing with joy. I run over, and am about to throw my arms around him. Gosh, I missed him.

But I am greeted with his fist instead. My head snaps back, and I clutch my face, blood spurting from my nose and lip where his fist connected. Blood stains my shirt and my hands as I look at them. Shocked, unable to process what just happened, I land on my back on the gravel. Lifting my head, I see his hand reach for me before seeing Kade's face contort with anger and his once handsome features are now twisted in a cruel sneer. His fist is covered in blood and his expensive suit is stained with it. He looms over me, his expression full of rage.

My mate grabs my hair, making me cry out as my neck arches back painfully. Kade says nothing, just rips me back toward the house; I clutch his hands, my feet slipping on the loose gravel as I try to stand. I feel the rough gravel scrape against my bare arms and legs as he drags me across it, and my scalp burns violently as he rips on my hair. I clutch the top step as he hauls me up it, only to earn a kick to the stomach when he is halted.

"Kade?" I cry out as he drags me across the ground and up the steps by my hair. What did I do? I don't understand. My hair tears painfully from my scalp when he tosses me inside. I scream in pain when I land on the hard floor on my hip. My hands jar as I throw them out, trying to break my fall. The metallic scent of blood fills the air as it drips from my nose and lips.

Kade kicks the door shut, and my eyes widen when he turns on me again.

"You fucking whore, who were you with?" Kade bellows at me. I scramble back on my hands and feet when he grabs my hair again, hauling me upright.

"What do you mean?" I shriek as he yanks me into the kitchen.

"Whose car was here? Do you think I wouldn't notice, wouldn't feel your infidelity?" he screams.

"He stopped in to visit me and bring food; it was just Gannon," I sob, trying to get him to let go.

He finally does let go, and I stumble back into the sink when he growls, grabbing the back of my neck and plunging my face into the water. I choke and sputter on the dirty water. My hands grip the sides as I try desperately to pull my face out, only for him to shove my face in harder. I scream choking on water only for him to rip my face.

"Kade, please!" I beg, gasping, trying to twist out of his grasp.

"You think you can just fuck around behind my back? You belong to me!" Kade snarls, his fingers digging into my skin.

"I'm sorry," I whimper, feeling like I can't breathe when he suddenly continues to hold me under the water. I thrash, my lungs screaming for air.

"Sorry doesn't cut it," he spits, finally pulling me up from the sink. I gasp for air, coughing, and wheezing as he grips my shoulders, shaking me violently.

"Please," I cry out, tears streaming down my face.

My throat burns and aches furiously from inhaling the water, making my nose burn, but before I can drown, he rips my head out, and I suck in harsh ragged breaths.

"Did you fuck him, you whore?" Kade screams in my face. I breathe harder, gasping for air. My hair and face are drenched, my shirt soaked, and the water in the sink is stained red.

"No! I swear," I sob, knowing that even if Gannon had made a move on me, I would never cheat on Kade.

"You're lying!" he roars before delivering a hard slap across my face. The force makes me stumble backward and fall onto the floor.

I curl up in a ball as Kade towers over me, his fists clenched at his sides.

"Lying slut!" he screams, grabbing my hair again, I scream and beg, my arms shaking as he pushes me toward the sink.

"No, no, please. I'm not lying," I beg.

He shoves my face back in the sink, and I claw and scratch at the bench, trying to get air. Water sloshes onto the floor at my feet as I struggle against him, only for him to rip me out at the last second again.

"He brought me food, that's all," I choke out desperately, wondering what he is talking about. Kade yanks my head back, ripping open the pantry and fridge.

He snarls, storming over to me and slamming my head into the bench again. Pain explodes through my skull, and I see black as my head pounds to its own beat. I collapse onto the floor, gasping for air as I try to shake off the dizziness.

Blood pools in my mouth from where he has split my lip open with his violent grip. I struggle to look around through my blurry vision, feeling the panic rise in me as he looms over me.

"What did you just say?" Kade growls, his hand still gripping tightly onto my hair.

"I-I said he brought me food," I stammer out weakly, trying to catch my breath.

"A man brings you food and you don't tell me? You hide it from me like some kind of secret?" Kade's voice is filled with rage and betrayal.

"I didn't think it was important," I whimper, tears streaming down my face as I try to defend myself.

"Nothing is more important than what happens in this house,"

Kade seethes, his grip on my hair tightening even more. "You're mine, and everything that concerns you concerns me."

"I know, I'm sorry," I cry out, feeling completely helpless under his wrath.

"You'll be sorry when I'm done with you," he sneers before slamming my head back into the bench again. The pain is worse this time, and I feel hot tears streaking down my cheeks as darkness starts to close in on me.

But before everything goes black, Kade lets go of my hair and turns away from me. Gasping for air and clutching at the bench for support, I watch as he storms across the kitchen and punches a hole into the wall.

I shrink back against the cabinets, fear coursing through me as he continues to vent his anger on anything in sight.

He starts ripping the canned food off the shelves, tossing them at me, and I shield my head, my body becoming bruised and battered, the bond screaming for him to stop, and my heart twists painfully in my chest. He snarls, picking up a bag of candy.

"Did you fuck him?" Kade snarls, and I shake my head, sobbing. My hands shake as he reaches for me, and I put them up to shield my face. Blood trickles down the side of my head, from my nose and eyebrow, my lip, my arms are bleeding from his claws and my blood stains the floor, my hands, and my clothes.

"Please, Please, I didn't do anything wrong," I shriek when he grabs my hair again, ripping my head back before stuffing the candy in my mouth. I try to spit it out, choking on it.

"Filthy fucking pig, you fucked him, didn't you? Thought you could get away with sneaking around behind my back," he roars in my face, spittle hits my face with his words.

"You want to act like a whore, I will treat you like one," he growls.

CHAPTER
NINE

ABBIE

    Kade rips me to my feet by my hair, and he shoves me toward the door. I see my phone and desperately try to snatch it off the counter when he punches me in the stomach, knocking the air from my lungs as I double over. He smashes it on the floor, my phone breaking into pieces while I try to catch my breath. He kicks me in the stomach, and I retch. The little food I had eaten bubbles up my throat and spills onto the floor along with my blood.

    Black dots dance before my vision, and flecks of gold as a wave of dizziness washes through me, the room spinning around me violently. My blood drips from the gash on my head. Kade's feet stop beside my face when hands grab me, and I am tossed over his shoulder. He kicks the door, sending it flying into the front of the yard before stomping down the steps.

    "Open the trunk," he snaps at one of his men, who rushes to do his bidding. I thrash, trying to get him to put me down, begging and pleading with him, though it falls on deaf ears when I find myself tossed into the trunk, and he slams the lid shut. The sound of the trunk closing echoes in my ears, followed by the sound of the car engine roaring to life.

The inside of the trunk smells musty and stale, with a hint of gasoline from the car's fumes. My own blood and vomit lingers in the air, making it difficult to breathe, and I taste bile in my mouth as I continue to retch, my stomach empty and churning with pain. My tongue tingles from the metallic taste of blood.

I can hear faint, muffled voices and the thud of the trunk hitting the pavement as the car drives away. My fingers scrape against the rough carpet lining the trunk, seeking any sense of stability as I am thrown around with each swerve and turn. My body bruises against the unforgiving metal walls, the pain radiating through my limbs.

I have no idea how long he drove, but I am sent hurtling into the rear seat when he slams on the brakes. My heart beats erratically, filling my ears with the pounding sound of it when I hear the car doors slam, and I suddenly can't breathe, panic consuming me, and I try to suck in a hiccuped breath as the trunk opens. One of his enforcers reaches in to grab me. I thrash, slapping his hands away and kicking when he punches me. My head whips to the side, and I feel my eyes swell shut instantly, and I groan, dazed from the blow.

"Hurry up," Kade snarls when I feel a needle jammed in my arm, it is like someone set my veins on fire as the poison rages an inferno through my bloodstream. "Don't worry, love, it won't kill you, but you won't be able to shift or heal, just a mild sedative," Kade mocks as I peer up at him through my swelled eye that feels like it is ballooning out.

The other man grabs me, tossing me over his shoulder, and I groan, feeling sick at the motion of him walking up steps before I am dumped onto the red carpet. I can't even sit up, wholly paralyzed yet wide awake. My mind races as I try to look around, yet all I can see is a bed with red blankets in the distance. Attached to it are different chains and ropes, and the room smells funny. The pungent aroma of incense burns my nose.

"Sit her up, and make sure she watches," Kade sneers when the man from before grips my shirt, leaning me against the wall. He grabs my head, which is now lolled forward; I notice I am dribbling blood and drooling down my chin. A woman walks in with barely any clothes on.

She is dressed in intricate black lace lingerie, with a matching garter belt and thigh-high stockings. Her hair is cropped into a short, edgy pixie cut, and she towers over me in her stiletto heels. "Yes, Alpha," she asks, yet I notice the tremble of her fingers and the shake of her voice.

"This is my mate, Abbie. She is being punished, so we are going to put on a show for her, get on the bed, Blaire." The woman gasps and spins when he motions toward me with his hand, and she stumbles back, her face paling.

"Your mate?" she gasps, and she goes to kneel, her hands outstretched like she wants to help me when Kade snaps at her. "Don't touch the slut. Now get on the bed," Kade snarls at her.

The woman looks horrified at Kade. "But she is your mate," the woman says, and Kade growls.

"Are you questioning your Alpha? You remember what happened last time you questioned me?" he asks, tilting his head to the side, and she whimpers, offering her neck to him and nods. "Get your clothes off, and get on the fucking bed," he snaps at her, she looks over her shoulder at me.

My eyes well up with tears when Kade starts removing his own clothes.

"If she closes her eyes, hit her," he orders the man holding my head up.

The woman, Blaire, quickly strips off her lingerie and gets on the bed, lying on her back with her legs spread open. Kade climbs onto the bed and positions himself between Blaire's legs, his eyes never leaving mine. The man holding my head up grabs a handful of my hair and pulls my head back so I can't look away.

"Watch," Kade orders me as he leans down and starts kissing Blaire's neck. She moans softly, but I can see the fear in her eyes. I feel sick to my stomach as I watch Kade touch another woman like that. Tears stream down my face as I am forced to watch every intimate moment between them.

I try to look away, but the man holding me slaps me hard across the face, making me cry out in pain. "No closing your eyes," he growls at me.

Kade continues to fuck Blaire while occasionally glancing over at me with a smirk on his face. I feel so violated and helpless, unable to move or protect myself from this humiliating display.

Pain ripples through every part of my body, my heart crushed to smithereens. Gannon was right; there is nothing wrong with me. The pain I feel now is worsened because I not only endured it for so long, but I am also now forced to watch it as he fucks this girl right in front of me for hours, the pain is excruciating, and I pray for it to end. Kade finally finishes, climbs off the bed, and walks over to me when he is done. Tears trek down my face when he stops in front of me.

"Open her mouth," Kade says, and my eyes widen. I try to move, but can't; I can't even speak. My tongue feels numb; I can only drool on myself. The sting of tears pricked at the corners of my eyes as rough fingertips grab my chin, forcing my mouth open wider. My panicked gaze flicks to the woman named Blaire, her sobs muffled by her hands as she lay on the bed. But my attention is quickly drawn back to Kade as he stuffs his cock into my mouth. Each movement feels like a violation, his touch alone making me feel dirty and used.

Kade's grip on my hair tightens as he begins thrusting into my mouth with an almost violent force. My tongue recoils at the taste of her, slick and bitter on my taste buds. He had already used her for pleasure, and now I am little more than a vessel for his release as he empties himself inside me. I can't help but gag and choke on it.

Finally, he lets go of my hair and I crash to the ground, gasping for air and feeling utterly violated. The taste of her lingers in my mouth, a constant reminder of what had just happened. My entire body goes numb, even my mind as I stare blankly at the dust underneath the bed.

I stare beneath the bed, no longer listening, going deaf to my surroundings. Closing my eyes, I pretend to be back in mine and Ivy's room at the orphanage, remembering the times we would lay on the hard floor gazing out the window at night making pictures of the stars, dreaming of what it would be like to be free. I never thought I would see the day when I would rather be back there than where I currently am.

Kade leaves me on the floor and walks out, and it takes hours before I can move my hand. Eventually, I brush my hair behind my ear. It had been annoying me, obscuring my vision for hours and tickling my nose. I try and blow it away to no avail, so I eventually use my hand, having regained some feeling back. My fingertips brush the scar behind my ear, and I suck in a shaky breath.

"More than my life, more than my life," I repeatedly whisper to myself as I cry because she is the only person I'm holding on for.

"More than my life."

CHAPTER

TEN

I VY
I leave Kyson in the bathroom; feeling terrible for scratching him and hoping it will heal quickly. I close the bathroom door and make my way back to the bed. Trying to clear my head, I snatch the phone from where I left it earlier and try to call Abbie again. Something must be wrong with Kyson's phone because it won't even ring, just beeps in my ear before hanging up. My anxiety about not knowing what is going on with her starts making me itch, an involuntary reaction I've always had to anxiety. Seeing Gannon *that* upset keeps eating away at me... what does he know that I don't?

I call her again, no luck. My eyes move to the bathroom, wanting to ask him to fix his phone, but also not wanting to argue with him again. So instead I walk to the door, growling as I open it and realize I can't walk past the damn threshold, like some barrier or force field prevents me. I growl angrily at his command and my inability to fight it. Dustin, noticing me, walks over.

"Something is wrong with it. Can you fix it? I want to call Abbie," I tell him, and he takes the phone from my hand. He fiddles with it and then tries to call her, but the same thing.

"Her phone is off. It isn't the King's phone, but Abbie's," Dustin says, and my brows furrow worriedly.

"Try her again," I tell him, but it is the same result.

"I'm sorry, my Queen, but her phone is definitely turned off," Dustin tells me. Why is it off? Nodding, I take the phone from him before closing the door; nausea rolls over me, and I don't know if I want to throw up or throw something. My instincts are all over the place, fear, and anger at Kyson, anxiousness, all of it bubbling up and beginning to spill over. Before I even register what I have done, I throw the phone, my hands clenching into fists and fur growing up my arms. I try to stop it and regain control.

Kyson opens the bathroom door at the same time I toss the phone at it, his reflexes are so much quicker and more controlled than mine, as he snatches it from the air before it smashes into the bathroom door. He looks at the phone, and I notice his face has healed, but has surprisingly left a faint scar down his face. Kyson growls, pocketing it while I try not to shift.

My wrists and ankles crack as the urge becomes overwhelming, and I have no idea how to stop it. "You need to calm down," Kyson says. That is easy for him to say, another thing entirely to actually do, especially when it comes to Abbie. I am out of my mind with worry.

Clutching the dresser, my claws slip out of my fingertips, scratching into the mahogany-stained wood. "Azalea, do you want help, or are you shifting?" Kyson asks, while I try to breathe through my fingers, stretching and growing longer. It is so odd hearing him use another name for me, but I prefer the name. Ivy is weak. I no longer want to be Ivy, but I also don't want to look weak by asking him for help because I really don't want to shift. It took ages for me to shift back last time.

"Such a stubborn little thing you are," Kyson growls just as the heat of his body presses against my back. My claws slice through the wood of the dresser, and I feel my canines elongate painfully. The stretching and moving of bones grosses me out but is nowhere near as painful as my first shift, but it is still unpleasant, though.

"Do you want help?" Kyson asks as his hands fall on my hips, and he tugs me flush against him. I growl and nod.

"Please," I grit out through clenched teeth, knowing I will be stuck in my Lycan form without his help until my body shifts back on its own. So, I allow it and melt against him when he purrs, the calling washing over me, making goosebumps rise on my flesh, and every nerve ending begins to buzz, as the urge to rub myself all over him becomes overwhelming. The urge to shift leaves as he holds me against him.

"Breathe, Azzy, come back to me baby," Kyson purrs, his hands rubbing along my ribs. My head rolls back on his chest.

"That's it, love, let go. Just breathe," Kyson soothes while I turn to putty in his arms.

"We will get Abbie back. We just have to be patient," Kyson purrs next to my ear.

"You should have told me," I snap before purring, anger and lust mingling and blurring the lines between both emotions, fighting a war within me.

"So you could be like this and worry about something you can't control?" Kyson asks, and his hand slips beneath my shirt to my stomach.

"You're the King, you can order him to return her."

"And start a war for the abuse of power? Just because I can, doesn't mean it is allowed. I may be King, Azalea, but we live by the law, and the werewolf and Lycan council members would look for any reason to take down a Lycan Royal. I can't break the laws that I created. She needs to leave on her own."

"But is she safe?"

"You spoke with her the other day," Kyson answers with a sigh.

"Then why is Gannon upset?"

Kyson growls, his arm tightening around my torso before tugging me toward the bed. "Alpha Kade has a wife and kids that Abbie doesn't know about, also a few girlfriends on the side," Kyson tells me.

"And you let her go with him!" I snarl, turning in his arm and shoving him off.

"Gannon tried to tell her, but she wouldn't listen."

"Then you should have told me. I would have convinced her. She would have listened to me," I yell at him, my anger spewing over, and fur grows over my arms, my neck cracks. Kyson's calling grows stronger, and I close my eyes, trying to catch my breath and calm down.

"You can speak with her on the phone. If she says yes, I will send Gannon to go get her, but until then, Love, my hands are tied."

"You're the fucking King. Order the council to be okay with it!"

"I can't do that. I will have every pack breathing down my neck if I do. Just because I am King doesn't mean I can make my own rules as I go, Azalea. Do you think I don't want to do that? Gannon is one of my best friends. I don't want to see him hurting just as much as you don't want to see Abbie hurting, but my fucking hands are tied."

"Hurting? What do you mean, Abbie is hurting?"

Kyson sighs and pinches the bridge of his nose.

"The chest pain she feels, her pain is caused by his infidelity, not something being wrong with her. The mate bond can feel it, but you two girls were never taught any of this sort of stuff, so she thinks there is something wrong with her, but it's because Kade is screwing other women who aren't his mate."

I growl, my anger emblazoned and so hot I want to hurt something.

"Shh, calm down. You can convince her to come home. She only needs to reject him, and it is all over. She can come home then. I promise we will get her back," Kyson says, his hands sliding up my arms and rubbing them as he steps closer.

"Her phone is off," I tell him, and he sighs.

"I will call Kade and ask him to get her to call you," Kyson says. He steps away, pulling the phone that I threw from his pants pocket. I follow him over to the bed as he climbs into it.

CHAPTER
ELEVEN

I VY

Kyson dials his number, and I crawl onto the bed when he pats his chest. With a sigh, I lay down, placing my head on his chest. I listen to the phone ring, and it doesn't take long before Kade answers it, and Kyson puts it on the loudspeaker, so I can hear better without straining my ears.

"Good afternoon, my King," Kade answers, his voice rather chirpy, and I growl when Kyson's hand clamps over my mouth.

"Kade. Abbie isn't answering her phone," Kyson says.

"Oh, yes, she dropped it in the sink accidentally. It got wet; I have ordered a new phone for her," Kade replies.

"Are you with her now?" Kyson replies.

"Ah no, I am working. She is at the pack house with my... Cassandra."

"So, you told her about Cassandra?" Kyson asks.

"Of course, she was shocked but is accepting since we have three kids together, they have been getting along great. Cassandra adores Abbie and is excited to have another woman in the house."

My brows furrow, and the growl that leaves me is loud and

unable to be stifled with just his hand as I reach for the phone, wanting to demand to speak with her. However, Kyson moves, rolling on top of me and nipping at my neck, the calling seeping into me louder, forcing me to relax beneath him, yet defiance rears its head within me, and I bite his shoulder viciously. Kyson, growls in warning to let go.

"You seem to have your hands full, my King," Kade says with a laugh.

"Hmm, well, I want Abbie to ring this number as soon as possible. I have a mate missing her friend and very concerned after learning you are already married," Kyson tells him.

"Ah, I see," Kade replies.

"Good because with them being so close, I am sure you can imagine how upset Ivy was to learn her friend ran off with a married man."

"Oh, Cassandra is fine with it. They will be like sister wives in no time."

"My mate's concern is for Abbie, not your wife. Have Abbie call us, or I will be coming down with Ivy to see her."

"Oh, no need. Abbie is perfectly fine. I will have her call you in the morning when I return home."

"Video call," I mouth to Kyson, who presses his lips in a line.

"Get her to video call, or we will come to visit, Ivy wants to see her," Kyson tells him.

"Certainly, my King. First thing after the ladies get the kids ready for school, I will ensure she calls," Kade answers swiftly, and I glare at the phone, wanting to snatch it off him and yell at Kade. I don't like his tone of voice, something is off, or maybe I am just too angry with the man because he tricked Abbie.

"Very well, we will speak soon," Kyson says, hanging up. He leans over and places the phone on the bedside table before looking down at me. "You bit me!"

"You used your calling on me, to try to shut me up!" I retort. I push on his chest, and he exhales but rolls off me.

"You will speak to her tomorrow, okay? He won't put her on if something is wrong, and she is now aware; he said she is okay with it."

"I know Abbie, and there is no way she would be okay sharing her mate or being lied to."

"Well, we'll see tomorrow, won't we?" Kyson says. I growl, and he rolls on his side, tugging me closer.

Just as he goes to turn me to face him, a knock is heard on the door, making him look at it, and the door opens a crack.

"My king, it is Trey. Clarice sent me up with your dinner," Trey answers, and Kyson sighs heavily at the interruption.

"Just put it on the coffee table," Kyson states, sitting up and swinging his legs over the side of the bed. He pats my hip with his hand.

"You should eat," he says. I glare at the wall, much too upset to eat.

"Thank you, Trey," the King says, and I hear Trey leave as Kyson climbs off the bed.

"Ivy, up and eat, or am I to call you Azalea from now on?" he says.

I roll my eyes, knowing he will keep nagging, and I force myself out of bed. I walk over to where Kyson is sitting by the fire and sit next to him.

"Azalea," I answer his question. "I don't want to be Ivy anymore."

He nods, sliding my plate over to me.

"Azalea, it is then. I will tell the staff too about the correction. Now eat," he says, pointing to my plate. I pick up my knife and fork to dig into the steak and salad. Whereas Kyson just has a different assortment of raw meat.

"You never eat salad?" I ask him, noticing how usually he only eats meat.

"I do, but rarely. Lycans are carnivores. Our sense of taste changes after a while," he says with a shrug.

"So I won't like salad and vegetables after a while?"

He chews his food and seems thoughtful for a second. "No, you still like all food. You will just prefer certain things to others, but if it makes you feel any better, Dustin is vegetarian and a Lycan."

"Huh? But everyone here is Lycan. How could he be a vegetarian?"

"Yes, but he chooses to be vegetarian, and I still like fruit, et cetera; I just prefer meat."

"I can't believe Dustin is a vegetarian?" I tell him, a little stunned by that information. Kyson chuckles, but it explains why I have never seen him eating meat now that I think about it.

"Huh, I never noticed," I tell him.

"I suppose you also never noticed that he is gay then?" Kyson says.

"He is gay?" I ask, shocked once again. I don't know what I thought a gay man would look like, but I always pictured them more feminine, and there is nothing remotely feminine about the man.

"Yep, which is why I assigned him as your guard, plus he asked to be placed as your guard when you came here... When I came to my senses," Kyson says.

"Why are the good-looking ones always gay?" I mutter. "Excuse me?" Kyson growls.

"What? You said it yourself; he is gay. I was just making an observation," I laugh.

"I don't want you checking out my guard, Azalea," Kyson warns.

"I wasn't, but come to think of it, Damian is nice looking too, and..." I tease, my words trailing off, seeing him become jealous. I have no interest in any of them, and none are as gorgeous as Kyson.

"Oh, and?" Kyson growls, and I laugh.

"Say one more word, and I will put you over my knee," the King growls. However, his words don't scare me, instead, they sent a thrill through me, wondering if he actually would.

"Gannon's alright, too. I can see why Abbie likes him," I snicker. He leaps over the coffee table, his growl ripping through the air as he lands on top of me, making me laugh.

"Are you teasing me, my Queen, because if you're not, I may have to kill my entire guard to stop your wandering eyes," he says, pinning my hands to the floor while he nips at my lips and rolls his hips against me.

"You can't kill your guard because they don't just belong to you. Besides, Dustin is my guard, not yours, so you can't kill him," I tell him.

"So not only are you claiming your title back, but you are now claiming my guard? Anything else, my Queen?" he asks, and I purse my lips.

"Hmm, I am yet to claim my king. I think I will claim him too," I tell him. The king growls, and his lips press against mine hungrily.

CHAPTER

TWELVE

IVY

My bond flares to life as he presses his entire body against mine. His tongue dominates my mouth, tasting every inch, his skin against mine makes my whole body tingle, his scent invades my nose, and a purr escapes me as I kiss him back with the same desire. I want to mark him, the bond screaming for me to forever tie him to me. My canines slip out, nicking his lips, and he growls, rolling his hips against me when there is suddenly a knock on the door.

Kyson pulls his lips from mine and growls at the disturbance. I tilt my head to look at the door and sigh when he climbs off me to answer it. Kyson speaks in a hushed voice to someone before shutting the door and walking back over to me.

"What is it?" I ask, seeing the troubled expression on his face.

"Another body turned up?"

"A child?" I ask, but he shakes his head.

"No, a woman's body. I need to go speak with the pack who located the body."

"I'll come with you," I tell him, getting to my feet, but he shakes his head.

"I won't be gone long an hour tops; I am not going to the scene; I will let Damian handle that," Kyson tells me, and I sigh.

"It isn't something you want to see; I won't be very long. Eat. Hopefully, I will be back before you fall asleep. Dustin is outside the door, so if you need anything, just call out to him," Kyson tells me, then bends down and kisses the top of my head. He walks into the walk-in closet and pulls on a black top and leather jacket before leaving.

After he leaves, I eat my dinner, then grab the tablet to fiddle with the writing and reading apps. I really love playing with the text and voice commands. However, I have to call Dustin twice to fix the tablet when I go into something I can't get back out of.

Grabbing my dessert off the tray, I go to sit on the bed, my back aching from being hunched over sitting on the floor in front of the fire. But once again, I begin feeling sick. The bond has me yearning for my mate, and my whole body feels uncomfortable. I squirm, my stomach turning violently, making me run for the bathroom.

Sweat glistens on my skin as I break out in a cold sweat. Rinsing my mouth, I go to lie down and crawl under the blankets, shivering. Hours pass, and I can't sleep. Instead, I toss and turn until I hear the door open, and Kyson quietly enters the room. I have the lights off, hoping sleep will take me, only it never does. Kyson, noticing I am still awake, comes over and presses his hand to my head.

"You skin is warm," he murmurs. "Do you feel hot?"

I shake my head; I feel like I am freezing, despite the sweat drenching me.

"I tried to get back as soon as I could; I thought you were sick; you felt off through the bond. Must be your heat coming on," Kyson says, sniffing the air, and I watch his brows pinch together.

He looks confused. "You don't smell like you're coming into heat, and your scent isn't affecting me, though, strange," he mumbles to himself. I wrinkle my nose as he leans down, pressing his lips to mine, and he chuckles.

"Sorry, the Alpha I met with is a chain smoker," he says with a laugh.

"You smell like an ashtray," I tell him.

"I will go shower, but I think I might call in a doctor to check you over," he says. I shake my head, not wanting to be prodded and poked by any doctors or stuck with needles. Besides, I am sure it has to be the bond.

"No, I think it's the bond; I started feeling sick not long after you left," I murmur, trying to close my eyes, which feels scratchy, like sandpaper. Kyson growls and doesn't seem to like my answer but nods anyway.

"I will be quick," he whispers, and I nod to him, tugging the surrounding blankets higher, trying to warm up. Just as he is about to leave, I call back out, wanting to know about the girl who was found, remembering why he left in the first place.

"The woman?" I ask, and he stops and quickly sits back on the bed.

"A rogue again, however, this one we found ID on, or a form of ID anyway, a library card," Kyson answers.

"Was she a sex slave?"

"We aren't sure, but we think so. She had a heap of condoms in her handbag, a few miscellaneous items, and no wallet, but tucked in the back of her handbag; we found the library card, though it is rather old and in a different state."

"Next of kin?" I ask. Kyson shakes his head.

"Unsure. Damian is going to see if the library still exists. We only have a name. The card is really old, and we can only make out the first name, Blaire," he tells me, and I nod. The name doesn't ring a bell but I still feel sad for the woman.

He hops off the bed and makes his way into the bathroom, and the light hurts my eyes, making me squint at the brightness. Yet, the motion of him climbing off the bed makes me queasy as his weight makes it dip and spring back.

I lay there for a few minutes until his scent wafts out the open door with the steam. I wiggle to the edge because my instincts want me to go to him. My teeth chatter and goosebumps spread across my body the moment I pull the blanket off. My hair is drenched in sweat and sticking to my face.

I climb out of bed and stagger to the bathroom, wanting his scent, knowing it would reduce the churning in my stomach. The bond is crying out for him to ease my discomfort. My vision blurs as I make my way into the bathroom and black dots flicker before my eyes. I can hear my own breathing in my head, each breath becoming harder to take as I force myself to breathe. Stumbling almost blindly with my hands outstretched when someone's hands grip my arms. Tingles spread up my arms.

"Azalea?" Kyson calls and I clutch my stomach.

"I don't feel good," I tell him, my voice barely audible to my own ears, and bile pools and fills my mouth. The taste is terrible, and I gag, throwing up everywhere. Kyson jumps, not expecting it when a wave of dizziness washes over me and everything goes black. Just before I lose consciousness, I hear the King scream out for Dustin then I no longer feel anything.

THIRTEEN

KYSON

I pace outside the small infirmary; the doctor kicked me out because I was becoming aggressive as they poked, prodded, and jabbed her with needles.

Dustin is inside with her because I feel like wringing the doctor's neck every time she cries out. Especially since he shoves a tube down her throat to pump her stomach, and she wakes abruptly. It caused me to shift and grab the man. Seeing the frantic look on her face pushed me over the edge. She kept slipping in and out of consciousness and freaking out each time she came to.

"Any news yet?" Damian asks as I pace out in front of the door. I growl and shake my head as he approaches, and Damian sighs.

"They locked you out?"

I nod, too angry to answer when the brown door suddenly opens, and the pack doctor from the small town outside the castle gates walks out. He scrubs his hand down his face and through his mud-brown hair. The doctor watches me warily, straightening his white coat before he steps closer to Damian. His eyes glaze over as he mindlinks my Beta. He is clearly frightened while I am in my Lycan form; however, I am focused and in control. So it irritates me that he addressed Damian first when she is my mate.

"Are you sure?" Damian asks him.

"Positive, her blood work showed it, and so did her stomach contents."

I snarl, making Doctor Rick jump. He hides behind my Beta, his eyes wide with terror.

"What's wrong with her?" I demand. Dr. Rick hands me her paperwork with shaky hands, and I snatch it, staring at it, but it looks gibberish to me.

"Fucking answer, me," I snarl, shaking the papers at him, commanding him.

"She has ingested poison. We found it in her system, my King," he stutters.

"Poison? Someone poisoned my mate?" I ask, startled. I wasn't expecting that to be the answer.

"Kyson, calm down and keep your head," Damian snaps at me, and I glare at him. How could he say that when someone tried to poison his queen?

"What sort of poison?" Damian asks.

"Water hemlock and wolfsbane are in her system. You should check who is working in the kitchens or, more importantly, with the Queen's food. I sent Dustin up earlier to check your food, my King. Your personal food was untouched, but the bowl of fruit had traces of both plants in it. Azalea was targeted specifically," Doctor Rick tells me.

"I want all the kitchen staff to be in the kitchen within ten minutes. Send all of my guards to wake them and bring them down; no one is to be unaccounted for," I tell Damian.

"I will send out the alert," Damian says, and I watch his eyes glaze over as he mindlinks our men.

"Is she awake?" I ask, turning my attention to the doctor.

"No, my King. We have given her something to counteract the

poison. She should be fine within a couple of hours," the doctor tells me.

"Tell Dustin to remain with her until I return," I tell him, stalking off toward the kitchen where everyone will be meeting. I am absolutely furious, and I now had a traitor among my staff, one that had tried to hurt Azalea. Now I have to figure out who is overseeing her food. They will pay.

Clarice is the first to walk in, rubbing her eyes and dressed in her floral nightgown. Her hair is in rollers; she yawns before flicking the lights on and jumping when she notices me standing in the kitchen center, leaning against one of the steel tables.

My anger refuses to let me shift back, and I can see she is startled by my presence but regains her composure quickly. All the guards were warned not to tell the kitchen staff about the meeting. Damian quickly marks her name off as he steps in with the folder containing a list of the kitchen employees, but Clarice is far from a suspect. I trusted Clarice with my life and Azalea's, but she will be able to tell me who cooked our meals tonight and who was stationed on since she handled the kitchen rosters.

"My King? What is this about?" she asks, looking at me worriedly, trying to fight the yawn I see taking over her. She fails to contain it and covers her mouth, yawning loudly.

Damian waves her forward to speak with her while I watch the 30 kitchen staff members file into the room wearing pajamas, looking confused and dazed at the late-night wake-up call. They all line up, the room filling quickly with the number of people in here.

My personal guard is stationed by all entrances, blocking the exits. They spoke among themselves in hushed whispers, trying to figure out what was going on.

"Who was responsible for cooking the King and Queen's meals tonight?"

"Me, always me Beta Damian. I don't let anyone else cook for them. Why?" Clarice asks.

"Azalea's food was poisoned, and we don't think it was the first time. She was sick also on the night of her shift, they found water hemlock and wolfsbane in her system."

"Is she alright?" Clarice asks, becoming instantly alert, and her eyes flick in my direction, the fear on her face was palpable, and her eyes glassy as if she is holding back tears.

"Yes, but we need to know who was in the kitchen when you were cooking, who had access to her food," Damian explains. She nods, looking worried.

"Only eight of us," she answers quickly.

"Point them out for me," Damian tells her, and she grabs the staff schedule off the wall, which had everyone's timesheets. She points out everyone, and I let Damian interview them while the others stand around nervously before I command them one by one to answer. I hope to weed out any liars, but we find none. Besides Clarice and Azalea's guards, no one has gone near her food. Turning to Clarice, since she is the only one I had not commanded to answer, she sighs.

FOURTEEN

KYSON

"It's okay, my King. I know you have to," she says, focusing on me. I feel terrible. Clarice has been with me since I was a kid, and I knew she never would, but I wasn't going to trust blindly when it came to my mate. My guards are under oath to protect my mate and future Queen and couldn't go against the promise; there was no way they could even if they wanted to.

"I'm sorry, but I have to be sure," I tell her. Clarice is under oath, but none of the staff know that. I need eyes on the staff, and I know no one would tell her anything or confide in her if they knew. I trust her, but for appearance's sake I have no choice, and she nods her head in understanding. Clarice is the oldest of my staff, besides Tanner, the gardener. My command drops all the kitchen staff in the room to their knees because they cannot fight it. A King's command is excruciating when used at full strength.

I swallow and nod to Damian, who grips her arms, so she doesn't hit the ground as the rest did. He looks away, and I knew he feels terrible. He loves Clarice like a mother. I am sure everyone in the castle does, since she raised most of us when she was still my nanny when I was a small boy. She has been by my side since I was a toddler. She raised half of those here in this room alongside me, everyone here taking their parents' places within the castle walls when they retired.

"Did you poison my mate?" I ask her, commanding the answer out of her. She shrieks and drops, but Damian grips her tighter. Tears spring in my eyes, and she shakes her head, gasping.

"No, my King," she rasps out.

"Do you know who did it?" I ask, and she screams, the sound so agonizing some of the staff break down, and others cover their ears. I cup her face in my hands and brush her tears away with my thumbs.

"No, my King," she answers.

"Do you suspect who might have tried?" I ask her, tears slipping down my cheeks, and she cries out before looking around at her kitchen staff.

"No, my King."

I sigh, dropping the command. She pants, her face flushed, trying to catch her breath, and Damian rubs her arms.

"It's okay, son. I know you had to," she whispers, clutching my hands in her shaking ones. Her words don't make me feel any better about using it on her.

"When I find out who did it, I will not just punish them for what they did to Azalea; they will get double for making me hurt the woman who raised me," I assure her. She nods, and Trey rushes over, grabbing her arms. Damian lets her go before getting her a glass of water and helping her hold the cup to her lips so she can drink.

"Help her back to her room," I tell Trey, and he nods his head quickly.

"One minute," I say, stopping him.

"All the food. Where have the orders been going out to?" I ask her.

"The fruit is from here, obviously; the rest are ordered in from town and the usual shipments we receive," she answers. She points a shaking finger toward the back wall.

"All order forms are pinned over there, Kyson," she says. A few of the kitchen staff gasp at the casual way she addresses me. In front of the staff, Clarice always called me by my title except when Azalea was around or my guards. Clarice recognizes what she did and quickly corrects herself, but I shake my head.

"You know you can call me anything you want, Clarice," I tell her.

"I know," she says, and the kitchen staff looks relieved that she isn't being punished for it. Not that I ever would punish her for the casual use of my name or anyone for that matter, not that I would tell them that. Everyone slips up from time to time but considering the woman who used to change my diapers when I was a baby, Clarice had earned her the right to call me whatever she wanted and has never been afraid to scold me either.

Damian fetches the paperwork down and the kitchen inventory lists from the noticeboard at the back of the kitchen where Clarice pointed.

"Everyone is dismissed for now," I tell them, allowing them back to bed. Damian hands the documents to me, and I shake my head. "You handle it; I want to go check my mate," I say, and he nods before following me out and back to the infirmary.

When I enter, I see Dustin sitting beside her in a chair while holding her hand, rubbing circles on its back with his thumb. He quickly stands, but I shake my head. He looks terrible, and I know guilt is eating at him.

"Has she woken up yet?" I ask him.

"Briefly, she asked for you," he answers, and I nod, brushing her hair from her face.

"Did you find who did it?" he asks, and I shake my head.

"No, but until I do..."

"Until we do, I will be cooking all the King's and Queen's meals," Damian says, cutting me off. I was about to say I would do it.

"I will be. You are to stay with our Queen at all times."

"Fine, you're a better cook than me anyway," I tell him, and he chuckles before sitting at the desk in the corner, going over the

71

paperwork he retrieved from the kitchen. I look down at Azalea, and my body starts relaxing. I suddenly shift back abruptly. Dustin clears his throat, averting his gaze before standing up.

"I will get you some clothes," he says, exiting quickly. Damian laughs.

"The only time I see that man blush is when one of us stands naked in front of him," Damian says, unfazed by nudity. Not like we hadn't seen each other plenty of times before. I am confident every person within the castle grounds had caught sight of me naked at some point. I take his seat before grabbing her hand and kissing it.

CHAPTER
FIFTEEN

G ANNON

Liam agreed to come with me. I had to make sure whoever I took with me had a strong stomach to handle what I have planned for the bastard that touched my Abbie.

Liam is part of the King's Royal Guard, and the man has an iron gut since he is the King's executioner. Liam is like a ghost, half the time you don't realize he is there; the man is silent as the night when he wants to be. He is also just as fucked up in the head as me, probably why we get along so well.

He is also the only person who knew of my mate. Liam is like a brother to me, he is older, not by much, but we grew up together, and he was raised by Clarice, just like most of us guards in the castle.

But just like Liam, I never speak about my past. It haunts me, but out of everyone, Liam and I have no secrets between us; he even helped me cover up what I did.

Kyson is aware that something had happened, yet I don't think he truly knows what or who she was to me. Or if he did, he never mentioned it or acknowledged it. One thing I do like about the King's royal guard, we all grew up together. It's why the king trusts us, we all know each other's secrets mostly, we definitely know the king's. We all know Liam's; it's why no matter how unhinged he becomes, the King can never turn his back on him.

Kyson, Damian, and Liam and I are best friends, but I know even Kyson and Damian have their limits. They would look at me poorly if they know what I did, especially after what I did to her, so I never told them. How I survived, I'll never understand. Most Lycans die without their mate or are driven insane, yet still, I'm alive, that's if you call my existence living. For so long, I have purely existed, my life holding no meaning until Abbie came along.

However, I am pretty sure Damian and the King suspected something was up because I never showed interest in looking for my mate, and that was because I had already found her.

I met Sia a year before Claire died, and she was a normal she-wolf. I thought it was a mistake, Lycans aren't usually mated to common werewolves. She rejected me the same day I met her. The only issue was that Lycans can't be rejected. The bond doesn't just go away for us. The bond doesn't end until one is dead. Werewolves can reject each other. While it's painful for them, the bond eventually severs.

Even so, it took years after her death for the bond to die out completely, something I never thought would happen. I assumed I was stuck with longing for a bond that didn't want me and was dead and buried for her betrayal. A betrayal I couldn't look past. I held out hope she would come to her senses. That was when I learned werewolves could reject their mates. That was one difference between our species that became so obvious to me the day she did it.

Ironically, she could reject me and feel nothing toward me while I would be left pining for her and feeling her betrayal, and in some cases, it can kill us. After 2 years of it, I killed her. Liam helped me destroy the evidence and I know Kyson and Damian would have forgiven me for it or convinced me to hold off longer, but I didn't want their pity; I didn't want their concern when it wasn't needed; I had it handled. And the King was grieving his sister.

At least I thought I did. It made me cold and unfeeling, and I detached from everyone. The only time I felt anything was when Kyson would send me to do the jobs nobody wanted, and usually, Liam came with me for those jobs; I relished it, relished their screams, and eventually grew an appetite for it.

Then Abbie came along, I didn't want her screams; I wanted her. I wanted her love, and I had never wanted another woman since Sia and was content forever to be alone. Yet, she stirred up feelings I thought I was no longer capable of. From the moment she came into my quarters accidentally, and an obsession was born, one in which I wasn't sure was healthy but still better than the void I have felt before she came into my life.

"So, we are going back for that headmistress?" Liam asks finally, something he doesn't do frequently. I look over at the man, surprised that he asked anything at all. He has a massive scar down one side of his face that went from his hairline to his chin, though it was barely visible. Liam is almost blind in that eye, which is funny considering he is our best gunman. Not that we had much use for guns, but they made things easier than risking the King when he traveled.

Like the rest of us Lycan men, he appears to be in his mid-thirties.

"Her and another," I answer him as he unrolls his knife pouch to make sure he has all his trusty knives. The man has a knife fetish.

"Who else?" he asks as he runs his thumb down the blade and lets it slice his thumb as he tests how sharp it is.

"The butcher when we find out who he is."

"A butcher?" he chuckles. "Well, that is interesting. I wonder how he will feel when he realizes it will be his meat you're cutting into," Liam chuckles, glancing at me then smirking.

"So the Alpha and his mutt son know we are coming?" Liam asks.

"Nope, but I have the paperwork if they kick up a fuss."

"To bring him in?" he asks, I snort and smile. He knows if I'm hunting, and he is with me, this isn't a catch and release mission.

"Well, I suppose they wouldn't have sent you if it was as simple as taking them in," he says, rolling the pouch back up.

"So, what did he do to the King?" Liam asks.

"Not the King, to Abbie," I explain, and he exhales, pushing his fringe from his eyes and turning in his chair to look at me.

"That's your girl, right? The one you buy that candy for all the time?"

"Yep, when I get her back," I tell him, and I will get her back even if I have to go behind Kyson's back; I wasn't losing her. For now, though, I will wait like he asks to see what he comes up with.

I know he will have to, for Ivy. I heard the call go out earlier in the night about her title change, yet I am used to calling her Ivy. The King likes to pretend he is in control, yet I know he would allow her anything she requested if she batted her eyelashes at him. She will learn he is putty in her hands. She just needs to recognize that, which is precisely why I let it slip about Abbie. Kyson can deny me, but he won't deny her for long.

Going at Kyson headstrong won't get her anywhere, but she has other ways to get what she wants. She just needs to come out of her shell and play on that, which I know Kyson is dreading when she figures that out.

He knows he is screwed when she does, especially with her bloodline. Landeenas were known to have certain gifts, so it would be interesting to see if she inherited any of those traits. She has her mother's eyes, so it will be interesting to see if she receives her mother's abilities or if she will inherit her father's. Or both? Only time will tell. But if she inherits either, she'll be a force to reckon with. The Azures and Landeenas were the two original kingdoms, and they were not just King's and Queen's they were so much more. Queen is not a title fit for Ivy, and when she realizes that Kyson is in trouble.

"So, what did this butcher do?" Liam asks. I growl at his words, and he nods, casting him a warning look.

"Enough said," he says. We spend the rest of the drive in silence. The long, windy roads are boring, and I pull over and swap with Liam when I feel myself nodding off. By the time we arrive, it is the early morning hours, the sun is just creeping above the trees of the sleepy town. A town I am about to wake with a monster's screams.

CHAPTER
SIXTEEN

G ANNON

Liam's forceful smack against my chest jolts me awake, instantly alert as I catch sight of the town limits unfolding before us. "Orphanage first," I command, and he nods, deftly steering the car towards our destination. Leaning over into the back seat, I extract my jacket from the bag, as a chill lingers in the morning air. We pull up in front of the dilapidated building.

The orphanage, a crumbling structure on the brink of condemnation, had been modified to accommodate the old hag's wheelchair-bound existence after our last visit. Today, however, she would no longer need to fret about her future, for hers would come to an end.

Liam pulls over to the curb, and I step out of the car, closing the door with a gentle click. The children remain asleep, their absence evident in the stillness that permeates the premises. They are all tucked away in their beds. I effortlessly hop over the small brick fence that encloses the front yard, while Liam opens the trunk.

"No need for those," I caution him, considering the presence of innocent children within these walls.

"Then why are we here?" he queries.

"Grabbing the old bat, getting a name and leaving," I tell him, and he sighs but shuts the trunk. "I'm still bringing my knives just in case," he mutters.

As I approach the entrance, I rap on the door, waiting in vain for a response. It is early; perhaps Mrs. Daley is the sole adult present. However, sneaking around to the back of the building, I discover that the door has been left unlocked — an oversight on their part. Stepping inside, I notice that it is colder within the orphanage than it is outside.

"Fuck, it's like the arctic in here," Liam snarls.

"I presume she no longer occupies an upper-level room," I remark, eyeing the worn spiral staircase.

"Not unless the old bat sprouted wings and learned to fly," Liam chuckles.

"Oh, she will fly alright," I tell him, walking through the bottom level, looking for where she may have had her room moved to. It was the sounds of banging around that alerted me to which one. It sounds like she has fallen out of bed, and her annoying screeching voice as she curses makes my upper lip pull back over my teeth as I push open the door. The room stinks of piss and shit.

"Fuck me, we haven't even touched her, and she already shit herself," Liam chuckles, and her head snaps up to look at us from where she was trapped beside her bed, her wheelchair overturned. Her eyes go wide, and she cowers away.

"Haven't you done enough?" she says, visibly shaking.

"Nope, but I will make it quick. All I need is a name, and address," I tell her, gripping her shoulders while Liam turns the wheelchair upright. I lift her, dropping her into the seat, and she clutches the armrests so tightly her knuckles turn white.

"How about a nice cup of tea, love? You look rather parched. I make an outstanding brew," Liam says, grabbing the handles and steering her out.

"There are children here," she stammers, flinching as she passes me when I hold the door open for them.

"Well, what would an orphanage be without children?" I retort, trailing behind as Liam leads her into the kitchen. He glides around the space with practiced ease, his theatrics serving to alleviate her anxiety — a prelude to her impending demise.

"What have I done this time? What did the King order you to do to me?" she asks, her lips quivering.

Liam chuckles, finding an apron hanging by the stove and putting it on before flicking the kettle on. "The children will be up any minute; I have to start making their breakfast soon," she claims. Liam snorts.

"You, you can't even reach the bench. What use would you be in a kitchen?" Liam asks her, and her eyes prick with tears.

"Regardless, today will mark the end of your suffering. Answer truthfully, and I will make it swift. Fail to do so," Liam interrupts, swiftly plunging a knife into her hand, his other hand clamping over her mouth as she gasps in horror.

"Understand?" I inquire, folding my arms across my chest, my glare fixed on her. She wheezes, her withered face turning crimson as she stares at her hand, the knife protruding through her flesh and impaling the wooden armrest.

"Oh, right. Almost forgot," Liam remarks, yanking the blade free.

"Ah-ah! No need for that. You're a big girl," Liam admonishes her as she opens her mouth to scream, wielding the knife before her face. He proceeds to wipe it clean on the apron tied around his waist. "I should get myself one of these," he muses, admiring the floral pattern.

"Do you have one with skulls instead of flowers? Not that I'm complaining, though," he adds cheekily.

Mrs. Daley shakes her head, fresh tears streaming down her cheeks as her mouth hangs agape. She bears an uncanny resemblance to those carnival clowns with gaping mouths waiting to catch balls.

"Never mind then; this one suits me just fine," Liam taunts, wiggling his jean-clad behind in front of the frail woman. "Does it make my ass look big?" he jests, prompting me to shake my head, attempting to stifle my laughter as he parades around the kitchen. She shakes her head in response.

"Well, that was a lie, wasn't it? No matter; I'll let it slide. One lump of sugar or two?" he asks, receiving only wide-eyed silence in return.

"You strike me as someone who prefers two. Let's make it three; you seem like a bitter old bitch," he remarks, turning back to prepare the coffee.

Once Liam finishes brewing the drinks, he hands me mine, and I take a sip, observing Mrs. Daley wince as he thrusts the cup into her injured hand.

"Bottoms up; it's piping hot. We wouldn't want it to go cold," he remarks, sipping his own coffee. "Ah, now that's a fine blend. What brand is this?" he inquires, glancing back at the counter where an expensive-looking jar is displayed.

"Hmm, where did you order this from?" he probes.

"Online," she stammers.

"Good. Write down the website before I end your life," he commands. Mrs. Daley whimpers, pointing to a card affixed to the fridge's cork-board. Liam strides over and plucks it off.

"Well, that was easy," he remarks, slipping the card into his pocket alongside the coffee jar's label. Meanwhile, Mrs. Daley sips her coffee as if it might somehow delay her inevitable fate. In an effort to entertain ourselves, Liam engages her in idle conversation while I finish my drink. Placing my mug in the sink, I wash it before setting it out to dry. Turning around, I lean against the counter, watching as the woman trembles like a leaf, her eyes fixated on Liam's every move.

CHAPTER
SEVENTEEN

G ANNON

Liam leans back against the fridge, a wicked grin spreading across his face. "So, I hear you have a mighty fine butcher in town," he taunts, causing Mrs. Daley's hand to freeze midair as she goes to take a sip from her cup. I observe her closely, noticing the sudden gulp that betrays her nerves.

"Now that looks like a guilty face, now doesn't, brother?" Liam says, nudging me.

"Very guilty. Do you have something to confess, love, want to get it off your chest before you meet your maker?" Liam taunts.

Caught off guard by Liam's comment, Mrs. Daley stammers

"What do you mean?" she says, and I click my tongue.

Her fake confusion only fuels our amusement.

I decide to play along, my voice dripping with phony innocence. "Oh, we were just hoping for a friendly chat, a little slaughter, but if you insist on being difficult, I suppose a little practice won't hurt." I extend my hand towards Liam, silently requesting his knives.

Liam, always prepared, retrieves a rolled-up leather pouch from the pocket of his jacket and hands it to me. I unravel it on the

wooden bench, revealing an array of gleaming blades. With deliberate movements, I picked up each knife, showing them to Mrs.
Daley. The sweat began to glisten on her forehead as her eyes darted
anxiously between Liam and me. Liam's sadistic smile grows wider,
and I turn my attention back to Mrs. Daley.

"Now, which one shall we use?" I inquire calmly. She shakes her
head vehemently, clutching her mug tightly in her trembling hands.
Liam takes the opportunity to snatch the cup from her grasp.

"Come on now, no need to be coy," Liam sneers. "Confess your
sins."

"I...I never... It was just that one time... I had to feed the children,
funds were low," Mrs. Daley stammers, her words tumbling out in a
rush of desperation. "She probably doesn't even remember..."

A cold smile plays upon my lips as I tighten my grip on the
boning knife. I twirl it between my fingers, relishing in the weight
and balance of the blade. Slowly, I move closer to Mrs. Daley, the
sound of her racing heartbeat filling the room. The blood from her
injured hand pools at her feet, a stark reminder of the power we hold
over her. With deliberate precision, I place the back of the blade
against her cheek, tracing a chilling path down to her chin. Tilting
her head up to meet my gaze, I hold her captive with my cold, gray
eyes.

"Name or the ear goes first, then the toes, then I will de-glove
your hand," I tell her calmly., my voice laced with a dangerous edge. I
have every intention of following through with my threats if she
refuses to comply. The horror in her eyes told me she knows this too.

"Doyle Mathews," she blurts out, her voice tinged with fear.

"And his address?" I press, my grip on the knife tightening ever
so slightly.

"3 Lincoln Way," she answers, her voice barely above a whisper.

"Any wife or children we should be aware of?" I continue, but she
shakes her head, tears welling in her eyes.

"Figures a pig like that would have no family," Liam sneers, his
contempt evident in his tone.

"Go check it out and load him up," I tell Liam, who ducks out quickly. When he leaves, I clean up the blood on the floor and wrap Mrs. Daley's hand in case any of the children wake up.

"Go check it out and bring him back," I command Liam. With a nod, he swiftly exits the room. As soon as he is gone, I turn my attention to Mrs. Daley, efficiently cleaning up the blood and tending to her injured hand.

Twenty minutes pass before the shrill ring of my phone pierces the silence. Pulling it out from my pocket, I answer the call just as a little girl descends the stairs, rubbing her sleepy eyes. Hastily grabbing a tea towel, I discreetly cover Mrs. Daley's wrapped hand.

"Yep," I answer the call, watching the child as she walks down the stairs. She looks up, hearing my voice, and I wave to her before kicking the wheelchair. Mrs. Daley smiles fakery and waves to her, earning a strange look from the child, who waves briefly as she steps off the last step.

"We've got him, and I'm on my way back," Liam's voice crackled through the phone.

"The trunk?" I inquire, anticipation coursing through my veins.

"Nope, he showed me to his store. He's tied up in the cold room," Liam chuckles wickedly.

"Even better," I respond, ending the call. Now it is time to focus on the little girl before me.

"What's your name?" I ask gently, bending down to her level. She hesitates for a moment before answering.

"Kimmy, sir," she replies, her voice filled with a mixture of shyness and curiosity. I scoop her up into my arms, holding her securely.

"Are you hungry, Kimmy? What do you usually have for breakfast?" I inquire, noting the furrow in her brows and the rumble of her empty stomach.

"We haven't had breakfast since Abbie and Ivy left, sir. You came with the King?" she whispers into my ear, her innocent question catches me off guard. I nod solemnly, glancing at Mrs. Daley, who lowers her head in shame. A low growl escapes my throat as I redirect my attention to Kimmy. Her hair resembles a tangled haystack atop her head, some strands matted and neglected for far too long.

"What did they usually make for breakfast?" I probe gently, hoping to ease the hunger that gnaws at her small frame, that's if any food is in this place, the cupboards looked pretty bare.

"Pancakes, but Mrs. Daley can't get the flour from the basement. The bag is too heavy for us to lift, we did try though," Kimmy explains.

"Very well, I'll fetch the flour. You go and do whatever it is you kids do in the morning," I instruct, gently setting her back on her feet.

"Can we watch cartoons?" she asks before her eyes go to Mrs. Daley, who purses her lips.

"Yep, and make sure you turn the volume all the way up," I tell her, just as a few more kids start rushing down.

Kimmy scampers off to join the other children, more little ones begin descending the stairs, their excited chatter filling the air when Kimmy tells them they are having breakfast this morning.

Within minutes, the room buzzes with activity as I make my way down to the basement. The sight that greets me is chaotic and an utter mess. Flour is spilled haphazardly across the floor, evidence of their futile attempts to scoop it out with cups. Shaking my head at their efforts, I grab a fresh, 50-pound bag of flour and climb the steps.

Liam reenters just as I drop the bag onto the bench, his eyes widening at the sight. "What's with the flour? Planning to batter the old hag?" he jests, a mischievous glint in his eyes.

A chuckle escapes my lips as I reply, "No, Liam, the kids are hungry." Turning my attention back to Mrs. Daley, I ask, "When does your staff usually arrive?"

"Katrina comes in at lunch," she responds hesitantly.

"Call her in early," I instruct firmly. Liam hands her his phone, and she dials the number obediently. As she carries out our orders, Liam takes it upon himself to count the number of heads in the room, determining how many pancakes would be needed.

"Who wants pancakes?" I hear him scream out and all the kids cheer.

"Alright, alright, settle down. Uncle Liam is going to make them, so settle down and watch your dancing puppet show," I hear him say. Suddenly, a little boy stumbles down the stairs, a tattered blanket trailing behind him.

"103, fuck me, that's a lot of pancakes," Liam says, coming back in. Liam's gaze shifts to him, and I catch a whiff of something familiar in the air. A rogue. Mrs. Daley growls softly before realizing who stands beside her. She flinches away, cowering in fear, and the young boy mirrors her reaction, whimpering as he tries to escape back up the stairs. Acting instinctively, I reach out and grab the back of his pants, plucking him off the steps. He can't have been more than three years old, dressed in worn-out pajama pants and no shirt. Goosebumps cover his exposed skin, and he clings desperately to his dirt-stained blanket.

CHAPTER
EIGHTEEN

GANNON

The rogue boy's little arm has a deep, purplish bruise, causing him to wail in fear as I take hold of him, making me wonder if it is fresh since my grip appears to hurt him. "Shh, shh. What's your name?" I whisper, attempting to soothe him. His gaze shifts anxiously towards Mrs. Daley, who sits nearby, emanating an air of intimidation directed at the child. The boy appears fragile, his emaciated frame attesting to a lack of proper care. Hollow cheeks and sunken eyes accentuated his desolate countenance, while his matted, knotted black curls cascaded down his shoulders.

"He doesn't speak," a young girl named Kimmy interjects, emerging from the dimly lit room in her tattered pajamas. She seems to be one of the older children here, a fact that struck me as peculiar because where are the older children?

However, seeing a rogue child is more bizarre, and I have a feeling it is just for show in case the King stops by. One thing is apparent - none of these children are cared for properly, and that really grinds my gears.

"Is he unable to speak, or does he not know how?" I inquire, my gaze shifting between Kimmy and Mrs. Daley. Kimmy shrugs, her eyes darting nervously towards Mrs. Daley. It is evident that she fears the woman.

"Mrs. Daley is leaving today; she's retiring. You can speak freely now; she won't harm you," I reassured Kimmy. Biting her lip, she hesitates before scratching at the tangled strands of her hair.

"I overheard Mrs. Daley arguing with Katrina. Katrina wanted to take him and his brother, but Mrs. Daley refused," Kimmy divulges.

"He has a brother?" I ask with surprise.

"Had; we haven't seen him in two days. He bit Mrs. Daley when she struck Oliver," Kimmy explains, pointing towards the boy in my arms.

"His name is Oliver?" I confirm receiving a nod from Kimmy.

"And the brother's name?"

"Logan, sir," she replies.

"What about Katrina? Does she harm you?" I press further. Kimmy shakes her head, her gaze darting nervously towards Mrs. Daley, who stares vacantly out of the window above the sink. She knows she has made a grave mistake and her death now will be painful.

"Mrs. Daley had the butcher hurt Katrina for defending them. He broke her arm, but she's okay now," Kimmy reveals, her voice laced with fear.

"Kimmy, could you find some clothes and socks for Oliver?" I request, to which she nods, extending her arms to take him. He timidly moves towards her, and she leads him upstairs while I maneuver Mrs. Daley's wheelchair with my foot.

"Where is his brother?" I demand, my tone sharp as I confront the withered old hag.

"The kid is nothing but trouble; he bit me like a savage," she sneers defiantly.

"Where is the boy?" I snarl, my patience waning. Liam glares at her, his knife twirling ominously between his fingers as a silent warning.

"You better answer him. We have no tolerance for child abusers, and you know that," Liam cautions, causing Mrs. Daley to gulp audibly.

"He's in the laundry room outside," she finally admits reluctantly. Fueled by anger, I storm outside searching for the room, eventually discovering it hidden behind the shed. The sound of whimpering grows louder as I approach the wooden door. Pushing it open, my eyes fall upon another small boy huddled inside a cage beneath a bench next to the washer. A surge of fury courses through me as I crouch down. He appears to be around the same age as Kimmy, his frail form shivering from the cold, covered with numerous bruises and signs of mistreatment.

"Did Mrs. Daley do this to you?" I ask gently, not wanting to scare him further. The boy shakes his head, retreating to the back of the cage.

"I won't harm you; I am here to help," I reassure him.

"My brother, please help my brother," he whimpers, flinching away as I break the front door of his cage open. Taking a step closer, I extend my hand towards him.

"Who put you in here? Was it Katrina? I promise I won't let them harm you," I say, removing my jacket and draping it around his emaciated frame. He hesitates for a moment before finally placing his hand in mine, allowing me to pull him out of the cramped enclosure.

"How old are you?" I ask softly.

"Eight, sir," he replies meekly. Nodding in understanding, I notice his bare feet and swiftly scoop him up into my arms.

"So was it Katrina?"

"No, she tried to help me."

"Who brought you out here, then? Daley couldn't have. She wouldn't have got down the back steps."

"The Butcher did, sir," he says as he stares at me, his entire body trembling.

"Come on, you and your brother are coming home with me; I

won't hurt you, but I need you to come inside where it is warm; Liam is inside. You will like Liam; he is making pancakes," I tell him.

I carry him inside before stepping into the kitchen.

"Where's Daley?" I inquire, noting her absence and Liam turns to face me, his eyes take in the boy, but he says nothing about his state.

"She went to get more flour," Liam informs me, offering a sly wink.

I smirk, taking Logan towards the living room, where I wrap him in the warmth of a blanket retrieved from the couch. Returning outside, I gather firewood and stoke all the fireplaces, trying to get some heat flowing throughout the space. The aroma of pancakes wafts through the air. Just as I finish setting up the living room fireplace, a woman who must be Katrina walks in, her presence announced by a sniff of the air. She glances at me nervously, her gaze fixates on my face.

"Who are you?" she inquires, her voice tinged with apprehension. Catching a whiff of her fear, I glance at her.

"I'm Gannon. Liam is out there. I assume you're Katrina?" I respond, observing her nod in confirmation as I set the fire poker down.

"Where's Mrs. Daley?" she asks nervously.

"In the basement, getting flour for the pancakes" I inform her, prompting a flicker of concern to cross her features. She opens her mouth as if to speak, but abruptly halts upon spotting Logan by the fire, causing her eyes to widen with surprise. Rushing towards him, she attempts to grab both him and Oliver. Instinctively, I reach out and grasp her arm.

"I won't harm them; I'm not like Daley," she assures me firmly, I release my grip. She hurriedly tends to the boys. Letting out a sigh, I make my way towards the door.

"Assist Liam in feeding the children; consider yourself promoted to headmistress," I instruct Katrina, receiving a nod of acknowledgment from her. As I walk towards the kitchen, the anguished groans and cries emanating from the basement grow louder.

"Do you need any help?" Liam offers, his body covered in a dusting of flour and pancake batter covering his hands.

"Nope," I reply curtly, seizing the knives from the counter before swinging open the basement door. The sound of the radio suddenly fills the kitchen as Liam switches it on, music blaring from its speakers.

Descending the stairs, I discover Mrs. Daley sprawled on the ground, desperately attempting to crawl away. Her legs tangled in the wheelchair, she claws at the floor in a futile attempt to escape.

"Change of plans. I want to hear you scream," I proclaim, my voice dripping with venom. Reaching down, I seize her hair and yank her head back by her hair. "And trust me, you will scream," I snarl, relishing the fear in her gaze.

CHAPTER
NINETEEN

ABBIE

Two long and agonizing days have passed since Kade abandoned me in this wretched brothel, leaving me to rot in the depths of my despair. Each day, he comes to torment me, a cruel reminder of the power he holds over my life and the little I can do about it. So, when the door swings open once again, I am not entirely surprised to see a woman step inside. However, my surprise quickly turns to shock when I recognize her as the woman who used to park outside my cabin.

Her heels click menacingly on the creaking floorboards as she makes her way towards me. Today, she wears a short black dress that clings to her every curve, the outline of her thong visible through the tight fabric. I avert my gaze, not wanting to subject myself to such a vulgar display. I can't help but wonder what purpose she serves here. Is she here to inject me with more of the vile substance that Kade has been using on me, so I can't shift? Or perhaps she has come to inflict some new form of torture upon me. I refuse to shed tears for her because by the sly smile on her face, she has come to witness my torment. She does not deserve the satisfaction.

Inwardly, I long for Blaire's return. I need reassurance that she is safe, I haven't seen her since that dreadful night when I was forcibly brought to this despicable place, yet I've heard whispers through the walls, and I can't get the sound of her screaming out of my head after Kade beat her when he was done with her that night. The woman crouches down beside me, her grip on my chin forcing me to meet her cold gaze. A sneer twists her lips as she shoves my face away with an air of distaste.

"Kade is on his way," she hisses, her voice dripping with malice. "And you better be on your best behavior for my husband."

I swallow hard, the sting of her words resonating deep within me. She's his wife? If she thinks I'll fight for him, she is wrong, she can have him. I want no part in the life she shares with that man, and I feel foolish for ever believing in the possibility of happiness or the strength of mate bonds.

"It seems that your precious friend, that bitch queen of yours, has been asking about you," she continues, her voice laced with venom. "You so much as breathe a word that jeopardizes the life I have with Kade, and it won't be him you need to fear. I'll order every pack warrior to tear through you, treating you like the home-wrecking whore you are."

A bitter laugh escapes my lips. Of course, Kade's wife would be just as depraved as he is. "It must have been quite a blow when you learned he had a mate," I retort, glaring defiantly at the woman.

Instantly, her hand strikes my cheek, the force of the blow causing me to grit my teeth in pain. And then she grabs hold of my hair, yanking my head back with a cruel force that makes me wince.

"Accidents happen, my dear," she whispers menacingly. "This is my pack. Kade is my mate. You will learn your place."

"My place isn't here," I spit, my voice filled with defiance. "Ivy will come for me."

She laughs, a sound devoid of any mirth, before tightening her grip around my throat. "Why do you think Kade is coming? To see you?" she taunts, clicking her tongue.

"Your friend won't be an issue after today. Kade is only keeping you around so he doesn't become weak. You would do well to remember that you are nothing to him—just a warm hole to fuck," she sneers, her words dripping with mockery.

"And what does that make you? His dishwasher?" I ask.

She grabs my hair and I grit my teeth.

Just as pain threatens to consume me, the door swings open once more, and his scent wafts towards me before I even lay eyes on him. A mixture of revulsion and an inexplicable longing washes over me as the bond recognizes him instantly. I despise the way he can still influence me, even now, when I hate the man more than anyone in this world.

"There are my girls, having a chat I see," Kade's voice echoes through the room as he saunters in, dressed in a tailored suit. The woman releases her grip on me and rises to her feet, a sickeningly sweet smile playing on her lips.

"Abbie dear, it seems you've met my wife Cassandra," he says, his voice dripping with possessiveness. He reaches out and brushes her hair off her shoulder before cupping her neck, his lips crashing against hers in a display of vulgar affection. I turn away, my heart aching at the pain that courses through my chest. Even after all he has done to me, I can't deny the hold he still has over my emotions, as much as I hate it.

"And now," Kade continues, venom lacing his words, "the Queen has decided she wants to video chat with you today. She found out about Cassandra, and you, my love, will convince her that everything is just peachy and that you are happy here."

With a firm grip on my arm, Kade yanks me to my feet. A flicker of excitement stirs within me. Nobody knows me better than Ivy. She knows my darkest secrets, my deepest fears. She will see through any facade Kade tries to make me put up.

He pushes me onto the bed and grips my face tightly. I struggle against his hold, tempted to sink my teeth into his filthy tongue when he forcefully kisses me. But I learned my lesson the hard way last night when he knocked me unconscious. My jaw still throbs from the blow.

"It won't work," I spit at him when he finally releases me.

"Oh, I had a feeling you would say that," Kade sneers as he whistles. A struggle ensues outside the room, accompanied by a woman's shrill cries and the desperate wails of a baby. My heart pounds in my chest as I rise to my feet, my eyes fixed on the woman being thrown to the floor, clutching a baby who couldn't have been more than a few months old. Anguish etches across her tear-streaked face, her mascara running down her cheeks, smearing her makeup.

I glare at the man who callously tosses her aside before turning my attention back to Kade. "I'll do it," I declare, my voice filled with determination.

"Now you will put on your best performance; Abbie, meet Stacey, Stacey, this Abbie," he says, and I swallow as he grips her hair, ripping her head back.

"Now, Stacey, Abbie over here is the one who decides if little Jacob here is going to get to live another," he says. Tears stream down the woman's face. The baby is bundled up, clutched in her arm, and tucked to her chest. Her mascara runs down her cheeks as she looks at me pleadingly. Her bright red hair stuck to her face as tears smudged her makeup and lines trekked into her foundation. "I'll do it!" I tell him as he moves to grab the child.

"You touch one hair on that baby or harm her in any way, and I will refuse to comply with anything you ask. Leave her be."

Kade's hand freezes in midair as he reaches for the boy in her arms. He stands there for a moment, clicking his tongue in frustration, before finally releasing the woman from his grasp. She crawls quickly towards me, clutching the baby tightly, seeking refuge at my feet. Kade snarls at her and moves to grab her, but I step in between them, shielding her from his reach.

"It seems you do have a backbone after all," Kade remarks with a twisted smile. "It will do you no good here. You fuck this up, you watch them die," he warns me.

95

"You harm them, and you do! I'll happily watch as your world crumbles around you," I warn him. I am the only thing standing between Ivy and the King's wrath. And if our roles were reversed, I know she would do the same.

Kade nods and looks at Cassandra, who smiles sweetly before tugging her handbag off her shoulder. She pulls a smaller bag out containing makeup. I sit on the edge of the bed, knowing exactly what will happen next. Mrs. Daley was good at this facade, too, when she wanted sponsors and had covered our scars plenty of times. If I can survive that bitch, I can survive anything.

Stacey cringes away from her, and Cassandra raises her hand to hit her when Stacey accidentally bumps into her. Rage courses through me, and I grip her wrist. We stand off for a few seconds. Cassandra is clearly shocked I would grab her, especially in front of Kade, who she was expecting to jump to her rescue, but he only chuckles.

"Now, now, ladies, no fighting," he says, sitting in the chair in the corner beside the bed.

"You don't want to jeopardize that future you want so badly, do you?" I ask her, and she glares at me.

"You are asking for death, girlie," she spits, yanking her arm away.

"Good thing I don't fear it, but I bet you do," I tell her, and she glares at me. I sit on the bed, and Kade clicks his fingers impatiently at her.

I shut down, letting her play dress-up, solely focused on keeping the woman at my feet and her baby safe from these monsters.

CHAPTER
TWENTY

A ZALEA

The jostling sensation of movement rouses me from my slumber, my eyelids fluttering open to take in the unfamiliar surroundings. As the fog of sleep dissipates, the memories of the previous night slowly trickle back into my consciousness. I find myself cradled in Kyson's arms as he carries me.

The warmth radiating from his body seeps into my bones, easing the residual wooziness that clings to me like a haze.

I release a shaky breath, my gaze meeting Kyson's intense eyes as he gazes down at me. With a gentle motion, he lifts me higher, his face burying in the crook of my neck as he inhales deeply. My hand instinctively finds its place on the side of his neck, fingers lightly grazing the skin, and a sense of calm washes over me. The wired and jittery feeling that had coiled within me begins to unwind, replaced by a soothing peace.

He moves me, allowing me to wrap my legs around his waist, and I laze against him.

"Thank god," Kyson breathes, his voice laced with relief and concern.

"I feel better," I murmur, a yawn escaping my lips. Yet beneath the surface, anger pulses through our bond, radiating from Kyson like an electric storm. Sensing the turmoil within him, I pull my face away from his neck to look at him, feeling his aura crackling with pent-up fury.

"What's wrong?" I inquire, my voice laced with genuine concern.

"Someone tried to poison you," Kyson reveals, his tone filled with determination. "I promise I will figure out who soon. Until then, you are to remain with Dustin or me."

Confusion knits my brows together as I try to comprehend his words. Why would someone want to harm me? I had done nothing to anyone here. Although the gravity of the situation should have sent shivers down my spine, a peculiar distraction captivates my thoughts. My instincts, normally so attuned to danger and survival, seem to be in a state of disarray. No matter how hard I try to focus on the gravity of the situation, all I can think about is the overwhelming desire to taste Kyson.

My instincts are going berserk. No matter how much I try to focus on what he was telling me, all I want to do is lick him.

Carrying me effortlessly, Kyson leads me to our bedroom. Though perfectly capable of walking on my own, an inexplicable yearning keeps me clinging to him, relishing in his warmth and intoxicating scent. My hand absently rubs the center of his chest, eliciting a chuckle from him.

"Something you want?" he asks, amusement etched into his features.

"You," I reply simply, my voice laced with need. My instincts swirl chaotically within me, demanding the presence of my mate. Before I can restrain myself, my teeth sink into his chest through his shirt, my claws finding purchase in his shoulder as others claw at his pec through the fabric.

A grunt escapes Kyson's lips as he hoists me higher, making me want to climb into his shirt.

Your scent is changing," he purrs, nipping at the mark on my neck as I continue to explore the taste of his skin. A shudder ripples through his body as he tightens his grip on me.

Finally stepping into our room, Kyson kicks the door shut with a deft movement of his foot. "You should rest; you had an eventful night, and Abbie will be calling this morning," he says, moving towards the bed and gently placing me down on its soft surface.

He attempts to stand up, but I swiftly wrap my legs around his waist, tugging him closer. My teeth break through his collarbone, drawing another growl from him as my teeth break his skin, and he starts to purr, the calling wrapping around me, and my claws slip out, shredding his shirt even more.

Kyson presses his weight down on me, the calling, the low rumble emanating from his chest as he rolls onto his back, pulling me on top of him. My lips trail over his chest, tracing a path of possessiveness, while his hands move with gentle precision up and down my arms and sides. I revel in the sensation of mauling him, my teeth seeking purchase wherever they can find it. His chin drops as I attack his neck, his stubble grazing my cheek, and a primal growl escapes me when he denies me the satisfaction of marking him.

"I thought you wanted to speak to Abbie?" he murmurs, kissing the side of my mouth. Abbie, it has something to do with Abbie and it's important; I just can't remember why. My tongue rolls over his chest, my hands clawing at his flesh.

"She should be calling soon, Azalea," he reminds me gently, his voice laced with patience and my teeth nip at him, making him groan.

Abbie...remember the thing about Abbie. What is it again? My tongue glides over his chest, soothing the marks I have left behind, while Kyson's scars remain.

A flicker of confusion passes through me as I realize that not all wounds heal at the same pace.

Yet is soon once again forgotten, my sole focus on my desperate need to mark him. I couldn't think of anything but wanting to crawl inside the man. Desire courses through me so strongly I can't think of anything else.

"Love, Abbie. She is calling soon," Kyson growls, nipping at my shoulder. I try to shake the fog, consuming me and muddling my thoughts. Kyson smashes me with the calling, and I melt against him, pressing my ear to his chest and listening to the sound emanating from him.

"Shh, Abbie is calling soon. You want to speak to her, remember?" Kyson says softly, the calling growing stronger and making my eyelids heavy. I yawn, pressing my face into his chest.

"Abbie! Think of Abbie, Azalea. If you don't answer her call, I don't want you to hate me for missing it, so you need to focus. You can mark me afterward," he purrs, kissing the top of my head. His finger strokes my hair. My claws slip out of his chest as his calling turns to a sedative.

"That's it, plenty of time for that later, but calm," he purrs, his fingers moving from my hair and trailing up and down my spine. I blink, fighting the urge to sleep, trying to fight the calling, and my breathing becomes harsher.

"That's it, love. Fight it. You can fight your urges; just focus on a different emotion or think of Abbie," Kyson says. Yet, my brain feels like mush.

"Abbie is with Kade."

I blink, the fog in my mind dissipating like a morning mist as I remember that I am waiting for Abbie's call. The name *Kade* slips into my thoughts, igniting a fierce growl that reverberates through me. The mere mention of his name fuels a surge of hatred within me, even though I have not yet met him.

I sit up, blinking, my claws sinking into his chest, and he hisses. I look down at my hands, and Kyson pulls my claws out, and his blood oozes down his side. I move to lick his wounds, wanting to heal them.

"It's fine."

I cut his words off, running my tongue over the puncture marks. They heal instantly, and I have no idea how I did it, but I can tell my saliva had changed. It tastes different on my tongue. Kyson looks at his chest. The scars remain, which I find odd. They are fresh wounds and should have healed completely. I glance at his face to see the faint scars from the other night.

"You're not healing, it scarred you?" I murmur.

"Worry about that later. It is because you were angry. See, these healed just fine," he says, pointing to the love bites I gave him. It makes no sense why they would heal so unevenly. They all should have healed. I feel my brows pinch together when his calling slips out once more.

"That's it, just focus on something else."

I blink. Clarity washes through me like a tidal wave as I remember I am waiting for Abbie's call, Kade slipping into my thoughts.

"What time is it?"

"Just after 10 am, so she should be calling any minute," Kyson says, lifting his hips and pulling his phone from his back pocket, handing it to me.

"Do you remember how to answer it?"

I nod, unlocking the phone and climbing off him. The moment I do, I immediately feel pulled back to him. I look at the phone in my hand and at Kyson on the bed. It's like a war in my head between what the bond wants and what I need, and that is to ensure Abbie was okay.

"Focus, think of Abbie."

I nod. It is difficult to keep a coherent thought. However, I am glad Kyson ignored his instincts to let me mark him, knowing I would regret it if I missed Abbie's call. The phone starts ringing in my hand, and Kyson, seeing me struggle, moves quickly, answering it, and her face pops up on the screen, snapping me out of my inner battle.

"Abbie!"

"Hey, Kade said you wanted me to call; I dropped my phone in the sink. You know I am clumsy," she chuckles.

My brows furrow. Abbie isn't clumsy. "Have you got makeup on?" I ask her, staring at her face, trying to figure out why it looks different. The urges coursing through me instantly stifle as I scrutinize her appearance. Abbie is far from girly, so her wearing a thick, coat of makeup is beyond strange. Something feels off.

"Yep, do you like it? Cassandra helped me," she says, turning the phone, and I see a woman who looked like she just stepped out of some magazine. Her face is made up perfectly and she looks immaculate. The woman smiles and waves enthusiastically before Abbie turns the phone back to herself.

"How have you been?" she asks, and I don't miss how her eyes move to someone past the phone. Kyson walks into the bathroom, and I move to the couch.

"Cassandra, that is-" I ask.

"Kade's wife, they have three kids," Abbie says, cutting me off and smiling, yet something doesn't feel right; her eyes aren't lighting up the way they usually do.

"And you're okay with that?" I ask her.

"Well, I can't punish him for marrying before he found me," she says. I squint at her, and Abbie then changes the topic of conversation, asking me questions this time. Eager to hear more about what's going on with her, I ask about the packhouse, but get only vague answers in response. Kyson comes up behind me and into the camera view.

"Hi Abbie, you look nice," Kyson says, sending her a wave. She smiles and waves, saying hello. At face value, she seems like her normal, bubbly self. But something is off. Kade says a quick hello over Abbie's shoulder.

"Well, my King and Queen, Abbie and Cassandra are about to go shopping," he says.

I nod, and he moves away from the camera's view. I can hear him talking to someone but can't quite make out what he's saying. Kyson has turned his attention to the tablet I was using last night, checking my writing.

"Well, I will try to call you again soon," Abbie says.

"I was going to ask if you wanted to come up on the weekend?" I ask her, and I see Kyson look at me out of the corner of my eye.

"That would be wonderful; I have missed you," Abbie says, her eyes lighting up for the first time.

"Not this weekend, Abbie. A driver won't be available," I hear Kade say somewhere off the side.

"I t's fine. I will send Dustin to come to get her and your wife, be a girl's weekend," I tell him. Not that I want to see his wife, but I know it might seem suspicious if I don't invite her to.

"The kids have a soccer match, and it's Abbie's first one. She doesn't want to miss it," Kade says, and Abbie nods before rubbing behind her ear.

"Yes, I promised the kids I would go; I forgot maybe the one after," she smiles, yet my focus was on her hand rubbing behind her left ear. My neck itches, and I instinctively rub the scar on the back of my neck where my hairline is as I nod. Something in the pit of my stomach tells me something is amiss. I cannot ignore it.

"Sounds great," I tell them, plastering a fake smile on my face. Abbie's smile waivers slightly.

"Well, I will let you go, call me tomorrow night," I tell her, and Kade pops back into view.

"I will make sure she does," he says, kissing her cheek in a show of affection. Abbie blows me some kisses.

"I love you," she says.

"More than my life," I reply.

"Yep, you know that" she says, smiling, and my heart hammers in my chest. I press my lips in a line as she rubs the spot behind her ear. She didn't say it back. *She always says it back!*

"I love you; I will speak with you tomorrow," I tell her. She nods, and we both hang up.

"She seems good. Hopefully, Gannon will get off my back now," Kyson says.

"She didn't say it back," I tell him, looking at the blacked-out screen.

"Pardon?" Kyson asks.

"She always says it back!" I tell him. Kyson's brows furrow.

"She looked fine, she said so herself."

T hey are making her say that Kyson. She didn't say it back!" I tell him, becoming angry.

"I know you miss her, but..."

"She didn't say it back. She always says it back. We are leaving now; we are bringing her home," I tell him.

Kyson growls and shakes his head. "Kade will bring her up the following weekend. She seems fine, looked great, and seems to be getting along with Cassandra," Kyson says.

Is he thick? Did he not hear what I said? Anger courses through me, the raging lust burning out. I know Abbie, and I try to explain about her touching the scar behind her ear. But Kyson looks back at me like I have three heads. I know Abbie better than I know myself.

Kyson reaches out for me, but I pull away.

"We need to go get Abbie, now!"

"I can't do that, Azalea. She wants to stay; she told me herself when I asked."

"I don't care what she told you. I am telling you; it was an act that was not Abbie, not my Abbie!" I yell at him.

Kyson reaches for my hand, and I jerk it away from him. "Don't fucking touch me. We need to get Abbie," I snap, and he growls at me.

"You are being ridiculous. She is fine," he retorts, stepping closer, but I take a step back.

"Azalea!"

"We need to go get Abbie!" I snarl.

CHAPTER
TWENTY-ONE

GANNON

Liam had to repeatedly crank up the volume to drown out the shrill cries emanating from the basement. Mrs. Daley's blood-curdling screams reverberated around the dimly lit space.

Eventually, her cries cease altogether, replaced by a ghastly silence. The stone floor is now a bright canvas, painted with the remnants of her life. The scent of raw meat permeated the air, mingling with the metallic tang of fresh blood. Her body is bloody and lifeless, having skinned the bitch alive. Oh, how I loved hearing them scream. Although I could have gone without the erection it gave me.

Washing my hands in the filthy sink, I dry them on a hessian bag I find sitting beside it before looking at the old hag's pelt hanging up on a hook from the ceiling, admiring my handiwork. I head for the stairs with a shrug. The rickety old steps creak under my weight as I climb them. Opening the door, I shake my head when I see Liam shaking his ass and dancing to the music he has blaring loudly. Liam is still wearing his floral apron, only now he is doing the dishes.

Katrina comes into the kitchen with another pile of plates clutched in her hands, a tea towel draped over her shoulder. She gives me a wary look. She hesitates for a second, then hurries past me toward the small kitchen. I watch as she sets the plates on the bench beside Liam. He grabs her hand and twirls her around, pulling her to dance with him, tugging her body flush against his.

Only then does he spot me standing by the basement door. He smirks, letting her go and drying his hands on the apron.

"About time; I thought you were trying on Mrs. Daley and wearing her skin as a suit with how long you were taking," Liam laughs. Katrina stares wide-eyed at me, turning my head to look at her, she hastily looks away.

Liam undoes his apron and sets it on the counter before pecking Katrina on the cheek. "Be seeing you later, doll face," he says, sending her a wink. I shake my head as he walks toward me and stops at the door leading out to the hall. "On second thought." He turns back and snatches the apron off the counter. "You don't want this, do you?"

Katrina shakes her head. I am pretty sure she would give him her kidney if it meant he would get away from her. Probably even cut it out herself.

"Good, good, it looks better on me anyway," he says, chucking it over his shoulder and sauntering out.

"Ah, Mrs. Daley?" Katrina asks me when I turn to follow him.

"No need to worry, I already hung her up to dry; just let her air out for a bit," I assure her, following Liam back through the house. We pass Oliver and Logan, who are huddled under a blanket, watching the other children play with puzzles. "I will be back in a few hours to pick you up; I have someone I want you both to meet," I tell them.

Oliver rests his head on Logan's shoulder, sucking his thumb.

"Who?" Logan asks me, hugging his brother closer.

"A woman named Clarice. You will like her, and she will love both of you. She will take good care of you," I tell him as he chews his lip while looking at his little brother. He nods, so I turn on my heel before walking outside. When I do, I am confronted with Alpha Dean and Alpha Brock, who must have been having a heated argument with Liam.

"Can I help you?" I ask them, coming behind Liam and stepping over the small brick fence that ran along the footpath.

"Don't you mean, can I help you? This isn't your pack, and we were called here about a disturbance," Alpha Brock states.

"Is that right? Well, last I checked, werewolves were lower on the food chain. So, I suggest you move along before you meet the real big bad wolf," I snarl. Alpha Brock looks at Liam and me before focusing back on me and looking me up and down.

"Well, the King never informed either of us that you would be showing up; if we had known, we would have prepared for your arrival," Alpha Dean adds, glancing around nervously.

"No preparations needed. If you will excuse me, I have a butcher who needs butchering," I tell them before smiling and shoving past them both. I open the driver's door, and Liam tosses me the keys, and I snatch them out of the air, about to climb in the car.

"Exactly why are you here?" Alpha Brock asks as I start the engine, I look over the roof of my car at Liam.

"Little slow, this Alpha is. No wonder the pack is going broke. Not one brain cell between the two of them," Liam says, climbing in and shutting the passenger side door.

"The two rogue boys inside will be leaving with me when I return; touch them, you will be hanging alongside Mrs. Daley in the basement," I tell them before climbing into the car.

They glance at the orphanage behind them as we drive off. Liam provides me with directions to the butcher's shop. It is a stroke of coincidence that this establishment is situated in the heart of the small-town square, where curious glances welcome our arrival as we step out of the vehicle and make our way toward the storefront entrance.

A huge glass display fridge is out the front, taking up half the store, but I can see a room out the back behind the till. Pushing through the hinged door beside the fridge display, I went out the back of the small store to the freezer room. I can hear muffled yelling as I approach the enormous steel door. Twisting the handle, I yank it open and step inside. The room is freezing, and I shiver instantly.

"Quite frosty in here," Liam remarks playfully, his voice laced with mirth. Yet, my focus remains fixed on the figure before me — the butcher himself. His gaze, wide and filled with a mixture of apprehension and curiosity, locks onto mine. A man in his mid-forties, he stands clad in plaid pajama pants, his disheveled hair defying order as it sticks out at odd angles. Chattering teeth and his lips tinged with a bluish hue betray the frigid temperature that surrounds him. His bare chest has goosebumps that adorn every inch of his skin.

Liam has skillfully bound him, ensuring there is no escape from his restraints. The butcher's eyes dart back and forth between us as Liam pulls out his charming floral apron, while I grab one of the rubber ones hanging just outside the freezer room door.

"Bring him out," I call to Liam, who obediently follows my command, his hands eagerly rubbing together in anticipation.

Untying the butcher, Liam sets him free, only to have the man bolt toward the door in a desperate bid for freedom. However, a swift blow to his windpipe quickly halts his escape. Gasping for air, he clutches his throat, but before he can gather his wits, I seize a fistful of his hair and forcefully slam his head into the unforgiving steel of a nearby table. He crumples to the ground at my feet, left defenseless and subdued. Liam emerges from the room, shaking his head disapprovingly before delivering a swift kick to the butcher's ribs, eliciting a pained grunt.

"Now, listen here, pork chop," Liam asserts with a weary yet firm tone. "I am old and tired, having just prepared over 100 pancakes. So do me a favor and hoist yourself up onto that steel bench. My back is aching." Liam tells him while tying the back of his apron.

The butcher's eyes widen with fear as he stammers in protest. "There must be some mistake! I don't even know what I've done. You've got the wrong guy!"

I fix him with an unwavering gaze, my voice steady as I inquire, "Is your name Doyle?" He nods hesitantly in confirmation.

"And do you happen to be acquainted with a young girl named Abbie?" I press further, observing the flicker of recognition in his eyes. "So, you do know Abbie?" I continue, watching as he glances between us before finally shaking his head.

"Well, now that's quite the lie, isn't it? Mrs. Daley spoke of you and your despicable act—how you paid her to violate that poor girl, robbing her of her innocence," Liam interjects, tilting his head slightly as he studies the trembling figure before us.

"No, I swear! I never took her virtue!" the butcher pleads, panic evident in his voice. "Mrs. Daley lied! Abbie is still pure, I swear it. If she claims otherwise, she is nothing but a liar. I know better than to defile her. After all, a girl like her loses her value if she's been sold off," he blurts out, his words hanging heavy in the air.

"What do you mean?" Liam asks, his expression mirroring my confusion. It was inconceivable to think that the king would deceive me or lead me on a wild goose chase.

"I'm saying that you didn't purchase damaged goods. I overheard rumors about how the Lycan King took her under his wing; she remains untainted, I swear it. If she claims otherwise, she must be lying. Inform the King of her purity; I know it to be true! I know better than to steal her purity." My eyebrows shoot up in surprise. Did this man truly believe that the King would stoop so low as to acquire a sex slave? Did he not comprehend that the King possessed the power to have any woman he desired? Though, truth be told, the King only wants Azalea.

"You know better?" I inquire, my voice laced with incredulity, and he nods seriously, his gaze pleading with me.

What in the world is wrong with this man? I thought my own mind was twisted, but he has taken it to an entirely different level.

"I'm a little confused here. Are you Gannon?" Liam asks, glancing at me. "Because he claims to know better, yet he seems to find rape acceptable," Liam interjects, his tone heavy with disgust. "Am I understanding correctly?" Liam asks, his brows pinching together, mirroring my confusion.

"What? No, I merely paid for the whore," he retorts callously, and a surge of anger courses through my veins at his vile words. Without hesitation, my claws slice down his face, cutting through flesh until they reach bone. In one swift motion, I seize his throat, hoisting him up before forcefully slamming him onto the nearby table.

"Please, I beg of you! She's still pure! I only fucked her ass. Her virginity remains intact. Buyers value that," he pleads desperately. Every fiber of my being bristles with rage at his words. Liam's claws sink into his thigh at his words.

My grip tightens around his throat as I growl, "You seem to be gravely mistaken. We couldn't care less about her virginity; what truly concerns us is whether or not you've caused her harm. But please continue talking; you're only making your demise more excruciating. There are two things we despise with every fiber of our being: rapists and those who harm children. And you, my friend, have committed both of these heinous acts. Now, you shall face the consequences of your crimes with your blood," Liam snarls menacingly, his claws digging into the man's thigh as his screams reverberate through the air. With deliberate slowness, Liam withdraws his claws, twisting them as he does so, causing the man's agonized shrieks to fill the room. Meanwhile, his hands clasp mine, reinforcing my grip around the man's throat.

"Help me move him, flip him on his stomach," I tell Liam, who walks off into the freezer. He returns, bringing back the ropes he had tied this scumbag with. We flip onto his stomach before binding his hands and feet to the legs of the table. He thrashes wildly and continues to scream.

Liam starts whistling as he cuts the vile man's pants off while he cries and begs. Walking into the freezer, I look for a broom, finding one in the back corner by the grate and drain in the floor. Grabbing it, I walk back out to find Doyle crying hysterically and begging Liam to free him.

His words cut off, and his head lifts, his mouth wide open on a silent scream as he gasps when I shoved the broom handle up his ass. His entire body shakes, his legs trembling uncontrollably. Blood trails over the steel table.

"I swear you're still pure. Anal doesn't count, right?" I ask him while I walk around the table. I grip his hair, yanking his head back. He pants, eyes wide, and I smile when Liam gives the broom a jiggle, and he makes a pained groan. I drop his head, and Liam walks over to the wall and pulls down a bone saw, chucking it to me. He then unrolls his pouch of knives, selecting one.

"So slice and dice, or will we be more creative today?" Liam asks.

"Please, please, just let me go," the man begs.

"Don't cry, beefcakes. Gannon here will make sure we tenderize your rump before we make you eat it. We can stuff it some more," Liam tells him, slapping his ass. "If you like. I reckon you could take another, pretty loose back there," Liam adds. The man whimpers and sobs before pissing himself, urine cascading down the sides of the table along with his blood.

"What's that?" Liam asks when Doyle mumbles something incoherently.

"Think he said he wanted the other broom," I tell Liam, who smiles sadistically while the man screams and thrashes as much as possible.

Liam comes out with a mop, and I shrug.

"It's alright, I will spit on it first," Liam tells him before shoving it up alongside the other one. His screams are music to my ears, ringing out loudly, and making me shiver.

"Now, do you like your meat medium, raw, cooked all the way through? How should we serve it to you?" Liam says, cutting a chunk of his ass cheek off with his knife. The butcher screams wildly, and I grab my saw before using a rag as a tourniquet. I know he will heal quickly, but the tourniquet will ensure he does before bleeding out. Wrapping it just above the knee, I pull it tight before grabbing my saw, and I start cutting into the back of his knee.

CHAPTER
TWENTY-TWO

A ZALEA

Kyson's refusal to listen only fuels my frustration. He accused me of being unreasonable, insisting that Abbie probably just forgot to say it back. But I know Abbie better than anyone else, she always says it back. She *knew* I would notice, so her failing to do so was clearly a message to me, something that only I would understand. Kyson offered to take me to see her on the weekend, but I can't bear the thought of waiting that long. Today is Monday, and I am unwilling to endure days of worry. What if she is in danger? He won't listen.

However, the searing heat coursing through my body leaves me with no choice but to confront the unbearable pain I'm in. It washes over me relentlessly, like a merciless tidal wave, intensifying with each passing wave. I feel crippled by the agony.

"This is absurd, Azalea. You're in pain. Let me help you," Kyson snaps, his voice laced with frustration as he reaches out and grips my shoulder, attempting to roll me onto my back.

His touch burns, lust trying to consume me. All I want to do is bathe in his scent, craving his touch and him like he is an antidote to crippling agony rushing through my nerve endings and making my entire body burn and ache for him. Sweat glistens on my skin and drenches my hair. My pillow is soaked as I squirm in pain and my core clenches. No matter how I lay, I cannot get comfortable.

His touch scorches my skin, igniting a potent desire within me. All I can think about is immersing myself in his intoxicating scent, craving his touch as if it were the only cure for my agonizing torment. Beads of sweat glisten on my skin, drenching my hair and soaking my pillow. I writhe in agony, unable to find any position that offers relief

"Bring Abbie home," I snarl, curling up into a ball on my side and turning away from him. My knees press tightly against my chest in an attempt to alleviate some of the pain, but nothing seems to bring relief. Kyson growls in frustration, but I pay him no mind. My stomach twists with cramps, and his scent continues to drive me to the brink of insanity. I cling to my burning anger, determined not to succumb to instinct until he either sends someone to retrieve her or takes me to her himself.

The bond between us tugs at my chest, refusing to settle, urging me relentlessly towards my mate. It whispers promises of comfort and relief if only I would surrender. Kyson growls, his grip on my shoulder tightening as he forces me onto my back.

I thrash beneath him, desperately trying to resist as he pins me down, his body presses against mine with an intensity that leaves me breathless. His hands tingle where they grip my wrists, his very presence a seductive lure that threatens to consume me. His calling rushes out of him, the deep thrumming of it resonates within his chest, as he tries to coax me into submission.

A moan escapes my lips, swiftly followed by a growl as realization hits me like a lightning strike jolting me. He tears my clothes away with a ferocity that leaves them in tatters, and in response, I sink my teeth into his chest, biting down with all the strength I can muster. Kyson growls fiercely as he slams me back onto the bed, my teeth tearing away from his skin. His canines press against my throat, a warning that makes me freeze, my breaths coming in harsh gasps. Anger surges through me at his attempt to force me into submission.

"Stop! Even if you're my mate, it's still rape. And I will never forgive you," I spit at him, defiance burning in my eyes. A whimper escapes his lips, a sound I have never heard before. His tongue traces a path along my neck, and he breathes heavily before burying his face against my skin.

"I would never," he growls, genuine hurt evident in his voice as I turn my head to look at him. Kyson's distress over my accusation strikes a chord within me.

"Then get off me," I retort, and his eyes flicker, his body tensing as he fights against the urge to shift. Jet-black fur begins to sprout along his arms, his skin rippling as he fights the urge to shift. His hardened length presses against me, sending a tingling sensation through my entire body, and my arousal coats my thighs.

"Get off me, Kyson!" I snap when he hesitates. With a reluctant sigh, he rolls off me, only to pull me on top of him. I push against his chest, desperate to create distance between us.

"Stop! If you refuse to mate with me, at least try to ease your own discomfort. Your heat affects me too, Azalea," he snarls, holding me firmly against him. I squirm and wriggle in an attempt to break free, but he is far stronger than me, his arms acting as restraints. After a brief struggle, I give in and relax against his warm skin, allowing it to offer some relief from the relentless agony coursing through me.

The heat subsides slightly, beads of sweat still clinging to my skin as the fever consumes me. It feels as if my very flesh is scorching hot, while my insides boil like a bubbling cauldron. A sigh escapes me as Kyson's hand trails up and down my spine, the mere contact causing my temperature to drop ever so slightly.

"We'll see Abbie on the weekend, I promise. I'll take you to her, Azalea. Please," Kyson pleads, his voice filled with genuine concern.

"Not until she's here. Go get Abbie," I murmur, licking his skin before quickly realizing what I am doing and clenching my jaw.

"I'm busy. The weekend isn't far away," Kyson purrs, burying his nose in my hair as he inhales my scent.

"Then send Gannon!" I plead, knowing that Gannon will drop everything to come to her aid.

"Gannon is occupied with another matter; he won't be available for quite some time. I'll contact him as soon as he returns," Kyson states matter-of-factly.

"What about Damian?" I ask, grasping at any possible solution.

"I need Damian here with me," Kyson says simply, and I curse under my breath.

"You won't be able to fight the heat for long, Azalea. Just give in. It is pointless. You will mate me, so give in! It doesn't just make you uncomfortable!" he growls, gripping my hips and rubbing my pussy along his raging hard-on. I moan at the feel of his cock gliding through my wet folds but still, I refuse, shaking my head and earning a growl from him.

TWENTY-THREE

KYSON

Azalea is so damn stubborn, her defiance pulsating through the bond that connects us. I feel her agony, every ripple of pain amplifying my own. Pressing my skin against hers offers a modicum of relief, but it's fleeting. With each passing moment she denies us both my patience wears thin, festering into frustration.

The waves of her heat crash against me, causing my muscles to tense involuntarily. I clench my teeth, fighting the urge to sink my canines into her flesh, forcing her to submit. She demands Abbie's return, oblivious to the fact that Abbie appeared perfectly fine—excitable and true to her usual self.

As the King, I bear the weight of consequences far greater than Azalea can comprehend. She is thinking like a child, desperate to see her best friend. But there are complexities she fails to grasp, such as the pact I have forged as the ruling monarch. She believes it's as simple as issuing commands to our kind, but the reality is more complex. I'm bound by obligation to provide the five founding council members with my blood each year, rendering them immune to my control and my command.

Lycan blood in itself holds power, extending lifespans well beyond their natural limits. But a King's blood? I can't command them even if I wanted to.

Azalea has tasted traces of my blood when biting me, and during those moments, she grows stronger, defying my attempts to rein her in. However, the council members have been consuming my blood for years, rendering them immune to my commands. It's a bitter pill to swallow, but a necessary one. What good are laws if the one who created them doesn't abide by them? It's what makes me a fair and just ruler.

Impactful decisions require input from all parties involved; I can't direct and enact laws without considering the council's perspective. They are immortal beings, advising and guiding alongside me for centuries, thanks to the immortal blood coursing through their veins.

This system is precisely why some packs have chosen to assist the hunters. They find it unfair that one individual possesses such absolute authority over all Lycan packs. If I were a tyrant, I could command them to take their own lives, and they would obey without hesitation. By having a council that can hold me accountable for any wrongdoing, we establish a balance of power. Consequently, only a handful of packs now side with the hunters in their quest to eradicate Lycans. The system was put in place shortly after my sister's death to ease tensions among the packs.

Now, though, I regret that pact, as Azalea perceives me as nothing more than a jerk for denying her. Little does she realize that the consequences for someone of my status defying the werewolf community go far beyond those faced by an ordinary wolf. They would come for me swiftly and relentlessly. Until Abbie explicitly instructs me to retrieve her, my hands are tied, and unfortunately, I can't solely rely on Azalea's gut feeling.

Eventually, she will understand once she encounters the council. Until then, I will have to endure her tantrums and her wrath.

Another intense wave of heat washes over Azalea, causing her body to tense against mine. Beads of sweat form on my skin where she lies atop me, her scorching heat growing more unbearable with each passing moment. She is burning herself from the inside out. Her teeth sink into my chest, her claws digging into my sides as she writhes, her bare pussy rubbing against my pulsating length, eliciting a deep groan from me. My blood surges hotter, and I instinctively grip her hips, grinding her against me. Azalea moans, but then her claws dig deeper into my flesh. "No!" she growls.

"Azalea, your temperature is dangerously high. Lycan women can die if they don't mate during heat!" I snarl, my frustration seeping into my voice.

"Then bring Abbie home!" she retorts, attempting to roll off me. The scream that tears from her throat as her skin leaves mine sends chills down my spine. Dustin's voice immediately echoes in my mind, responding to that soul-shattering sound.

"My King?" he calls through the door.

"Fetch the pack doctor," I snap at him. I can't afford to let Azalea continue like this for much longer; it will jeopardize her life. How she resists succumbing to the instinctual urge to mate in this state baffles me. I have never heard of a Lycan female enduring such prolonged heat without giving in. Her stubbornness will be the death of her.

"Yes, my King," Dustin replies as I seize Azalea's arm, pulling her back on top of me. Her temperature drops slightly, but not enough to alleviate my concern for her.

She is leaving me no choice but to stop her heat forcefully. Either she surrenders to save her own life, or I intervene at the risk of endangering myself. Undoubtedly, she will choose Abbie over me—I know that much. The day I discovered them together, it became apparent that they are a package deal. They are both willing to die for the other, preferring death over a life without the other one. Their bond is unbreakable, unreceptive to any outside interference, which right now has my anger rising.

Azalea struggles to free herself from my grasp, but I growl menacingly, sinking my teeth into her shoulder, eliciting a moan and shiver from her. I press the points of my teeth near her mark, acutely aware of the laboring breaths that reverberate through my sensitive ears, amplified by her heightened state of arousal.

"Move, and I will make you submit," I growl in warning, retracting my teeth. "The doctor is on their way. Stay put. If you move off me again, I will mate you!"

She nods against my chest, and I glare at the ceiling, cursing her stubbornness. It will only worsen when she discovers the extent of her power—the ability to defy my commands through her Alpha voice. Especially once she realizes what power is running through her veins. She is half Landeena and half Azure and those two blood-lines are in history books for a reason. She is not merely royalty, she is so much more, and that thought frightens me most.

"Azalea, I am not above begging," I plead with her as she continues to squirm, her desire and heat coating my throbbing length. She buries her face in my chest.

"Not until I have Abbie back," she snaps, sinking her teeth into my arm. I groan, half in arousal and half pain at the feel of her teeth. She is acting on instinct, she wants my blood, my bond, me, but still, she refuses.

As sparks rush up my arm, I hiss as my cock twitches against her. She growls at the feeling like she thought I would pin her down and force her, not understanding for Lycan men, it is involuntary. Our urge to mate is just as painful as her heat.

"Stay still then," I tell her, gripping her hips and holding them in place. My control slowly wanes, and I hope this fucking doctor gets here soon. Although parts of her are turning savage and running off of instinct, she remains where she is, unable to fight my command.

She could resist my commands. She may not be able to resist my calling, but my orders she can and until she trusts me, I can't risk using the call to make her submit. Azalea needs to understand I will only use it to calm her or for her safety. Unfortunately, I ruined her trust and now am stuck earning it back. My father used it on my mother constantly for the same reasons once he forcibly marked her since she wasn't his mate and it was an arranged marriage, she didn't want to marry him, he gave her no choice and after a while it just became easier to get his way and a breach of trust after a while, not that mom noticed, or he did anything wrong to her. Still, it wasn't always necessary, and I didn't want that with Azalea. I rather she sought out my calling than me use it against her.

It was a big mistake for me to not see how close Azalea and Abbie really are. It took me too long to understand their bond. They've both been through so much pain and horror together. When things became too much for one, they leaned on other to keep going. They shared and endured everything.

For so long, they needed each other to survive. It's like they're two pieces of the same puzzle, each reflecting the other's pain and being the other's strength. Without the other, they both seem lost. They've been through so much abuse that it's made them depend on each other more than anything else. They protect each other fiercely, ready to face anything rather than see the other get hurt. The saddest part is that they refuse to live for themselves, choosing only to live for the other.

They're each other's safe place in a world that's been only cruel to them. Being apart isn't just hard; it's unthinkable for them. They're like mirrors to each other's experiences.

Their connection goes beyond friendship. It's a lifeline. They are each other's anchor, holding on tight in a storm. They've built an unbreakable bond from their shared pain, a bond that gives them the strength to keep fighting.

Understanding how much they rely on each other shows a deep kind of sadness, a darkness that they face together. Their bond is their way of fighting back, their promise to each other that they'll never have to face the world alone again. They see each other through everything, sharing both the pain and the hope for something better.

I should have noticed the depth of their connection from the very moment Azalea threw herself at my feet, her desperate pleas for Abbie's life echoing in my ears hauntingly. It gives so much more meaning to their words: More Than My Life.

They truly believe life isn't worth living without the other. They stopped living for themselves. That speaks volumes to me, how much did someone have to break, that they only kept breathing out of obligation to the other, knowing taking their life meant taking the other's?

As I ponder upon this revelation, I realize that their bond is unlike anything I have ever witnessed before. It transcends the realms of mere friendship or a mate bond that I have come to associate with pact bonds or the brotherhood forged over centuries, or through blood ties like the unyielding connection I share with my guard. No, Azalea and Abbie's relationship is something altogether different. It's a fusion of survival and an inexplicable reliance upon one another.

And now, as I stand at this precipice of understanding, I know that I can never hope to win if I were to force Azalea to make a choice between us. Her loyalty to Abbie runs deeper than any mate bond she might have felt towards me. It's a bond forged through anguish or love, a bond that defies reason and surpasses all expectations.

Hearing a knock, I sit up. Azalea groans as she slides lower on my lap. I rip the blanket over her naked body to cover her.

"You can enter," I call to him. The moment his scent wafts to me, Azalea growls at the intruder in her nest, which is currently me, as she burrows under the blanket, her claws scratching my sides.

Doc approaches cautiously. She is dangerous in this state. You never intrude willingly on a nested she-wolf, let alone a Lycan. I grab her arms, wrapping them around my waist before laying back down, trapping her arms underneath me, and wrapping my arms around her shoulders, pinning her as she goes to attack him.

"Be quick," I tell him, feeling the mattress shred beneath my back. The growl that leaves her is more predator than prey. I smash her with the calling when I feel her start to shift, and she melts against me. Doc's eyes are wide as he stares at her and watches me. He was not just intruding on her nest but looking at my heated mate. Not a scenario anyone wants to be in.

"My King, what you're asking..." Doc tries to say.

"Will stop her heat, now do it!" I tell him.

"Yes, but my King, it isn't..."

"I said do it, stop her heat. I will not force her," I snarl at him, and he seems perplexed.

"She is resisting?" he asks, and I growl. He shakes himself, startled by that information just as much as I was that she could resist it.

"You want to argue with me, do it through the mindlink. I know what's at risk, do not make me order you, doc," I warn him, and he sighs, looking at her as she purrs, licking my chest, having forgotten we had people in our presence, unable to fight my calling as it has lulled her into a sedated state. Doc pulls herbs and vials out before making the concoction up in a bowl and extracting it with a syringe.

'My King?' Dustin asks through the mindlink, and my eyes move to him over Doc's shoulder.

'I know, but I won't force her,' I reply through the link. Dustin nods once but looks away. We all knew what I'm risking, but I'm not willing to guilt trip her into giving in because I knew she would, but then she would resent me afterward or may accuse me of lying.

Doc clears his throat awkwardly, and Dustin averts his eyes while mine go to Doc's. "My King, I have to... the injection site, I have to..." he stutters, and I growl, knowing he had to inject it into her ovaries. I had seen it happen to a Lycan woman who was in heat just as her pack was attacked. It stopped her heat and saved her until the bond was severed when her mate was killed. She ended up killing herself not long after her mate died, anyway. She went insane after about a month.

"Which one?" I ask him.

"Either," he states, averting his gaze while I rearrange her by pressing my leg between hers to cover her. My hands and the blanket tangle around her to cover her nakedness. Yet, the moment he turns, the savage growl he received from me had him jump back. I can't help but to covet and protect, my instincts are going haywire. Knowing he can see what is mine and is about to touch her while she is in this state is sending me overboard.

TWENTY-FOUR

Doc is shaking at my outburst, and before I can stop myself, I am shifting. Dustin only just rips him back in time before I slash his eyes from his head, the needle dropping from his hand. I tuck her under me. Azalea's eyes roll in her head, the calling wearing off, and I only just manage to flood her with it as she comes to. No doubt she would lash out at someone so near her nest.

"My King?" Doc stutters. I have never struggled with control like this. Most of my guards had caught her in some state of undress before, but never while she was in heat. My instincts tell him he's trying to take her, even though I consciously know I asked him here. Reason tries to calm me, but it doesn't abate my urges.

Dustin bends down, scooping the needle off the ground. My eyes track his every move as he approaches the bed. Though his scent near her doesn't seem to faze me, probably because she reeks of him constantly or maybe because I know he's not a threat. Plus, Dustin has no reaction to Azalea; she's not his type. The doctor on the other hand, I can sense his testosterone levels rise around Azalea because she's in heat.

"Ovaries, right, doc? I'm not good with female anatomy," Dustin admits, and Doc moves toward the end of the bed, watching from afar, careful not to come too close. His nostrils flare, earning him a growl. Dustin's hand shakes as he stops beside me at the edge of the bed. He bares his neck to me, and my eyes flicker as he offers his neck to me.

"No threat, Alpha King," Dustin says steadily as I sniff his neck, turning my nose away from him to sniff my mate. Dustin reaches over, tugging the surrounding sheet over her legs and mine covering her.

"He needs to move his leg," Doc says, glancing away when my eyes snap to him. Dustin's hand taps my leg. The man deserves a bravery award coming near me like this. I don't think Damian would be game enough to try while she was in heat. I move my leg, and Dustin quickly tucks the blanket between her legs, careful not to touch between her legs. Azalea's eyes flutter, and I bury my nose in her neck and lick the hollow of her throat.

"Focus on your mate, my King. I am no threat," Dustin says as I feel him moving her slightly, and I keep my face in her neck; she shivers, my whiskers tickling her neck.

"If you push hard enough, you will be able to feel it. The Queen is in heat. Her ovaries will be swollen. You won't miss it once you feel it," Doc murmurs.

"Feel what? I don't even know what I am feeling for," Dustin whispers.

"Hand on the back of her hip. Use your other to push down, no lower but above the pubic bone," Doc says, and I growl.

Dustin fiddles around then jumps. "Ah, that's wrong, so wrong, shit, sorry, my King," he says when my head snaps to look at his hands on my mate.

"Not gross, just didn't think ovaries could expand like that," he rambles, remaining still while my eyes remain on his hand touching her.

"She isn't human. Lycan anatomy is far different from human

anatomy," Doc explains, my eyes going to the man, who averts his once again under my glare.

"Fascinating. You could only feel the ovaries internally by lifting the ovary, and with a hand on the stomach. Still not 100% accurate on humans, Lycans are a little different," he says, turning his head. Dustin moves too quickly to pluck the needle from between his teeth. He freezes when I growl, offering his neck to me to sniff. I turn my attention back to Azalea and hear him breathe.

"Now I inject it into the ovary?" Dustin whispers. I feel relieved he is doing it, I don't think I could.

"Yes, but move quickly. The King will feel it. I have heard it isn't a pleasant feeling. He may lash out."

"Wait, will I hurt her?" Dustin asks.

"Not if the King keeps her sedated, no, but he will feel it," Doc says, my ear pricking on top of my head at his words.

I feel it alright and clench the sheets. Dustin moves quickly, but I am more focused on Azalea, watching her. I hear the door click as they rush out, and will have to remember to thank Dustin later.

It takes around 30 minutes until the side effects die down in her. Her breathing eventually evens out, her cheek is no longer a rosy red, and her skin is no longer blistering hot. However, it has no such effect on me. Her scent nearly drives me insane. The pain is pure torture for me, and now she lay asleep as exhaustion takes her after relentless hours of heat. She's vulnerable to me in her calm, sleeping form. I know I have to get out of here before I mate her.

Another hour passes as I pace and drink an entire bottle of whiskey, trying to force myself out of the room. Growing tipsy rather quickly, I snatch another bottle off the bar and stagger out of the room. Dustin grips my arm as I stumble toward the steps.

"Stay guard," I tell him.

"My King," Dustin murmurs.

"Don't, I know what I am risking? I am fine," I tell him.

"Do you?"

I growl at his question. "Yes, my life and I will be fine. I won't force her, and none of you are to tell her. She will come around." I stop, losing my train of thought.

"You have three days, my King," Dustin argues.

"I need to go. Not a word," I tell him, clutching the handrail as I head for my office.

CHAPTER
TWENTY-FIVE

AZALEA

My body groans in protest as I shift onto my back, the dull ache spreading through my limbs. My memory, like a grainy photograph, leaves me slightly confused. Wasn't I in the throes of heat just moments ago? Yet now, inexplicably, I feel perfectly fine and well-rested, devoid of any telltale signs of a feverish temperature. I had been in pain and discomfort so long that relief feels strange.

However, rolling over, I find the bed empty, making me get up.

Casting a quick glance around the room, my eyes search for any trace of Kyson's presence. Spotting the closet, I shuffle towards it, my footsteps muffled by the plush carpet beneath my feet. Inside, a limited selection of clothes awaits me, remnants of my tendency to shred them during my restless episodes. Most of them are Kyson's, but I remember he started keeping a stash in his office, away from the destructive reach of my claws. A bemused chuckle escapes my lips at the thought of him safeguarding his clothes against my unpredictable nesting habits. Such a bizarre thing to do, making me realize how little I know about being a Lycan.

I meander around the room, trying to wake up before hunting down Kyson when I notice my tablet. I pick it up to check the time before noticing Kyson's phone nearby. Furrowing my brows, I recall Abbie's promise to call back last night. Or was it still the same day? The boundaries of time have blurred for me lately, days blending into nights and vice versa with disorienting regularity.

I unlock his phone but notice he has no notifications on it or messages, not that I could read those anyway without typing them into my tablet. I toss the phone on the bed and head for the bathroom with a shake of my head. Eager to see Kyson, I shower quickly, eager to see Kyson, so I can try to convince him to take me to visit Abbie.

When I get out of the shower, I towel dry my hair, not wanting to use the hairdryer because my hearing is super sensitive right now.

Even now, every sound seems amplified, from the flickering of lights to the gentle rustle of curtains caressed by a passing breeze. My senses, already acute, seem to have reached an unprecedented level of intensity.

Slipping on a pair of comfortable flats, I turn the doorknob and step into the dimly lit corridor. There, leaning against the wall, yawning and rubbing his tired eyes, is Dustin. A small chuckle escapes my lips as I take in his disheveled appearance.

"You look exhausted," I remark, causing Dustin's eyes to snap open and his posture to straighten.

"Good morning, my Que—" he begins, but I raise an eyebrow, cutting him off before he can finish.

"Azalea," he corrects himself. It was stupid.

It's rather silly how he tries to maintain formality when he follows me around like a faithful shadow. I'd like to think of him as more than just a duty-bound friend. He's seen me at my worst.

"Do you know where the King is?" I ask him, and he yawns again.

"I will take her," Trey says, appearing seemingly out of nowhere, and Dustin looks at him. I hadn't even noticed him standing there.

"Why are you here?" Dustin questions, a touch of confusion lacing his words. "It's not your shift today."

"Damian instructed me to relieve you. I don't mind taking over your duties," Trey responds, shrugging his shoulders. My gaze shifts between the two men, realizing that Dustin had covered Trey's shift multiple times. Has Dustin been working tirelessly for the past three shifts? That's nearly forty hours without rest.

Dustin shakes his head and waves him off. "I am fine. You can go." Dustin tells him, waving him off.

"No, Dustin, you really should get some sleep," I interject, concern lacing my voice as I take in his exhausted appearance. His well-being matters to me; after all, he's more than just a guard, he's my friend.

"I'm fine, Azalea. The King is in his office, but I wouldn't advise going down there. He's in one of his moods," Dustin informs me with a hint of exasperation. But when isn't he in a mood? I can't help but wonder if it's just his personality rather than a temporary state of mind.

"You said Damian is back?" I ask Trey, and he nods.

"Go and rest, Dustin. Trey will accompany me to see the King," I insist, squeezing his arm gently as I pass by him. However, just as I'm about to join Trey, Dustin grips my arm, causing me to give him a puzzled look. With a sigh, he speaks up.

"It's fine. I'll take you myself. You're dismissed, Trey. Your presence isn't required here," Dustin asserts firmly, his voice tinged with authority. Trey growls in frustration, shaking his head in disagreement.

"But..."

"I am her personal guard, and I dismissed you. Now go!" Dustin's voice snaps with authority, his eyes filled with a steely determination. Trey growls in response, a low rumble that echoes through the tense air. He shakes his head in frustration, his lips curling into a snarl.

"Trying to help, gee," he mutters under his breath before stomping off, the sound of his retreating footsteps fading into the distance.

Turning my attention to Dustin, I see a mixture of anger and concern etched on his face as he watches Trey leave. His gaze follows the disgruntled figure until he disappears.

"Hey, what's got into you?" I inquire, my voice laced with curiosity and worry. Dustin shakes his head slightly, his fingers absentmindedly tracing circles on my shoulder as he drapes his arm over it, pulling me closer to him.

"Something's off about him," Dustin responds, his voice tinged with suspicion. "I haven't liked him since he came here eight years ago; he rubs me the wrong way." He lets out a sigh, his grip tightening ever so slightly. "However, he took a bullet for the King about six years back, earning a spot on the royal guard. Damian put him on personal guard duties alongside me; he is trusted." Dustin's words hang in the air, leaving an unsettled feeling in their wake. "I don't trust him, though; a few things don't add up for me."

My brows furrow in confusion as I try to process Dustin's concerns. Trey seems harmless enough, perhaps a bit brusque at times, but nothing that would warrant such skepticism. Then again, I remind myself, I trusted Dustin implicitly. If he sensed something amiss, it couldn't be ignored.

"What do you mean?" I ask softly, my voice filled with genuine curiosity.

Dustin's gaze meets mine, his eyes searching for understanding. "Just, I don't know. How he came to be here doesn't seem right to me," he explains. There's a hint of unease in his voice, a shadow of doubt that hangs heavy between us.

"So, where was he before?" I press on, my desire for answers growing stronger.

"The Landeena Kingdom," Dustin replies, his tone tinged with sadness. "About 20% of the pack here were originally your family guard or those from your Kingdom, survivors of the massacre. After your parents were killed, King Kyson's pack was the only remaining Lycan pack. For safety, Lycans stick together. We are a dying species, so the King took them in." Dustin nudges me gently with his elbow before stifling a yawn. "My Queen, those people are your people."

"And Trey was one of these people?"

"Yes, he came here eight years ago, he was here briefly, but he spent two years with the Landeena guard looking for you. I know he was high up in the Landeena Kingdom, yet he never speaks of his time there. None of the Landeena guards do, I know Kyson knows everything about Landeena and the guard, but I also know Landeena even to this day have kept your families secrets whatever they are. I am not sure why, but Trey, for some reason, has alarm bells ringing for me. He always appeared obsessed with finding you."

The revelation hit me like a bolt of lightning. *People survived?* I had assumed that in the aftermath of the horrific events that had unfolded, everyone had been lost. But now it made sense that there would be survivors, scattered remnants of a once proud and noble lineage. This knowledge makes me feel more connected to a past I don't recall than ever before. There's walking, talking evidence of my birthright, of my parents in this castle right now.

"How about we stay in the room for a bit?" I suggest softly, my concern for Dustin's well-being evident in my voice. "You can sleep. Since you don't want anyone else as my guard."

"I am fine; I can take you," Dustin assures me, but I grip his arm and pull him back toward the room.

"Sleep on the bed if you'd like. I promise I will remain here, I won't sneak off on you," I tell him, my voice soft and reassuring. Dustin shakes his head, a slight frown creasing his forehead. Instead, he follows me toward the couch, his eyes lingering on me with a mix of curiosity and uncertainty.

I retrieve my tablet and open it up and book, deciding to do something educational.

Dustin stands there, watching me intently, as I raise an eyebrow at him, silently questioning his disobedience.

"You are supposed to be sleeping," I remind him gently, patting the cushioned surface of the couch as an invitation. He purses his lips, a hint of defiance flickering in his eyes.

"Don't make me try to order you. It will just embarrass me when I can't," I chuckle softly, and his lips tug in the corners, but he reluctantly sits, and I put the throw blanket over him.

"Now, sleep," I tell him.

"Yes, boss," he laughs, closing his eyes. It didn't take him long before he fell asleep, and after an hour, he fell sideways into me, his head resting in my lap while I was trying to work out how to do the strange letter in the book. It had a dash above it, but I can't figure it out on the tablet. Giving up, I move to the following sentence when Damian comes in, and I hold a finger to my lips, pointing to Dustin, who is sleeping soundly.

"He should be on guard," Damian growls, and I growl back at him, shooting him a glare.

"Thirty-six hours he has been rostered on for," I snap at him, and he seems taken aback.

"No, Trey is his relief," Damian says, his eyes narrowing as he observes Dustin's slumbering form.

"Trey was here earlier. Dustin didn't trust him and sent him off," I explain.

Damian's confusion is evident, his brow furrowing as he tries to comprehend the situation. Eventually, he sighs, a resignation settling over him. "Fine, I will speak with Dustin when he wakes; I brought your lunch up," Damian says, passing me a plate. I sit my plate on the arm of the armchair.

"The King?"

"In a foul mood," Damian replies with a hint of weariness in his voice. He straightens his black shirt, brushing away breadcrumbs from the sandwich he had hastily made for me.

"Can you take me to see..." I begin to ask, but Damian raises a hand, cutting me off before I can finish my request.

"I know what you are going to ask. The answer is no, I have to go with the King to check out something. We will be gone for a few hours," he explains, and I huff, annoyed.

"The King said he would take you on the weekend. He will, Azalea, just be patient."

"I can't be patient when I know she is in trouble."

"The King said she was fine."

"It was an act!" I growl, becoming angry that no one will listen to me. Why won't they believe me?

"My Queen, I don't know what else to say, the King..."

"Yeah, the King said," I mock, glaring at the plate.

"He has his reasons," Damian defends him with a growl. If he has reasons, why not tell me those damn reasons? I just want to see her, that's it. If she is fine, I will apologize for wasting his time, but until I do, I will keep pestering him because I know I am right!

I place my plate on the coffee table before carefully slipping out from under Dustin's head.

"Azalea?"

"No, he won't take me, then that is fine! There are plenty of others here who can," I tell him before stomping off out of the room. Excuses, always an excuse.

Damian chases after me as I stalk down to the office, telling me I should leave him be. That he was in a mood! I roll my eyes and pull my arm from his grip when he tries to stop me from going into the office.

Pushing the door open, I step inside to find Kyson by the window, whiskey in hand. He looks at me and smiles, his eyes going over my shoulder as Damian steps in behind me, looking somewhat flustered.

"Everything okay?" Kyson asks.

"Yes, I was trying to take Azalea back to her room," Damian says, grabbing my arm, and Kyson snarls ferociously, making him let go.

He shakes his head, and his eyes flicker. Damian backs away from me with his hands up. What is wrong with him?

"Can I speak to you, please?" I ask Kyson, who is now glaring at Damian. Kyson turns his attention to me before waving me over and dismissing Damian. He glares at the door as it closes, and I slowly approach him.

Kyson sits in the armchair, flopping heavily into it, his whiskey sloshing over the sides of his glass. I take it from him, placing it on the lamp table beside him, just as Kyson grabs me, hauling me onto his lap. He buries his face in my neck and starts purring, tugging my shirt up.

"Stop. I need to talk to you," I tell him while pushing off his chest. He growls, ignoring me, fondling my breast, and nipping my shoulder through my shirt. His skin is scorching hot.

"Are you alright?" I ask him, but he growls again, tugging at my clothes, trying to undress me. With a sigh and I speak.

"Damian said you were leaving for a few hours, so can you get one of your other guards to take me to see Abbie, or even Dustin could take me?" I ask him, pushing his face away that was currently buried in my neck.

"I will take you on the weekend," he mumbles, licking my neck, his hands pawing at me. His grip feels rough as he tugs and pulls me.

"Kyson, stop. We will be quick straight there and back."

"No, it is too far to go on your own on the weekend. End of discussion," he snaps at me. I growl at him before shoving him off and standing up.

"Then Trey can come too?" I tell him.

"I said no!" he snarls, his eyes flickering dangerously.

"Abbie never called last night," I tell him.

"She was probably busy," he says, earning me an eye roll. I storm off toward the door. Fine, I will go by myself.

"Azalea?"

"If you don't take me, I will go myself," I tell him while walking toward the door. I barely have a hand gripping the door handle when the sound of snapping bones reaches my ears, and his hand falls on the door beside my head. The growl that rips out of him makes me spin around to face him.

It reverberates through the air, its deep and menacing timbre resonating with a haunting intensity. Goosebumps ripple across my flesh, each hair on my head standing at attention as an icy shiver slithers up my spine, sending a chill that pierces to the core. It is a feeling that engulfs me instantly, as if I have taken a leap off a towering building, my stomach plummeting with a sickening lurch. A sense of terror grips every fiber of my being as I come face to face with him, his face twisted in rage, his eyes pitch black.

Kyson, the man I once knew, has vanished, replaced by a savage creature. His voice emerges as a harsh growl, causing me to instinctively step back until my body collides with the door. The raw power coursing through him is palpable, his entire frame quivering with unrestrained anger. At this moment, I comprehend why everyone held such fear for him; even when he dismissed me with callous disregard, his rage had never been this consuming. It is something far beyond human emotion, a manifestation of a monstrous and primal nature that surpasses any semblance of humanity.

"Mine! You will submit..." His words hang in the air, abruptly ceasing as he blinks and shakes his head. His claws scrape against the door behind me, their grating sound akin to nails on a chalkboard. I grit my teeth, refusing to succumb to the overwhelming fear that threatens to overpower me. And then, a sudden transformation overtakes him. He stumbles backward, his expression one of bewilderment and vulnerability, as if he has lost control over his own ferocity.

The mood changes slightly. "Where is your guard?" he says, turning away from me and putting some distance between us.

"Outside," I lie, not wanting to get anyone in trouble, especially Dustin. Damian is angry enough at him earlier.

"You should go back to the room, Azalea."

"But Abbie..." I protest.

"I said room, now go. I have to leave anyway."

"Dustin and Trey..."

"I said no! Now get out!" he screams at me, and I shake my head, turning on my heel and rushing out. Damian stands by the door and jumps when I come rushing out.

"I told you he was in a bad mood," Damian says, and I growl at him before stalking off down the corridor toward my room. Just as I reach the doors leading toward the stairs, they burst open, and Dustin crashes through them, looking frantic. The look of relief on his face when he spots me is evident as he clutches his knees, trying to catch his breath.

"You said you wouldn't leave!" he says, coming over to me and gripping my arms.

"Sorry, I had Damian with me. I didn't want to wake you," I tell him, taking the arm that he offers me when Damian calls after him.

"Dustin, a word."

I chew my lip, hoping I didn't get him into trouble. Dustin sighs loudly but stops, walking back down the hall when Clarice comes up with the King's lunch. She stops, looking at Damian and Dustin, who are talking.

"Azalea, how are you feeling?" she asks, cupping my face with her hand. Before I can answer, I hear Dustin growl before yelling at Damian.

"Fucking bullshit!"

"It's an order. You need sleep," Damian snaps back at him.

"I will lock the door and sleep on the couch."

"Trey is her other assigned guard. The King trusts him, and so do I," Damian says.

"Get anyone else; I am telling you something is off with him!"

"Oh, for fuck's sake, if this is over the assignment last year, are you still pissed about that? He proved he had nothing to do with sabotaging you."

"No, it's about her safety. I couldn't give a fuck about that. But..." Dustin argues back.

"What happened?" Clarice whispers to me, and I turn my attention back to her.

"I'm not sure. Dustin keeps taking Trey's shifts, Dustin said he doesn't trust him," I tell her when I hear a growl.

Dustin curses under his breath, stomping back over to me. "Come on," he says, looking furious. My brows pinch as he grips my elbow, leading me away from Clarice, who glances at us confused.

"Are you alright?" I ask him.

"Damian pulled me from shift for the next 8 hours."

"It's fine. You need sleep," I tell him as he pulls me up the stairs.

We make it back to the room in record time, with his long strides as he tugs me after him. "Slow down!" I tell him, stumbling on the top step. His hand gripping my arm is the only thing stopping me from falling.

"Sorry," he says, leading me to the room. He pushes the door open.

"Just sleep; I will be fine."

"Damian ordered me back to my room to ensure I sleep. Just be careful around him. I am setting the alarm and will speak to some other guards to keep an extra up here," Dustin almost looks frantic. "Don't trust him, Azalea. Just stay in your room the moment I can come back; I will be here, just..." he curses, shaking his head. "Make sure you keep the door locked. Promise me you won't let him in here!" Dustin says, gripping my arms.

"Okay, I promise, I won't let him in the room with me." Not that I would; I barely know Trey. So I doubt he would try to come in here, anyway.

"It's fine. I will see if Clarice will stay with you while the King is gone; Gannon can't be too much longer, surely. I'll mindlink and ask Liam," Dustin mutters, rubbing his chin.

"I'll be fine," I tell him.

"You know where my room is, right? Wake me if you need me. You also have my number on the phone; just press number three, speed dials straight to my phone."

I nod, wondering if the lack of sleep is making him paranoid. He sighs, kissing my forehead and hugging me, something he had never done. "Don't let yourself be alone with him," he whispers before walking out when I nod. I watch him leave, wondering why he felt so strongly about Trey.

CHAPTER
TWENTY-SIX

KYSON

I have no idea what came over me; I almost attacked her. Her heat is still intense despite her no longer suffering its effects. I didn't mean to snap at her, but I would have bent her over my desk if she didn't leave. It takes twenty minutes before I calm down enough to shift back. Back in my human form, I snatch the bottle of whiskey off the lamp table and swig from it.

"You bloody idiot, are you trying to get yourself killed!" I snap at Damian.

"I'm sorry, I thought you had control, or I wouldn't have grabbed her."

I click my tongue and curse, shaking my head while tipping the bottle to my lips.

"Just let me explain to her," Damian says, and I shake my head.

"No, I want her to give herself to me when she wants to, not because she feels forced because my life is at risk," I tell him.

"Kyson?"

"The injection only lasts two days. We have some leeway. Azalea will change her mind," I tell him, not so sure whether she would.

"And if she doesn't?"

I bite the inside of my lip. "She will."

"If she doesn't, I'll tell her," Damian snarls, and I growl at him.

"You die, then what? You let her live with that guilt. No one can protect her the way you do, Kyson. Think this through."

"I don't want her to feel obligated to mate with me," I tell him.

"And I won't let you die, and neither will she!" he snaps. Damian tosses me some pants and a shirt, realizing I am still naked I take them, slipping them on and doing up the buttons.

"We should leave. I want to get back before tomorrow."

"We shouldn't go, not while you're like this..."

"And that is precisely why we are going. I am struggling to hold myself back. Now grab the keys. We are leaving," I tell him, grabbing my wallet off the desk and stuffing it into my pocket. I push the doors open and walk out toward the front of the castle. I need to get away from her for a little while, just until I get these urges under control.

However, when I reach the door, I stumble, vertigo washing over me, and the room tilts and slants, making me stumble. My hand goes out, catching myself on the wall as my vision begins to tunnel. "Kyson?" Damian worries.

A cold sweat causes sweat to bead on the back of my neck. Thankfully, Damian grips my upper arm, I blink, trying to force the effects away.

"We should stay," he murmurs, but I shake his hand off. "I'm fine, we will be gone only 12 hours max, plenty of time, and by the time we get back, the medication should be nearly worn off," I tell him. Damian growls disapprovingly but says nothing as I start walking out.

"Gannon is on his way back. He should be here before we get back," Damian assures me.

~*AZALEA*~

An hour has passed when I hear a knock on the door. I look toward it before hearing the handle twist, but they do not open it.

143

"My Queen?" Trey calls out from the other side of the door. I stick my lip between my teeth as I get to my feet and walk over to the door. I twist the lock and crack it open to peer out the door.

"Clarice said to bring you down to have afternoon tea. The King doesn't trust anyone to bring your food to you, so you will sit with Clarice," Trey tells me, and I nod, slipping out the door. I follow behind him as he leads me toward the kitchen. Once I step in, I see Clarice has some sandwiches made and she smiles warmly at me before wiping her hands on her blue apron.

"I have got everything out. You can see it all sealed," she says, pointing to the jams and spreads, and I nod before grabbing a butter knife. Clarice hands Trey a salad sandwich while I make myself a jam one.

"I know the jam is probably not what you had in mind, but Kyson doesn't want you eating anything unless he or Damian prepared it," Clarice tells me, and I nod before taking a bite of my sandwich. I start packing the spread and bread away while Clarice fusses that I shouldn't be cleaning. I ignore her before we all stand in awkward silence. Clarice continues to glance at Trey, and so do I after what Dustin told me. He must have noticed the tension because he swallows down a bite of the sandwich Clarice made him.

"What? Do I have food on my face?"

Shaking my head, I turn my attention to Clarice, who also seems a little stiff.

"Want to help me outside?" Clarice asks. Smiling, I nod. Anything is better than wasting away in the room.

"The king wants her to remain in her room," Trey says with a shrug.

"I will deal with the king. He has no reason to worry," Clarice chimes in before I have a chance to say anything.

"Yeah, I told Damian that when I took over from Dustin. Not like she can drive on out here to go after her friend," Trey chuckles. Clarice's eyebrows furrow at his words, and so do mine.

"I can't drive," I tell him.

"Exactly, and there is only one way out, which is to drive out the front gates. Unless you use the back exit, but no one goes down there, the road is too rough," he laughs.

Clarice sets her sandwich down on her plate and places a hand on her hip. "What? Are you trying to give her ideas?" she asks, raising an eyebrow at him.

"What? No, of course not, and she said it herself, she can't drive. Besides, there are guards at the front gate. She would never get past them. I am just saying he is worrying for no reason!" Trey says, sighing heavily.

The tension in the room becomes thick between them as they stare at each other. "Is everything okay?" Trey asks, glancing at us before he sighs.

"Is this about me taking over for Dustin? I swear I had nothing to do with that. I get you don't like me, but I would never place you in harm's way, my queen. Dustin and I just have history," Trey says, and my brows pinch.

"Pardon?" I ask.

"Ah, I probably shouldn't say, I know you're close with Dustin, and I don't like gossip."

"Well, you can't say that and not say it now, can you?" Clarice says.

Trey glances between us both and rolls his eyes.

"Dustin used to have a thing for me, and I turned him down." He shrugs like it's no big deal. "Not because I don't like Dustin, but I'm straight," he says, pointing to himself.

"Anyway, we had the competitor trials last spring for the guard position. Dustin blamed me for sabotaging him by setting the clock back, so he missed the trials and didn't make the cut," Trey says.

"Ah, yes, I remember that caused quite a stir."

"Well, did you?" I ask him.

"What? No, of course not. He forgot to put his phone on daylight savings time. He slept through the trial, somehow I got blamed for it because his phone was near me."

"What are the trials for?" I ask Clarice.

"Just a competitor thing between the guards, makes them compete each year for ranking within the royal guard," Clarice clarifies.

"Yeah, I don't understand why he blamed me. Nobody could beat his track time anyway from the year before or any of his scores, so his job was never in jeopardy," Trey shrugs.

"He holds the record?" I ask.

"Yeah, there is a reason he is your personal guard. He even beat Damian's record one year. Damian got it back, obviously, but it still shocked everyone. Especially with Damian's Beta genes," Trey states.

I chuckle, happy for Dustin. Although I never pictured Dustin to be so competitive, then again, he looks like he lives in a gym and is the most observant out of all the guards I have. Also, the most protective. Interesting.

"Want to help me garden?" Clarice asks. I nod excitedly, grabbing my plate and placing it in the sink.

"Is she alright with you for a few minutes? I want to go use the bathroom," Trey asks Clarice.

"Of course," Clarice says. She leads me outside. We spend the afternoon gardening, all while my thoughts remain troubled, fixed on Abbie. When it is getting dark, Trey leads me back to my room. Once again, Abbie never calls. Yet, all I keep thinking about is that back exit he mentioned. Rummaging around the room, I find some maps and try to read them, chewing my lip. I glance at the door, wondering if I can trick Trey into showing me on the map.

TWENTY-SEVEN

IVY

Pushing the door open, I pop my head out before wandering over to him. He instantly straightens. "Everything okay, my Queen?" he asks.

"Do you know where Alpha Kade's pack is? I want to post a parcel to Abbie," I tell him.

"You want to post a parcel?" he asks. I nod, biting my lip. He takes the map from me.

"Ah yeah, here, but you need her address, not just the suburb. Do you know the address?" he asks me.

I shake my head.

"You can use street view; I can show you if you want."

"Street view?"

"On Google, you type an address in the maps on the phone. You can pull up a street view of it. You would be able to see the pack house."

"The phone has maps?" I ask, incredulous. He nods, holding his hand out for the phone.

"Yep, like a nav man, it will even tell you how to get there, may I? I will show you," he says. I glance at the phone in my hand before passing it to him. Trey fiddles with it before pulling up some apps, and maps pop up. He then types in the address and goes to some link, and I see a picture of the packhouse, which is a huge white mansion with fountains out the front.

"That's where Abbie is?" I ask him.

"Technology is pretty cool, huh," he laughs. I nod.

"Oh, Dustin told me he will be up soon. He got permission from Damian to return to his post," Trey tells me.

"I hope he slept," I mutter.

"Yes, hopefully, he will be in a better mood," Trey laughs, and I nod, wandering back into the room. I lock the door before racing around the room. Rummaging through the closet, I grab a jacket while casting a nervous glance at the door, being careful not to bump the phone and get out of the address. Stopping next to the door, I listen for any movement while moving to the window.

I nudge the window up and peer out into the setting sun. Looking at the side of the window, I notice vines and give them a tug to see if they will hold my weight. Briefly, I wonder what my chances of not breaking something are if I were to fall when I notice a drain-pipe at the next window over. Closing this one, I move to the next. I put the phone in my pocket before throwing a leg out the window.

My heart pumps frantically as I pull myself to sit on the edge of the windowsill. I gulp, looking at the drop. My hands shake as I grip the copper pipe. Minutes pass, and I finally manage to build the courage to let the pipe take my weight. When the pipe doesn't pull away, I sigh and slowly climb down it until I get a safe enough distance from the ground to jump.

Once down on the ground safely, I do a happy dance looking at the window from which I escaped, which is cut short when I heard a guard's voice and race around the corner out of view.

I know the road Trey mentioned, but I thought it was a dead end.

Making my way to the garage behind the stables, I peer in the glass window to see if anyone is in there. Finding no one, I twist the handle and rush to one of the cars. Tugging the handle, I am relieved to find it unlocked and quickly climb in before looking for the keys, which are tucked under the visor. They fall on my lap, and I take the steering wheel.

"I can do this, I can do this!" I whisper, trying to figure out where the key goes. Finding the ignition, I jam the key in and twist, the noise of it making me jump when it makes a weird noise from holding the key on for too long. I duck behind the steering wheel, worried someone might have heard. After a few moments, I sit up, putting my seatbelt on when no one comes.

After a few seconds, I push my foot on the accelerator. The car goes nowhere. I push on it harder, still nothing, before I glance down to see what I am doing wrong, I find something strange between the seats.

I briefly remember seeing the driver once fiddling with it. I squeeze the button and move it, forgetting my foot is still on the pedal, and the car flies backward and hits another vehicle behind me when I jam my foot on the brake.

"Whoops."

The alarm blares, and I panic, moving the stick thing again, only for the car to jerk forward. How do people do this? I growl, pushing it forward again, only to hit the car again. On the plus side, the alarm turned off with the second crunch of metal on metal.

Moving it again, I take my foot off the accelerator and slowly press it, and the car moves forward toward the open roller door. As I put my foot down, my heart lurches into my throat, and the car plunges forward. I take it off, easing it on and scraping the brick wall as I leave the garage. I clench my teeth at the noise. The phone person on the Navman tells me I am off route and to move back to a road as I follow the dirt track at the back.

My hands shake as I move out into the open to see guards

running in my direction, and I floor it only to jam on the brake, trying to navigate the dirt path. Hearing a tap on the window, I jump and see Dustin walking beside the car. He points to the buttons on the door handle. I press them, the roof opens up, and the window rolls down.

"This would have to be the worst getaway I have witnessed, also the slowest; I can walk faster," he laughs, and I growl, ignoring him, the car moving at a snail's pace.

"Azalea, stop the car."

"I am going to get Abbie!"

Dustin looks toward the guards, but waves them off. He clicks his tongue, walking beside the slow-moving car.

"He'll kill me anyway. Stop and move over. He will be home long before you leave the driveway at this speed," he says, and I look at him, wondering if he is trying to trick me.

"Seriously? You'll take me?"

"Hurry before I change my mind," he says, and I jam on the brakes.

He reaches into the window, moving the thing in the middle, putting it on the P.

"Move, climb over then."

"Really?" I ask him.

"Well, you will keep trying to leave, and if you are going to, I would rather be with you," he says, opening the door.

"The guards?"

"I will tell them I am teaching you to drive. Clearly, you need teaching. Kyson will murder you. This is his favorite car. It never leaves the garage," he laughs, and my face falls as he peers up the side of the car.

"If he is going to kill us, might as well before something worth dying for, right?" I nod, and I climb into the passenger seat. He gets in and glances at me.

"Put your seatbelt on," he says, and I do. He shakes his head before continuing along the path but at a quicker pace.

"We have an hour before one of them mind links to find out I am full of shit," Dustin says as we reach the road far from the castle view. He floors it, shoving me back in my seat, and whistles as the engine screams as he tears onto the street.

I laugh, even though the speed he's driving terrifies me.

"Now, let's find Abbie," Dustin says with a wink.

CHAPTER
TWENTY-EIGHT

A BBIE

A gnawing hunger twists my stomach, relentless and cruel. I am absolutely starving, my body weakened by the relentless denial of sustenance since I arrived in this wretched place. The mere thought of food sends a surge of longing through me, but the girls who dared to offer me a morsel of anything were met with brutal beatings. I can't bear to witness their suffering, not when my torment is unbearable. So, when the heavy door creaks open, I release a weary sigh and reluctantly disentangle myself from the bed, knowing all too well what awaits me.

Slumping onto the cold, unforgiving ground, I lean against the rough wall, seeking a smidge of comfort in this wretched existence. Only Kade enters the room this time, his imposing figure halting in front of me. Usually, it would be Cassandra who made her periodic visits, injecting me with some vile concoction that prevented my ability to shift. But today, she is nowhere to be seen.

"Get up!" he barks, his voice dripping with malice.

"Pardon?" I respond, confusion clouding my senses. This is not the usual routine, which scares me. Kade always derives pleasure from forcing me to watch as he indulges in indecent behavior with those poor girls before forcing himself upon me afterward, making me taste them on his cock. Yet now, his intentions seem different. A flicker of unease tingles in the air as he kicks me once more

"Get up and get on the bed," he commands, his tone laced with an unfamiliar urgency. Before I can comprehend his words, he reaches down and seizes my arm, wrenching me to my feet. My body rebels against his grip, instinctively fighting against the impending violation. My hand lashes out, delivering a stinging slap across his face, but it is futile as he retaliates with a vicious blow to my face. Pain ricochets through my body, blurring my vision and leaving my face throbbing with agony. Blood spurts from my nose, staining the air with a metallic tang as I stagger backward, my hair ripped painfully from his grasp.

In a daze, I gaze up at the ceiling, disoriented by the chaos unfolding around me. Kade's furious growls reverberate in my ears as he lunges at me. Desperation fuels my actions as I lift my leg, quickly striking his balls. The impact elicits a grunt of pain, affording me a momentary respite to roll away and escape his clutches. But he is relentless, gripping my hair and wrenching my head back with brute force.

"You will obey your Alpha," he snarls, his voice dripping with venom.

"You are not my Alpha!" I scream, defiance surging through me like a wild flame. He responds by shoving me back to the unforgiving floor. Crawling towards the wall, I pull myself up, feeling the weight of his snarls bearing down upon me. And then, unexpectedly, he stops.

"Get on the bed!" he bellows, his command echoing through the room. But this time, it washes over me like a wave crashing against an impenetrable fortress. It doesn't stick! A surge of disbelief courses through my veins, mingling with the hysteria bubbling inside me. And so, I laugh. Uncontrollably.

I cannot fathom why laughter spills from my lips, but it only serves to intensify my mirth. The furious expression etched upon Kade's face takes on a comical quality at that moment, or perhaps I have simply lost touch with reality. He regards me as if I am insane, but there is no way I will comply and climb onto that bed. I would rather endure another merciless beating, for pain is familiar and something I can handle. Throughout the years, pain has been my constant presence, and I have developed an unbreakable pain threshold.

A beating, I could take one of those. Shit, I spent half my life taking those. So, if I had to choose. I would take a beating over, letting him take more from me.

The pain reverberates through my body, a slithering serpent of agony, yet I find myself unable to suppress a taunting smirk. "What's wrong, Alpha? Can't put your Luna in line?" I jeer, my voice laced with defiance.

His face contorts with fury, turning a shade of red that mirrors the rage burning within him. "Get on the bed!" he screams, his voice cracking with desperation. But his command holds no power over me; it is feeble and pathetic, only serving to amuse me further.

As I wipe the blood from my nose, crimson stains smear across the back of my hand, "What's wrong, Alpha? Can't put your Luna in line," I taunt.

"Get on the bed!" he screams, turning red-faced. I giggle at his pathetic command.

My muscles tense, a wave of pain coursing up my spine like a relentless tidal surge. It engulfs me, threatening to consume me entirely. Yet still, I laugh. Pain has become an unwelcome constant in my life, an unyielding presence that no longer holds the power to break me. Years of enduring nothing but anguish have forged within me a limitless tolerance for suffering. I had anticipated this torment, braced myself for its arrival, and ultimately survived it.

Once again, I feel myself disconnecting from my surroundings, growing numb to everything around me. *Let him hurt me, for pain is something I can endure.* But can he? I know it must inflict its own brand of torment upon him, but as for me? No, pain resides in the realm of the mind. It is something I can switch on and off at will, desensitizing myself to its cruel touch. And so, that is precisely what I do.

Most would call me mad for what I intended to do. Calm washes over me as I let my mind float. I go on autopilot, then I poke the wolf.

"Surprised you even have a pack," I taunt, my laughter echoing through the room. His eyes darken, shifting in a tempest of rage at my words. "Mrs. Daley's commands packed a better punch, and she was an omega!" The venom drips from my words, stinging his pride with a potency that cannot be ignored. His wolf lurches forward at the disrespect, his egotistic side coming forward wanting to force me to submit; I'll die before I do.

His malt-colored wolf charges at me. Paws hit my chest, sending me flying back against the wall. My brain rattles inside my skull as it smashes against the brick wall. He snarls, stalking toward me, and suddenly, I am seeing double, yet not a sound leaves my lips. Not even when his razor-sharp teeth tear through my flesh as he mauls me.

Don't cry, tears won't save you, I think, willing myself to remain silent. *I am done shedding tears for this monster,* I remind myself. When he gets no reaction from tearing into my thigh, he tears into my shoulder and arm. Blood drenches and pools around me. My body shakes, but I do not make a sound; I just stare a silly smile on my face. Instead, I go back to my safe place. Zoning out, my mind taking me to a place where no one can touch me. A place I've been many times before.

I exist as an empty shell, only coming back to my surroundings when his teeth snap at my face. His fur puffs out as he growls when I hear a sob. In the commotion, my eyes flit toward the door to see a woman. Tears stain her cheeks, but none fall from my eyes; I feel nothing as I stare back at her fear-stricken face.

In this life, every corner seems to hide something ready to knock me down. It's been one hit after another, each punch harder than the last; every bit of hope I try to hold on to gets smashed before it can even take root.

Being fearless? Being strong, being hopeful? That's not about being brave for me. It's more like I'm just too tired to be scared anymore. Life has beaten me up, taking everything that mattered – my innocence, my dignity, the chance to love, to really live.

What's left is just me, stripped bare, down to the broken, cracked, and charred bones of my existence; those bones are painted red, black, and blue, red for my blood that's been spilled, blue for the pain endured, black for my soul they have broken, barely hanging on, a shadow of who I used to dream of being.

And what I dreamed of wasn't ego-based, wasn't selfish, wasn't materialistic; it was freedom, freedom to be more than I was yester-day. A name, not rogue, whore, slut, slave, but Abbie, yet as each day passed, I eventually forgot who she was, beaten into silence, stripped of all rights, pillaged of everything.

So death doesn't scare me now. It doesn't make my heart race or fill me with dread. Instead, it feels like it's calling to me, promising a break from all this pain.

Instead, it beckons with the gentle allure of freedom, a release from this nightmare that has become my existence. Where life has been a relentless teacher of pain, teaching me the brutal lessons of loss and despair, death whispers of peace, of the end of suffering.

I've learned to embrace the void, to look into its depths without flinching. The prospect of no more tomorrows, of no more waking to the nightmare that is my reality, offers a strange comfort. For in death, I see not an end but a beginning—a chance to escape the chains that bind me to this tortured existence.

So, I stand on the precipice of death, gazing into the abyss, unafraid. Not because I'm brave but because life has broken me to the point where continuing to exist, to endure this endless cycle of pain, is the true horror.

Kade growls and I turn my attention to his enormous wolf standing over me. He whimpers when he backs up, sniffing my thigh where he tore it apart, and I glance down. So much blood; no part of me is left unstained, left unmarred.

"Are you done?" I ask. My voice comes out unwavering, yet I can't recognize it as my own. Kade turns his furry head to the side, examining me, and I stare back, unblinking.

Kade shifts back, his bones snapping as he crouches before me. For a second, I think I see guilt flash across his features. "You will learn. You only had to get on the bed," he says, his eyes scanning over my mauled flesh. "It didn't have to be this way," he snaps, making my eyebrows rise. I laugh and shake my head, yet I can feel my blood draining out of me. Feel the blood leave my face, the cold sweat beading over my skin, and I smile.

"Get the Doctor," Kade screams as I feel myself fading, the room becoming dull.

"Abbie? I... you need to stay awake," Kade says, and I feel the tingles spread across my skin as he tries to stop the bleeding. I am bleeding out and dying, I know, and he knows it.

"Get the Pack Doctor NOW!" screams Kade as my mark burns my neck, and I relish the pain of the bond dying along with me.

"Does it hurt?" I murmur, my eyelids closing. My head falls forward, unable to keep it up when he grabs my face. His fingers pry my eyelids open, yet I only see white.

"What?... Hurry up!" Kade screams, and I hear people running up the steps toward us.

"Does it hurt?" I repeat.

"You think I wanted to do this? Of course, it hurts, I..."

"Because I feel nothing!" I giggle.

"Hang on, Abbie," Kade says, and I snort.

"For what? Certainly not for you," I mumble, my lips going numb.

"Hang on for me. I didn't mean it. You should know better; I...I..." he stutters frantically.

"Just hang on," he says as my body feels more and more limp.

"I'm sorry, Ivy," I whisper.

"Yes, yes, hang on for Ivy, please, Abbie, hang on for Ivy," Kade begs, shaking me.

"I already did. She's safe now," I breathe out as I slide down the wall I am leaning on, my face pressing against the carpet, and I can hear the frantic beating of my heart drumming in my ears. I focus on that sound, waiting for the moment it would stop when everything goes black.

CHAPTER
TWENTY-NINE

G ANNON

      For two days, I listen to his screams until they finally cut out. Liam, his face contorted with a mixture of disappointment and frustration, lets out a deep sigh and pouts, his words dripping with sadistic delight, "Pussy! I wanted to feed him his own bowels first." His eyes narrow as he gazes down at Doyle's limbless body.

"Perhaps you should have considered the consequences before you heartlessly ripped out his beating organ." I point accusingly at Liam's hand, still clutching Doyle's lifeless heart. A flicker of realization crosses his face as he glances down at the heart in his hand.

"Oh, yeah, that would have done it," he says, tossing it over his shoulder.

My skin itches from all the blood caked on it.

The thick, congealed substance clung to me like a grotesque second skin. Thick like gravy.

Surprisingly, he had endured far longer than I had anticipated. If it weren't for the blood bags Liam had procured, he would have perished long ago when we mercilessly severed his arms. As if

159

possessed by a demented euphoria, Liam whistled gleefully at the sound of the bell ringing—a signal that someone had arrived.

"Ah, customers!" he exclaimed with perverse excitement. "I've missed my true calling, I must admit. I reckon my steaks look pretty good. Wonder if they want to try my marinated Doyle steaks or the Doyle sausage," Liam says, excitedly taking the tray he had been placing his were-steaks on.

He had taken his role as a butcher to an entirely new level. I couldn't help but chuckle at his twisted dedication as he snatched up the tray, rushing eagerly towards the front of the store.

Suddenly, a shrill scream pierced the air, followed by the jingling of bells as a frightened woman fled from the premises. Liam's disappointment was palpable as he called out to her, his voice tinged with a hint of desperation, "But it's a delicacy! I marinated him myself for twelve agonizing hours!" Shaking my head at his deluded persistence, I peel off my blood-soaked rubber apron and hang it on the hook beside the freezer door.

Liam comes in with his tray in hand, looking rather upset that the woman, whoever she was, didn't want to try his Doyle steaks.

"Wasted all that time marinating those," he says, tossing the tray on the counter. He washes his knives and places them in his satchel. Grabbing the soap, I scrub my hands clean when Liam growls. I peet over my shoulder to see him glaring down at Doyle's lifeless form.

"Bloody bastard, look what you did! You owe me a new apron. You better hope I can wash this out," he snarls, taking off his apron. I raise an eyebrow at him. The man is absolutely bonkers.

"What? He got his filthy blood on it. Look at this," he says, trying to clean his apron in cold water. "He turned it pink. I'll just say it is salmon. I can pull off salmon, right?" Liam growls, scrubbing the apron that he has come to love.

"I'd like to see someone tell you couldn't," I laugh before looking at my jeans. Not even the apron could save them. I sigh, walking out through the shop to the car and retrieving the bag from the trunk. I always bring spare clothes. The town square is pretty quiet as I finally get outside. There were plenty of stares, but no one dared say anything. I am kind of waiting for them to break out in a dance, like a flash mob, with the way the noise has stopped abruptly, everyone frozen.

Shaking my head, I pop the trunk, grab a fresh shirt, and pull it on. Hearing the butcher's shop bell jingle, I glance over my shoulder, and a scream rings out from an elderly lady sitting out the front of the bakery eating a scone under a blue and white umbrella.

Liam struts out naked, drenched from head to toe in blood. He shakes off some congealed blood that has plopped on his foot as he shakes his head. His apron is clutched in his hand, and he shakes it out.

"That is not coming in the car. Put it in the trunk," I tell him.

"But how will it dry?" he whines.

"I gotta grab Logan and Oliver. The kids will freak if they see you like that," I tell him when a shriek reaches my ears and a crowd forms around the old woman.

"Are you itchy?" Liam asks, scratching his balls. I chuckle, shaking my head when people rush over to the small bakery. Liam glances over there, and so do I, to see the old woman choking. Another woman pats her back frantically, and Liam sighs and shakes his head before stomping over to her.

He starts performing the Heimlich maneuver on her, which is a sight to see. Everyone scatters as he grabs her. His arms wrapping around her, his naked ass tensing as he performs the task. A piece of scone flies from her mouth, and she sucks in a breath before he lets her go. The woman collapses on the ground, and Liam clicks his tongue, sitting her up, his junk right in her face. She gasps, her eyes going wide when she realizes his dick is like an inch off her face. She looks up at him as if she's going to faint.

Liam winks at her. "I've got something you can choke on, love," he says, blowing her a kiss. She looks at him, appalled, his dick slapping her cheek as he turns to walk back to the car. I snort and shake my head as he leans into the trunk to retrieve some clothes.

He pulls on some shorts and a tank top before moving toward the passenger side, and I jump in the driver's seat, starting the car. As I tear out of the town square, the engine revs loudly, headed for the orphanage. Liam lights a smoke, and I click my fingers at him before he growls, pulling the smoke between his lips, handing it to me, and lighting another. I draw back on the smoke while weaving through the streets to get the kids.

"So what do you intend to do with them, anyway? Since when did you become all fatherly?" Liam asks, and I shrug. I never gave much thought to kids until I met Abbie. Maybe I could keep them? I shake the idea away. Abbie might not want kids. I suppose we will see each other when I get her back.

"I'm not keeping them," I tell him.

"So, why are we taking them?"

"Clarice," I tell him.

"Ah, I see, a fine woman. Too bad she could never have kids. She would have been an excellent mother," Liam says.

"Well, she is a mother. She practically raised Kyson and half the servant's kids. Clarice will look after them, love them," I tell him, and Liam nods.

CHAPTER
THIRTY

ABBIE

The steady beep of hospital equipment reaches my ears as I blink up at the white ceiling. My eyes feel heavy, my limbs immobile. Tears brim as I try to understand where I am and why I'm here.

Why? How could life be so cruel and bring me back? I remember the pain, the darkness, and then nothingness. Complete oblivion was what I expected; I had made my peace with it. I was ready to go. But here I am, alive.

I try to move my arms, but they feel like dead weights. Panic starts to rise in my chest as memories flood back. Kade shifting, the pain, and then everything going black. Was it all a dream? Or am I really alive?

"Abbie?" A soft voice breaks through the haze in my mind, and I turn my head to see a blurry outline of Kade, looking worried and disheveled. *No!*

"Thank god," comes his rasp of a voice before he's above, hovering over me. His hands paw at me, and I look away from him.

"I thought I lost you; the Moon Goddess must have heard my

prayers," he gushes, fussing over me like he was some fantastic mate and not the person who did this to me.

"She heard yours, but mine fell on deaf ears," I groan. Fuck, if she had heard mine, I would have been dead years ago. But here I am still, the so-called Moon Goddess fucking shit up and not giving me the luxury of death.

Kade grabs my face in his hands. Sparks rush over my entire body and make my whole body heat up. The bond reacts despite knowing what kind of monster he is. I gasp in horror as I become aware of the throbbing in my neck. Instinctively, I reach up and touch my mark to find it fresh.

Kade remarked me. Our severed bond is now stronger than ever by the feeling of the sparks that course over my entire body. Kade purrs while I think of how I failed to sever the bond and am again stuck with the miserable bastard.

"That was close," Kade sighs, kissing my forehead like he is some loving mate. I just blink and say nothing.

"Well, at least you have learned your lesson. Then, after all this mess, we can go home. Cassandra said she would make you a nice dinner. Need to get you up to full strength so we can complete the mating process; I will ask the Doctor to give you something to bring on your heat," he says before walking out. This can't be happening.

I swallow and try to move my hand to brush my hair back to find I am handcuffed to the bed by one hand. I tug on the handcuff, yet it doesn't budge. Sitting up, my entire body starts aching.

Panic bubbles up inside me as I remember what happened before passing out. Kade must have brought me here after he shifted back into his human form. I take a deep breath and try to calm myself down. My mind races as I try to come up with a plan for escape.

My leg burns the most, and so does every inch of me. Using my other hand, I tug the hospital gown down a little, groaning as I do. My shoulder is covered in stitches. Rolling the skirt up, I see my leg is the same. His mark may have saved me, but it didn't heal me. That's when I noticed the drip attached to my hand. I follow the line to see a blood bag and another bag filled with some kind of clear liquid.

My heart races as I realize what Kade must have done. He's keeping me alive by feeding me his blood and using whatever drug is in that other bag to keep me subdued and unable to fight back. The thought sickens me, but there's nothing I can do about it now.

I try to sit up more, wincing at the soreness in my body. My head spins, and spots dance in front of my eyes, making me dizzy and disoriented.

I choke when I realize it had the same label as the shit Cassandra had been pumping into me. No wonder I look like Frankenstein. Kade is still preventing me from shifting, and God knows how long that drip had been attached to me because it's not dark outside. I don't even know if it's the same day.

I lay back down when I hear Kade talking to the Doctor and hearing their voices grow nearer. Kade saunters into the room, a massive grin on his face.

"The Doctor said you can come home tomorrow. Isn't that great? He will prepare the injection just before you are discharged," he tells me.

"Why are you doing this? Why keep me alive like this?" I demand, glaring at him with all the anger and fear inside of me.

Kade's expression turns serious as he looks at me. "Because you're mine."

His words send shivers down my spine and make bile rise in my throat. I shake my head in disbelief and disgust. "You're insane if you think that means I belong to you. You're a monster, Kade."

His face twists in anger, and he goes to say something when suddenly the door opens. A nurse comes in with a tray of food. She glances at Kade nervously, and I can tell she fears him with the way she averts her gaze to the floor and drops her head, her curly dark hair covering her face.

"Hurry, hurry," Kade snaps at her as she wheels a small table over that slides under the bed before turning the tabletop so it sits above me. The smell of food makes my belly growl hungrily. My mouth salivates. She sets a tray on the table, and Kade clicks his tongue and growls.

"It's too much; I said something small until after her heat," Kade snaps at the woman. Taking the tray, which smells divine, he takes a pudding cup off it before thrusting the tray at her. She glances at me, and my stomach screams in protest as he takes whatever is under the plate cover from me. He slaps the pudding cup on the table. The woman bites her lip but takes the tray, looking at me apologetically. She goes to hand me the spoon, but Kade slaps it out of her hand.

The more I stare at her, for some reason, she reminds me of someone, I just can't think of who? It is her eyes and cheekbones. They look familiar. I have no idea why I feel that way.

"Idiot. It could be used as a weapon," he snarls at her. The woman blinks at him.

"She is handcuffed, Alpha. Where would she go?"

"Until I complete the mating process, no utensils. I don't want my mate to harm herself," Kade growls.

"Maybe I can feed her. You said she hadn't eaten in days; the Doctor recommended this meal to help strengthen her," she tries to argue, and I notice the malicious glint in his eye.

"It's alright. I'm not hungry, just thirsty," I tell her, not wanting to get her into trouble. Yet, my belly rumbles loudly. We all hear it in the quiet room.

"See?" Kade says, snatching the pudding cup off the tray. He thrusts it at me, and my hand shakes as I take it from him.

"Now leave. You are the last person I want to see in her room," he snarls, and she nods, rushing out. I stare after her as she runs out.

"Bloody fool, are you alright, my love?" he says, and I look at Kade and nod.

It is like his personality switched back and forth. He takes the pudding cup and pokes a hole in it before returning it. I try to figure out why the woman looks so familiar. I know I haven't seen her before, but something about her gives me déjà vu.

Shaking the thought off, I slurp my measly portion down. Kade only allows me half the pudding cup and watches me dig it out with my fingers before taking it. He tells me he doesn't want a fat Luna. It is humiliating, especially given the fact that I'm now skin and bones, but I remain quiet, hoping he will leave soon. After about an hour of sitting in silence, watching Kade fiddle with his phone, he stands up from the blue chair and walks over to me.

Leaning over the bed, he grips my chin, tilting my face up to his before shoving his filthy tongue down my throat. The bond reacts, but I just go to my safe place, go to the darkest parts of my mind, and float.

"I need to go, but I will return first thing in the morning. The Doctor will send someone in to give you some drugs to help you sleep," he says. I nod my head robotically.

Once he leaves, I try as hard as I can to get out of the handcuff, but nothing works; it is so tight that the tips of my fingers are going numb from putting strain on it trying to break out of it. My will to escape is dying, along with the last part of my will to live when the crippling pain washes over me.

Tears prick my eyes as I feel his infidelity wash over me once more. Life is cruel, and the Moon Goddess, if she exists, is determined to make me suffer. Rolling on my side, I hug my belly with my free hand. Half an hour later, the pack doctor comes in again. The man is an older gentleman. He looks over my notes and shakes his head. He checks my drip when the woman from before comes in.

"Alana will give you something to help you sleep, and in the morning, I will give a small injection into your ovaries to bring on your heat. You were fortunate. You almost died; if it wasn't for Kade's quick thinking of remarking you, we would have lost you," the Doctor says.

"Yes, so lucky to live with my pig of a mate," I sneer, and he nods, having not paid attention to what I was saying, too busy looking at the charts in his hand.

"You can give it to her, Alana, then observe every two hours," he tells her, and the woman approaches me. She smiles sadly as she walks around the bed and takes my arm in her hand. The Doctor watches as she stabs the needle into the cannula port in my free hand.

The Doctor sighs when I feel the top of my hand become wet, and I look at her. Her eyes meet mine, and I look down to see her hand covering the needle as she squirts the contents on my skin, not through the cannula, spilling it all over the bed. She then places my hand over the spot.

"Hurry, I haven't got all night," the Doctor complains.

"I'm done, Doc," she says, dropping the syringe into the small green plastic bowl she brought in with her. He nods, and she makes her way over to my drip, changing the bags out while the Doctor walks out.

She waits a few seconds before rushing over to me and grabbing my hand just as the Doctor walks back in. I feel something metal brushing my palm, and she quickly makes out she is tucking the surrounding blankets around me.

"You may feel a little groggy; don't fight it," she says, staring at me before glancing at the hand she had placed a key in, and the Doctor clears his throat.

"Alana, bed four needs changing again. Mr. Masters wet himself again," he groans.

"Yes, right away, Doc, just need to change out her bag on the drip," she says, and he nods, walking back out.

This time, when he leaves, he doesn't return. Alana rushes over to me and starts unplugging the machines attached to me. I wait for the beep, only to peer at the monitor and see that she has switched it off.

"I found a spare key in Doc's office. You have two hours to run east," she whispers.

"Why are you helping me?"

"My sister, Blaire, told me about you; now, don't waste any time;

he will feel you once you get too far away," she says before glancing over her shoulder.

Alana pulls a piece of paper from her cleavage and tucks it under my bottom. "I got your friend's number. Blaire gave it to me. She stole it from his phone and sent it to me. He then killed her for touching his phone, but I wrote it down. You must have been worth dying for, or she wouldn't have sent it. Blaire wanted to call whoever it was. She never said who in the message. I would give you a phone to call for help, but all calls are monitored and listened to. East there is a town there, you can ring from there. You try before you leave the town limits, and he will know about it."

"What about you?" I ask.

She doesn't answer; she just rushes over to the window and opens it before running out, closing the door behind her. I swallow, pulling the paper out with a number scribbled on it. Waiting a few minutes to make sure no one is coming in, I then use the key to undo the handcuff. I rub my wrist before forcing myself off the bed.

My legs collapse under me when they touch the floor, and I clench my teeth to stop screaming. Pain ravages me from my injuries and Kade's infidelity, but I force myself up and over to the plastic bag sitting on the chair that Kade brought with him.

Opening it, I find a man's shirt and some jeans. I swallow when I realize they must be Cassandra's jeans. I looked over my shoulder at the door, but no one seems to be in the hall. Pulling my hospital gown off, I pull the shirt on before gritting my teeth as I pull the jeans on.

My stitches tug and pull painfully. Sweat coats me with so much effort. Walking to the window, I try to figure out where the east is. She could have pointed that out, or I should have asked. My skin burns as the jeans rub my mauled leg, and I struggle to lift it over the windowsill. Breathing harshly, I pull the other over before sitting on the ledge.

After a few seconds, I brace myself for the pain and jump. It is only about a two-meter drop, but it feels like I had jumped from a lot higher when I hit the ground. Pain rattles through me as I land on my bad leg. Choking on a sob, I fight the urge to pass out as I rise to my feet, using the wall for support.

I see no one around and take off running as fast as my legs allow. My legs are killing with each movement and the bad one dragging behind me, but I still bite down on the instinct to stop and push on. The pain will not stop me. Ivy will come for me. I know she will come; I just need to get to that town.

THIRTY-ONE

K YSON

The drive is taking forever as we head for the borders of Landeena Kingdom. Someone had hung rogues along the castle walls so we were going to investigate. My entire body is vibrating from the effects of the bond and Azalea's heat. The effects are no different, even miles away. If anything, they're getting worse, as the urge to turn around and go home grows stronger.

Sweat coats my skin. I removed my shirt an hour ago, which hasn't helped seeing as my temperature continues rising, along with my anger. Poor Damian has remained quiet most of the trip, careful not to disturb me. Just the noise of the tires on the wheels aggravates me.

Not even three hours into the trip, the mindlink opens and Trey's panicked voice flits through my head.

'I can't find her,' he rushes out, and my stomach plummets to somewhere deep inside me. I fight the urge to immediately shift at his words. My claws sink into the leather seats, and the stuffing sprays everywhere. Damian glances at me nervously out of the corner of his eye.

'*What do you mean you can't find her?*' I snarl, my voice strained with anger and worry.

'*I mean exactly that,*' Trey replies, his voice shaking slightly.

'*Excuse me?*' I snarl back through the bond.

'*The Queen, she ran off with Dustin. He said he was teaching her how to drive. One of the guards said, but it has been an hour and a half, and we cannot find either of them or the car,*' he tells me.

'*Dustin said he was teaching her to drive, and you didn't think to fucking question that?*' I snap at him, seething. Damian glances at me, and I growl, my fist connecting with the dash, setting off the airbag. My claws slash through it, and Damian jumps, nearly swerving off the road.

I growl low in my throat as I try to process this information.

'*I thought she was in her room. She was...I didn't even know she had climbed out her window until Clarice went to bring her dinner in and found it wide open,*' Trey explains.

Turning to Damian, he looked at me. '*Damian, turn this car around,*' I order, my voice laced with a dangerous edge.

Damian nods and quickly takes an exit off the highway, turning the car around towards our kingdom. I have no doubt where she would have gone, but when I get my hands on Dustin, he is dead.

'*Check the footage to find out which road they took,*' I snap at Trey.

'*Already did. They left out the rear exit that runs along the river and headed for the highway.*'

I growl, knowing I am right. Azalea is going after Abbie even after I told her not to. The damn girl can't fucking listen to save her life. Bloody foolish, and Trey will be in for it when I get back for not paying better attention to his guard.

'*Is Gannon back yet?*' I ask him. Gannon will drop whatever he is doing and go if he knows.

'*No, sir, he shouldn't be far out, though.*'

I cut the link before feeling for Gannon's link. It opens immediately.

'*Where are you?*' I demand.

'*10 minutes out. What's up?*'

'*I am on my way back home, but further out, I need you to get Azalea and bring her home.*'

'*Azalea?*' he asks.

'*She ran off with Dustin to go after Abbie. You need to get to her until I get there.*'

'*Fuck! That bloody idiot should know better than to take Azalea into hunter's territory at night,*' Gannon growls. I know the pact he made now would overwhelm him as strongly as a command would. Pacts aren't taken lightly and require my blood, and hours of orders are forced on them so they can't break them. The only one who can break it is me.

I can force them to break it, but that would also be extremely difficult and take hours of me breaking their will. They would still run back for her the moment the command would drop. Which is precisely why they all turned on me when I banished her out of the castle. Most that signed up for it passed out and couldn't pass. Only 11 made it through the process, two of whom are dead now. It works similarly to the council not being able to be commanded, only it is directed to a specific person; I hoped I wouldn't have to, but Azalea has now left me no choice. I know she won't like it, but I won't put her life at risk.

She will be blood-tying herself to her guard; I won't let this mistake happen again, and Dustin will learn from this mistake. I trusted only Damian, Gannon, Liam, and him with her, completely followed by Trey. They lasted the longest during the trials, and that is exactly why they hold the positions they do.

The urge to protect her will be running through all my royal guards. No doubt, the others will be frantically searching the forests for her and Dustin. However, they wouldn't have expected Dustin to do something so stupid, and being fourth in command, they wouldn't have questioned him. I growl. He will pay for betraying me!

'*Which road?*' Gannon asks with an angry edge to his voice. Azalea's stupidity not only endangers herself, but likely Abbie as well. He would want to kill Dustin, and Dustin would know precisely what he would be coming home to.

'Highway,' I answer, and he growls. That is the worst road to travel on at night.

'Abbie?' he asks.

'Perfectly fine, seeing her on the weekend. You can come but bring my fucking mate home!' I tell him.

'I will bring the Queen back to you. What of Dustin?'

'Leave him for me,' I growl, cutting the link.

"What's going on?" Damian asks, ripping the car around. Our entourage follows and spins around after us.

"Azalea has run to go to Abbie," the moment the words leave my lips, Damian starts flooring it.

"Fuck!" he curses, knowing how bad that area is predominantly at night. Dustin should have known better, and he will pay dearly for his mistake. How he can agree to something like that is beyond me.

My eyes flicker, and I open the bond, feeling for her and what direction she went. Heat smashes into me. She may not be able to feel it, but I indeed do, and its intensity forces the shift in me. Damian slams on the brakes, and I only just rip myself out of the car before destroying it.

Cars screech to a stop, some skidding onto the grass to avoid hitting me, but I had one thing on my mind: to get to my mate. So I head for the forest, running, the trees blurring past me, and I let the bond guide me to her. She will be in serious trouble when I get my fucking hands on her.

THIRTY-TWO

ABBIE

My feet ache from running, my muscles protesting, and my lungs burning. I want nothing more than to collapse onto the cold concrete beneath me, to catch my breath and rest my weary body. But I can't stop, not when I know my window of opportunity is small. I have no idea if I am even running in the right direction or how far the town is, making decisions at each corner harder.

I run blindly through deserted streets, ignoring the pain and exhaustion. My heart races in my chest, fear and adrenaline pumping through my veins. The fact I couldn't read any of the signs makes it even harder. Yet still, I run, praying that Ivy is on her way to me. Praying she picked up on my subtle message; hope is all I have, especially once the howls ring clearly through the sky.

His voice booms into the mindlink, hurting my brain, demanding I return home. When the screams and threats don't work, he tones it down. When that doesn't work, he yells again.

"You tell me your whereabouts, love, I will come get you. You stop at anyone's door and hand yourself in, and we can go home and put this behind us," he tells me, and I wonder if he actually thinks I'm stupid enough to believe him.

"Fucking whore! When I find you, I will make sure you can never run from me again!" he snarls angrily after a few minutes. Then back to the coaxing in gentle tones, only for his true colors to shine through once again.

By the time I am out of the town and on a long stretch of road, my feet are bleeding, my shirt is drenched with blood, and I am limping worse than when I started. My hand presses firmly against my side as I try to stem the bleeding. Yet hope comes in the form of a service station. Its light is a burning beacon in the night, and I pick up my pace, nearly there, yet I'm not oblivious to how the howls grow closer, and the sound of revving engines of cars tear up the town behind me, heading my way.

The neon lights of the service station sign illuminate the dark night, casting an eerie glow on the deserted pumps and flickering windows.

Reaching the service station. I burst through the door of the run down little building, panting heavily and my heart beating a million miles an hour. The man behind the counter jumps at the sudden commotion, his eyes widening in shock as he takes in my bloodied appearance.

"Ma'am?" he stammers, stepping back as I move towards him.

"Someone is after me! I need your phone!" I gush, desperation and fear evident in my voice. I frantically scan the area outside through the windows, expecting to see my mate hot on my trail.

The man seems stunned by my bloody appearance before shaking his head and looking for his phone.

"I have a first aid kit," he tells me after passing the phone. He asks questions and unlocks the door while peering out. I reach into my pockets to find the piece of paper with the number on it that Alana had given me while trying to answer his questions. My hands shake as I punch the number into the corded phone to call Ivy. When the phone starts calling, I hold it to my ear.

"Pick up. Pick up," I whisper, not realizing the call had already connected.

"Abbie?" she asks.

"There should be a microphone picture. Press it so I can hear," Dustin says in the background; it sounded like they were in a car.

"Are you there?" I ask while glancing around the windows.

"Yes, can you hear me?" Ivy asks, the phone volume turning a little static and crackling.

A sob escapes me. "Ivy! Oh please, thank God!" I gasp.

"I'm right here," Ivy tells me. And I can't seem to get myself together enough to speak.

"Did she answer?" the man from the service station asks.

"She answered," I tell him, peeking over at him as he watched out the window.

"Thank you so much," I quickly tell him before listening to the static through the phone.

"Are you there still?" I ask.

"Yes, I am. I am..." The phone crackles before the phone drops out of reception. I curse and call again. It immediately starts ringing again, and Ivy answers it.

"Abbie?" she asks.

"Listen, I need you to come to get me. I was wrong about Kade, Ivy. Send Gannon. Please! I want to come home! I am..." she falls silent. "I don't know where I am. I can't read the sign. I am... Where am I?" I ask, turning to the service station manager.

"Metro service station. It is in Langley," he tells me.

"Metro Service station in Langley. Abbie is there!" Ivy tells Dustin, obviously hearing him in the background.

"Are you okay, Abbie? We are nearly there," Ivy tells me, and I sigh.

"You have to be quick. I know he already knows I ran. Wait, you are nearly here?" I ask.

"You never said it back," Ivy tells me, and I break down sobbing into the phone. She knew something was wrong. I hoped she picked up on it during the call. Immense relief floods me.

"I thought you didn't figure it out!" I choke, wiping my eyes on the back of my hand, and the phone goes grainy again.

"You always say it back," she tells me, and I nod.

"What sort of car did you say your boyfriend drives?" the man asks beside me when a car pulls into the service station. Kade's car. I gasp. "A black one," I murmur when I see him climb out of his car, and I duck before I hear a bell chime as the door opens.

"Get down behind the counter," the man says, and I hold my breath, dropping to sit and lean against the counter, with the phone still clutched to my ear.

"He found me! Hurry!" I whisper into the phone. I hear the service station attendant speak above me and glance at him.

"Can I help you, sir?" he asks before I hear Kade's voice.

"I'm looking for a girl. Abbie, come out. This human won't save you from me!" Kade's voice growls, and I flinch at his tone.

"Sir, I have not seen a girl," the man says.

"I can smell her. Now come out, Abbie, before I kill this man!" Kade's menacing growl threatens.

I swallow, and my skin prickles with goosebumps as his footsteps grow closer. The man is suddenly grabbed by the collar of his shirt and ripped over the top of the counter. I scream, jumping to my feet in time to see Kade snap the man's neck.

His eyes dart to mine, and I drop the phone. I race toward the rear of the building, where the man had gone to retrieve the first aid kit. Kade snarls and gives chase, and I find a door. My palms hit hard, and it bursts open. Once outside, I look around briefly before taking off across the road toward the mountain to hide in the forest.

"Abbie!" Kade snarls, and adrenaline pumps through my veins, dulling all my pain as I run for my life. The howls grow louder in the distance as his pack closes in. I slip on the loose dirt and twigs as I force my body to climb the mountain, only to be tackled. Kade's fist slams into the back of my head before my side, making me wheeze, and I feel my ribs crack. My scream is deafening and hurts my ears.

"Think you can run from me! Who were you on the phone to?" he says, ripping me backward by my hair.

"Fuck you!" I spit at him just as I hear a loud crash, like a car accident coming from above. I kick and thrash while screaming for help.

A furious growl tears out of Kade, and he tosses me into a nearby tree. Pain washed over me as all the air leaves my body. I get to my hands and knees, only for him to grab my hair.

"Ivy!" I scream out clearly through the forest, praying she could hear me, when he starts dragging me down the mountainside with my flailing and thrashing.

Kade drags me out, down the hill, and onto the grassy patch. I escape his clutches and begin running again when his body hits mine from behind, and he pins me to the grass of the small meadow at the bottom of the mountain.

My eyes try desperately to scan my surroundings, my vision attempting to correct itself. But everything looks extremely fuzzing except the neon sign, which blinks frantically. All I can hear is the static noise emanating from it. The service station is about 300 meters from me and across the road. I scream when Kade starts ripping me backward from the woods. Kicking and screaming, I thrash around, trying to loosen his grip, begging him to let me go. Those pleas fall on deaf ears, however. Kade ignores me and rips me out of the tree line again.

CHAPTER
THIRTY-THREE

AZALEA

Dustin doesn't slow the car down once but glances at me nervously when we come to a particular spot on the winding roads. We know the castle is already aware of us leaving because Trey had mindlinked Dustin. I'm nervous, knowing the King will be furious. Plus, I'm scared for Dustin. "What?" I ask him, seeing him suddenly becoming nervous.

"We are about to drive through no-man's-land. I need you to get in the back. We aren't sure if the hunters know about you yet, but it won't surprise me because they have eyes and ears everywhere. Nowhere is safe," he tells me. My heart beats erratically at his words, and I swallow. We were deep into the forest and heading toward a range that leads between the mountains.

"Climb in the back and put your belt on. Stay low; the hunters have wild-game cameras in the trees, and I don't want you spotted. We cannot stop along this stretch, especially without the royal guard with us," Dustin tells me, and I glance at the backseat over my shoulder. I unplug my seatbelt before climbing between the seats and into the back. Looking around the back on the floor, I notice some tools, recognizing one to be a wheel brace. Also, some duct tape and rope. I bite my lip, not wanting to know why they are in the car. The wheel brace, sure, but why the duct tape and rope?

"Seatbelt, Azalea," Dustin says firmly before shrugging his jacket off, only leaving one hand on the wheel at a time. I quickly plug it in and see him glance in the rear vision mirror. He tosses me the jacket.

"Now, get down! Pull that jacket over you. The windows aren't tinted in this car," he says, and I sink down in my seat just as he floors it, accelerating even more. I am shocked at how much speed this car has; I honestly think we are moving too fast. Everything zips by in a blur. Dustin is driving so fast; we are passing cars like they are standing still. I remain quiet, letting him focus on driving along the steep, winding road leading into the mountains.

When we come to the top, it is a harrowing drive back down the other side, and he never slows, if anything, he speeds up more. I start to feel queasy from the motion. The car slides around the corners and makes me hit the door. His eyes flickering to me in the rear vision mirror occasionally makes my heart jolt when he takes his eyes off the road, even if only briefly.

After another half an hour of driving, I hear him let out a relieved sigh, so I know we must be coming into Alpha Kade's territory or at least off no-man's-land.

"How far out are we?" I ask him, and he looks back at me.

"About thirty minutes from the packhouse," Dustin says. We drive a little further, and I see a sign saying we are coming to a town when my phone starts ringing. Dustin glances at it, where it sits in the center console. We are coming to another steep incline, and I wonder why anyone would live far out into the mountains, hoping this one wouldn't be as winding as the last one. Leaning over, I grab it and answer it. What I wasn't expecting was to hear Abbie's voice.

"Pick up, pick up," I hear her say, not realizing the call had already connected.

"Abbie?" I ask, and Dustin glances at me in the mirror, his brows furrow, and I know he must be listening in on the call.

"Pull the phone away. Now on the screen. There should be a microphone picture. Press it so I can hear what she is saying," Dustin says. I quickly do as I am told before staring at the phone, wishing I could see her. "Are you there?" I hear her ask.

"Yes, can you hear me?" I ask her, the phone volume turning a little static and crackling.

A sob escapes Abbie. "Ivy! Oh please, thank god," she gasps.

"I'm right here," I tell her, and she cries into the phone, trying to contain herself.

"She answered?" I hear a man's voice say in the background.

"Yes, thank you so much," I hear her gush, her voice lowers slightly so I know she has turned her face away from the phone.

"Are you still there?"

"Yes, I am. I am..." The phone crackles before the phone drops out of reception. It immediately starts ringing again, and I answer it, putting it on the loudspeaker once more.

"Abbie?"

"Listen, I need you to come to get me. I was wrong about Kade, Ivy. Send Gannon. Please, I want to come home; I am..." she falls silent. "I don't know where I am. I can't read the sign; I am... where am I?" I hear her ask the person with her.

"Metro service station, it is in Langley," I hear a man's voice tell her in the background.

"Metro Service station in Langley. Abbie is there!" I tell Dustin, and he nods, having already heard.

"Are you okay, Abbie? We are nearly there," I recite that to Abbie, and she sighs.

"You have to be quick; I know he already knows I ran. Wait, you are nearly here?" she asks.

"You never said it back," I tell her, and she breaks down, sobbing into the phone.

"I thought you didn't figure it out." Abbie chokes out, and the phone goes grainy again.

"You always say it back," I tell her.

"What sort of car did you say your boyfriend drives?" I hear the man ask in the background before listening to Abbie gasp. "A black one," she says when I hear a bell chime in the background.

"Get down behind the counter," he says, and the phone goes deadly silent.

"He found me. Hurry," I hear her whisper into the phone. I hear the service station attendant speak close to her and realize she must be behind the counter with him.

"Can I help you, sir?" I hear him ask before hearing Kade's voice.

"I'm looking for a girl. Abbie, come out. This human won't save you from me," Kade's voice growls.

"Sir, I have not seen a girl," the man says.

"I can smell her. Now come out, Abbie, before I kill this man," I hear Kade growl out. I swallow, listening intently before hearing Abbie scream along with loud banging and grunts. A furious growl tears out of Kade, and my heart sinks to my stomach. I place the phone to my ear, and the phone goes dead. "Abbie?" Yet, all I got is the dial tone.

Dustin floors it, driving faster toward the town when suddenly, he screams at the cars swerving off the road. It's like time is slowing right down. My eyes widen when Dustin tenses and clutches his head. My gasp sounds so loud as we hit the gravel and the side rail.

The car becomes airborne as it bounces off the guardrail and flies toward the forest. Dustin turns his head to look at me. I see a horrified look on his face as the car careens over the side rail, turning upside down in the air. Dustin's eyes are glazed over, and I can see someone has mindlinked him, which caused the accident.

The sound of metal on metal reverberates as the car flips and smashes into trees, rolling down the hill. My stomach lurches into my throat, and I am tossed around like a rag doll in the back seat, the windows smashing out, and the noise is so loud it makes my ears ring. The crunching of metal and breaking windows rings out into the night as the car bounces off the tree.

My head smashes against the roof lining, and the car lands

upright beside an enormous tree. Dazed, I groan, clutching my head as I look around to see Dustin slumped forward in his seat, knocked out. Blood is dripping from his head. Frantically, I tug on my seatbelt, trying to unclip it. I try to open my door, but it is crushed from the roof, and the other door is pinned against the tree that has stopped rolling further down the hill. Finally getting free of my seatbelt, pain ricochets through me with each movement.

Reaching forward, I grip the back of the front seat headrest, pulling myself forward, my fingers slipping off the leather fabric made slippery with my blood. Blood trickles down the side of my face, some getting in my mouth and filling my left eye. I blink, wiping my face with the back of my hand and shuffling forward in my seat.

Climbing over the seat into the front passenger seat, I see the footwell is no longer there as the dash is pushed right into the chair. My knee brushes something that sends shooting pain through my abdomen. Falling in the passenger seat, I choke when I see a massive piece of metal embedded in my hip and stomach.

A gasp leaves me when I try to pull it out before choking on a sob and deciding to leave it. Sickened, I touch my back to find it has gone through. I have an overwhelming urge to pull it out but I know it's probably best to leave it. Grabbing Dustin's head, I tilt it back, and he groans; his shoulders drop, his head falling forward when I let him go before it snaps upright. Dustin looks around at me frantically, twisting in his seat. He clutches my arms before looking down at the metal that is stabbing through me.

"I'm fine," I tell him, though I can feel my pants and shirt soaked with blood.

Dustin looks around. "The King ordered me to stop," he says, clutching his head. He tries to open his door, but it's stuck against the tree. I gasp in pain, and Dustin tries to pull his legs out from under the steering wheel, which is pressed to his stomach. The whole front end of the car pushed into the front seats.

"Hang on, I will get you out," he says while groaning when he tries to unpin himself. My head pounds and my eyes pulse to their own beat. My vision blurs as I look around at the dark forest, only to spot the glimmer of lights among the trees at the bottom of the incline.

Those are town lights, and I gasp. "Abbie!"

"Azalea, no," Dustin hisses, attempting to free himself.

"That's where she is," I tell him, and he tries to grab my arm as I turn in my seat.

"Wait, the King and Gannon are on their way," he tells me, grimacing.

I shake my head, looking at him, but he looks fine despite being a little banged up and trapped. Abbie is right down there; I could just make out the service station's enormous neon sign blinking like a beacon straight to her.

"No, Azalea. They are twenty minutes behind us. Wait."

"Huh, we left hours ago," I tell him. There is no way they could have caught up to us by now.

"Lycans can outrun even the fastest cars, Azalea. The King is running through the forest to get here, and Gannon is even closer. Just wait. You can't even shift from the drugs in your system to stop your heat," Dustin growls at me, punching the steering wheel in frustration because he couldn't get out.

"But Abbie, she is right there," I tell him. He shakes his head. I sigh before nodding. "Fine, at least let me climb out and see if I can open the door for you so you can slide out," he sighs, glancing at his trapped legs and then nodding.

"Be careful. That rod is all the way through," he says, peering at my stomach. I touch it and hiss, wondering where it came from before realizing it was a wheel brace on the back floor. I gulp, but carefully climb through my broken window and out of the car. Blood drenches me from the movement, and I hit the ground hard, coughing and sputtering.

"Azalea!" Dustin shrieks.

185

"I'm fine," I choke, getting to my feet and walking around the wrecked car when I hear a blood-curdling scream.

"Ivy!" her voice rings out clearly through the forest, bouncing off the trees. My blood goes ice-cold, and I glance through the broken windshield at Dustin. He shakes his head. His eyes go wide when I hear her scream again. My heart rate spikes, and I feel adrenaline pulse through me.

"Don't you do it," Dustin screams as I take off, running to wherever I hear her voice screaming out into the night.

THIRTY-FOUR

A ZALEA

Once I start running down the hill, I find I am unable to stop. The incline propels me down, and even as I try to gain traction, I am sliding, underestimating how steep the mountain is, and I can't stop my feet. I try to grab a tree trunk, only for my grip to slip straight off, and the air leaves my lungs as the motion of attempting to stop myself sends me hurtling to the ground at an angle. The wheel brace pushes through me further, stealing my breath as pain courses through me.

A scream tears from my lips at the agony, and I begin rolling down the hill, smashing into trees and becoming airborne. I tumble down before hitting the bottom and seeing black as my head bounces off the hard ground.

It is only moments when my surroundings return. I am too dazed and in too much pain at first to realize what's going on. The wheel brace has been ripped out somewhere along the way. My vision blurs and doubles as I get to my hands and knees, trying to catch my breath. The trees look more like a wall encasing me as I stagger to my feet. I stumble around blindly for what feels like forever until the vertigo and blurriness abate. The forest is deadly silent. Not even the sound of crickets can be heard. Stumbling out of the tree line, I find myself in a grassy area beside a road.

My eyes try desperately to scan my surroundings, my vision attempting to correct itself. But everything looks extremely fuzzing except the neon sign, which blinks frantically. All I can hear is the static noise emanating from it. The service station is about 300 meters from me and across the road. I am about to make my way over to it when Abbie's scream rings out loudly and sends my head turning to my left to see Kade ripping Abbie backward from the woods. Abbie is kicking and screaming, thrashing around wildly as she struggles against him. Her pleas fall on deaf ears, however. Kade ignores her as he rips her out of the tree line near to me.

A gasp escapes me as I pivot and head toward her, only to trip in a small dip in the grass, landing face down in the dewy grass.

My heart races as I struggle to get to my feet. My breathing is harsh as I stagger determinedly toward Abbie and Kade. I keep falling, unable to keep my legs under me, and hitting the damp ground. The air leaves my lungs in a long wheeze on the fourth fall. I feel like I am trying to walk on the moon or like I am drunk. The ground is moving under me, and I clutch my stomach, trying to stem the bleeding. My head pounds against my skull as I make my way over to them.

"I reject you; I reject you!!" Abbie screams. I groan, the sound barely audible to my own ears over her screaming. Kade tosses her to the ground, and she crawls away from him as I struggle to get back to my feet.

"Doesn't work like that, love. That is not how you reject someone," he growls at her, stalking toward her. On my hands and knees, I see a rock and grab it before getting to my feet, and I hear a scream. It takes me a few moments to realize it is my own war cry when I rush at him, and he suddenly spins around, deflecting my raised hand about to hit him with the rock.

Kade and I crash to the ground. The rock flies from my grip as he lands on top of me and rolls away. Kade growls, trying to pin me.

"What are you doing here?" he snaps, holding me down on my back. I thought it odd. He could easily kill me, yet he only tries to pin me. Kade abruptly freezes before he growls and looks over his shoulder. His eyes dart to the tree line in a panic. Suddenly, I hear a thud, and Kade tenses above me.

I spot Abbie behind me, the rock in her hand, and Kade's blood drips on me, where she had hit him with it. Kade turns to attack her, but I grab his ankle, tripping him, and Abbie smashes him in the head with the rock again, and he goes limp on the ground, face down and unmoving.

Sitting up, I look at her, and she rushes over to me. Tears streak her face, blood coats her skin, and she has twigs in her hair.

The rock drops from her hand as she steps over Kade and moves toward me to help me sit up. My hand went immediately to my stomach, which is bleeding a steady stream and saturating my torn and filthy pants.

"Ivy!" Abbie gushes, clutching my arms as she hauls me upright. A sigh escapes me, and she grabs my face in her hands, sobbing uncontrollably. Only the moment she does. I see Kade get back to his feet, and my eyes go wide as he stumbles, looking around.

"Abbie!" I gasp, and she looks briefly behind her before ripping me to my feet with a strength I wasn't sure she possessed, given the state she was in.

"Can you shift?" I ask her, but she shakes her head.

"You?" I look down at my bleeding wound and also shake mine. Abbie whimpers, and Kade seems confused. Suddenly, howls in the distance ring out loudly, sending my blood cold. An icy shiver slivers up my spine.

"The pack! He called his pack!" Abbie panics.

"We need to get to Dustin; I can't shift," I choke out, nodding toward the tree line. She looks up at the steep incline. Suddenly, a dark, blurry figure pops out of the corner of my eye, tackling her to the ground. I scream when I see Kade sink his teeth into her neck, re-marking her and reinforcing their bond. Wolves burst from the trees and across the road, coming from behind the service station and racing toward us.

"You can't touch the girl!" Kade screams at them while pointing at me, then turns his attention back to Abbie. He grips her shoulders, slamming her onto the ground. Adrenaline courses through me. Suddenly, I am no longer on the ground, and I find myself standing.

"Submit!" Kade screams at her. Abbie's face goes slack under his command just as my body crashes into his.

Abbie shakes her head, trying to fight it off, and I hit the ground beside her. Kade rolls over the top of me.

My eyes go wide when I see wolves rushing straight at us, snapping their teeth, and snarling at us. I close my eyes, waiting for my death, when Abbie grips my fingers, and my head rolls to the side to find her looking at me.

"More than my life," she whispers, tears filling her eyes and her lips quivering.

"More than my life," I murmur, closing my eyes as I watch her close hers. Together, we wait for death, like we have before. Their paws on the earth grow closer when I hear a feral snarl rip through the air, bouncing off the trees, and I hear the wolves' claws digging into the soft ground as they skid around us.

My eyes fly open to find Dustin stepping over the top of us in his Lycan form. Dustin kicks Kade in the face as he tries to stand. Blood drenches him where he has pulled himself free from the car, but he doesn't appear to be bleeding anymore. Dustin growls, but it comes like more of a roar. The wolves jump back, and Kade gets to his feet and staggers backward, trying to get away from him.

"Kill him," I murmur to Dustin. My eyes flicker as I fight to remain conscious.

"If I do, it may kill Abbie," he growls, and I look at Abbie, tears glistening in her eyes.

"Reject her now!" Dustin tells him through gritted teeth.

However, there is no command behind it. Rolling on my side, I grab Dustin's leg, and his hand reaches down, gripping my arm to pull me upright.

"Order him," I choke out as blood fills my mouth from having bitten my tongue.

"I can't," Dustin grinds out, and I look at him, not understanding.

"You're Lycan," I whisper to him.

"I'm under oath being a royal guard. I can't break a mate bond. It is law and pact sworn to be upheld; I am bound by that oath, Azalea!"

Kade laughs, getting to his feet. I glance at Abbie as she sits up.

"Come here, Abbie," Kade orders, and I see her eyes glaze over. She obeys, taking a step toward him. My heart skips a beat as she dazedly starts walking over to her mate. Dustin grabs her arm, and Kade clicks his tongue.

"I wouldn't do that if I were you," Kade says, his pack of wolves circling around us. We are severely outnumbered. Dustin glances around nervously. Lycans are lethal, but against fifty-plus wolves, I am not sure how we would fare when Dustin is the only one that is shifted.

"You are aware of the repercussions, Dustin. Don't be foolish," Kade snarls. I peer up at Dustin, hanging onto Abbie's arm, preventing her from going to Kade, and his other hand holding me against him.

I move behind Dustin and rip Abbie backward and away from Kade. Gripping her arms, I shake her, but her fresh mark seems to have done something to her willpower; I can see she has multiple mate marks on her neck from him.

"Abbie, reject him," I murmur, shaking her.

Kade laughs and steps forward, which makes Dustin growl threateningly.

"You can't touch me. I am just collecting my mate. I haven't injured your Queen; I only tried to hold her. Though by law I could, considering she tried to take my mate from me by force," Kade says cockily. "You do anything, and I have a lot of witnesses," Kade says, motioning around to his pack. Dustin moves in front of us, but even I know if he attacks Kade, the rest of those wolves will rip us apart.

"Abbie, reject him," I beg.

Kade laughs louder and claps his hands. "She really doesn't know, and she is expected to be our Queen, pathetic! Foolish, you would expect the King to have more sense to pick a mate more suited to the position and keep his whore on the side. She can't run a pack, noble blood or not; she isn't fit for the title," he chuckles.

"Hold your tongue, mutt. You do not know what you speak of," Dustin snaps at him.

"No, your oblivious Queen isn't aware of the law. Should I educate her simple mind?"

I glance at him over my shoulder. "For Abbie to reject me, I have to accept it. Which I won't. She will leave with me."

"No, she rejects you. She can come home," I tell him. Kyson promised she could come home; she just had to ask.

"Wrong. A minor flaw in the King's law. Both parties must accept, and if one doesn't, it is decided by the council. Only then is it forced, but until then, she is mine, and I would like to collect her now!" Kade says, moving toward us. I look at Dustin, whose entire body tenses, and I glance back at Abbie. I shake her, anger coursing through me.

"Reject him!" I snap at her, trying to get her attention. "Abbie, reject him!" I yell in her face. Something I said clicks, and she suddenly straightens. She blinks, shaking her head.

"I don't know how. It didn't work," she murmurs, coming out of whatever stupor she was in.

"He is an Alpha you have to reject as your mate and as your Alpha. State your full name and reject him using his title," Dustin murmurs, not taking his eyes off Kade.

"But he is right, Azalea," Dustin glances at me. "I can't force him to accept it," Dustin whispers.

"Reject him," I tell her, shaking her. Kade just laughs evilly. Stepping toward her, his hand goes to grab her.

"Come, Abbie," Kade says, clicking his fingers at her. That same glazed look washes over her face at his command. I swallow, and she pushes past me when anger courses through me. I grab both her arms, jerking her back to me.

"Reject him!" I growl, and much to my astonishment, she does. My aura slips out, and I don't know how I managed to do it, but she looks at Kade and speaks clearly.

"I, Abbie Marie Barker, reject you, Alpha Kade, as my mate and Alpha," she says. Kade growls, clutching his chest, while Abbie shakes her head and blinks rapidly.

"I, Alpha Kade, reject your rejection," he snarls, and she whimpers. My fury becomes emblazoned by the fire burning in me at his words, and I turn on him.

"Accept it!" I roar, and it is like a burst erupting out of me. My words didn't feel like words but something else entirely. All the surrounding wolves yelp and cry out. I feel the tingling sensation wash over my body and out of me as the command takes hold of him and makes him tense.

"I, Alpha Kade, accept your rejection as my Luna and Mate," Kade blurts out, unable to fight the command. Abbie screams, clutching her chest and falling to her knees, and Kade staggers backward, clutching his chest, looking dazed.

CHAPTER
THIRTY-FIVE

AZALEA

Rattled by what has happened, Kade shakes his head. "You stupid girl," he snarls, lunging at me. Dustin is quicker, however, and punches him, sending him flying backward when all the wolves suddenly run towards us menacingly.

"Run!" Dustin screams as he starts fighting them off and keeping them from us. The sound of flesh tearing mixes with the horrible sound of whimpers and broken bones as Dustin grabs any wolf that gets too close. The sounds are savage, but as he gets rid of one, another comes in its place.

My heart thuds painfully in my chest, and I grab Abbie, pulling her to her feet and nearly passing out from the pulling as it strains on my abdomen when I pull her up. We run for the trees, and I hear Dustin fending them off. Wolves start dropping like flies as he takes them out. We start racing up the hill, only for one to slip past him, pounce on us, and knock us down.

The moment we both hit the ground, the wolf's weight lifts abruptly, and a furious growl rings through the air; pain rattles through me from my wound that is bleeding everywhere. His feet are next to my face, and I gasp, looking up to see Kyson in his Lycan form. The wolf that attacked is held off of us by his hand wrapped around its throat. Kyson squeezes his hand, and I grit my teeth when I hear the sickening crunch of its neck breaking when he flings it away. The wolf hits a tree, Kyson tossing him aside like he weighs nothing.

Kyson glares at me, and I drop my gaze to the ground at the angry look on his face when he steps over us. Gannon is right behind him, and he grabs both Abbie and me, pulling us to our feet and away from the fighting.

"Thank god," I hear him murmur, clutching us tightly in his arms. I look down toward Dustin, who is now fighting the wolves. Suddenly, Kyson's aura ripples out of him, and his voice booms around us, echoing through the night.

"Enough, now stop!" he bellows, and everyone freezes under his command. Dustin clutches his knees breathlessly. Kyson stomps past him and shoots him a glare as he makes his way to Kade.

Kade backs away from Kyson, hands up in surrender. At this moment, Kyson truly looks like a Lycan King. He towers over everyone, standing tall and intimidating. Power oozes off him in waves, and his aura feels deadly, suffocating the wolves pinned to the ground by it.

"I have done nothing wrong; I was merely getting my mate," Kade chokes out. He falls backward as Kyson's massive Lycan form growls menacingly, stalking toward him with calculated steps.

"Wrong!" Kyson says with a deadly calm. Somehow, that makes him even more sinister as I watch him approach Kade. Kade shakes his head, and the wolves all look away from him, cowering and whimpering.

"I hereby sentence you to death for treason!" Kyson tells him, stepping on Kade's foot and making him fall on his ass.

"Treason? But I didn't commit treason," Kade stammers, his voice more of a petrified squeak.

"Wrong, you touched my Queen. Your pack just tried to kill her!" Kyson snarls, grabbing the front of his shirt and jerking him forward.

"And for that, I sentence you to death," Kyson snaps before punching him square in the face. Or I thought he hit him until I heard Kade gasp and the sickening sound of flesh on flesh and a gross tearing noise. The wolves near him wail, writhing on the ground in what looks like pain. Kyson shoves him backward, letting him go.

His back is tense when he drops something on the ground, his breathing loud while the muscles of his back flex. Kyson looks around at the wolves as they all run for the trees, and then I notice a woman standing out in front of the service station. I can't make out her features with my blurry vision, but seeing her for some reason makes goosebumps rise all over me as she watches. She then simply turns and walks away, disappearing into the night.

Bile rises in my throat when I realize what Kyson dropped is Kade's heart. Kyson then turns toward us, and his eyes go to Dustin. I struggle in Gannon's grip when I watch, horrified, as Kyson stalks toward him like a predator hunting its prey.

Dustin doesn't even move; he simply accepts the repercussions. Lycans burst from the tree line, forming a circle around us, looking for any threat, having caught up with their King. Damian is among them. I turn my attention back to Dustin.

"You fucked up!" Kyson snarls furiously. Dustin swallows and nods once while my heart beats like a drum in my chest. I struggle against Gannon's grip, trying to escape him. Kyson merely nods once before Damian grabs me around the waist. My legs flail in the air as he pulls me against him.

"He disobeyed his King," Damian warns me.

"No, he didn't do anything wrong! Kyson, please!" I scream.

"I'll deal with you once home," Kyson growls, just as I am handed off to Gannon, who grabs me. This time, his grip tighter, ensuring I don't escape his clutches again.

"No, let me go, please, Damian! Don't let him..." only my words are too late, and I turn my head to see Kyson punch Dustin so hard it knocks him out cold. Dustin drops at Kyson's feet and just takes it. He doesn't even fight back.

I whimper, seeing my friend hurt, and Kyson's head snaps in my direction. He snarls, his upper lip pulling back to reveal his razor-sharp teeth. He moves toward me, and I press closer to Abbie, who cries hysterically while Gannon tries to soothe her.

"Grab him," Kyson snaps at Damian as he passes him on his way to me. His eyes do not leave me, and my heart beats faster as he draws closer. Damian rushes to do his bidding and grabs Dustin, tossing him over his shoulder. Kyson nods to Gannon, and he lets me go as the King approaches. His eyes look me up and down, and a furious growl tears out of him. I stumble backward, trying to get away from him, but Kyson grabs me. Despite his fury, his grip is surprisingly gentle, though his next move isn't.

"You disobeyed me!" Kyson growls. "And now you're injured!" he snaps. I groan in pain and try to defend myself.

"But Abbie," I try to say before he cuts me off.

"I don't want to hear it," he growls before his teeth sink into my neck. I grip his shoulders and choke on a sob when I feel them pierce and slide through my skin. My eyes burn with tears before they roll into my head as I am sucked under. Kyson forces me to submit, and I have no strength left to fight him.

CHAPTER
THIRTY-SIX

K YSON
No words can capture the depth of my fury when I learned she left with Dustin. My rage simmers, a violent undercurrent threatening to erupt. The urge to throttle them both for their recklessness pulses through me.

"You disobeyed me!" I growl, stalking toward her. My eyes scan over her to see her drenched in blood. Her worst injury is the gaping wound in her hip that was running a blood trail down her leg. "And now you're injured!" I snap at her.

"But Abbie," she tries to say before I cut her off with a growl. Her eyes widen as I reached her, and she cowers away, pressing closer to my gamma. But he knows better than to get in my way. He is also furious with Dustin for allowing her to put herself at risk despite being relieved to have Abbie back.

"I don't want to hear it," I snarl, ripping her closer, her tiny body smacking into my hard chest a little harder than I intended. I was frantic the entire run here, and now I know she is by my side. It was overshadowed by my anger and her heat that had returned. She struggles against me, which only makes my instincts want to claim

HIS LOVED LYCAN LUNA

her and heal her, and I regret not explaining almost instantly when I feel her betrayal hit me. She thinks I am making her submit. In a sense, I am. Although not for the reason she undoubtedly believes.

She would bleed out long before we got home, and I would mate her if she remained awake. Her scent is potent, as the effects of the drug Doc gave her have nearly worn off. So I sink my teeth into her neck, remarking her. Her body falls limp in my arms, and I barely scoop her legs up before she slips from my grip. I lick her neck, holding her tighter and attempting to lift her shirt when I am suddenly hit repeatedly by tiny fists in the back.

I snap out of my trance as I feel tiny fists pounding into my back. My head snaps around to spot Abbie standing there, glaring at me with a fierce protectiveness that catches me off guard.

"You fucking asshole, you prick! You didn't even let her explain. You just made her submit," Abbie screams, punching into my side in a fit of rage. I look over my shoulder to find her hitting me with her tiny fists like they will do something. Gannon grabs her around the waist, tugging her back when she falls forward in his arms while flailing as he restrains her arms. She snarls angrily, leaning forward and biting me like a damn savage.

I blink down at her, her teeth embedded in my arm just as Gannon rips her backward, making him fall on his ass, her teeth ripping out of my arm painfully. *She bit me!*

"I will fucking kill you, you savage Neanderthal," she screams as she turns red-faced, landing on top of Gannon.

"Deal with her, or I will!" I warn Gannon. I'm not in the mood to tolerate such disrespect. They both put themselves at risk tonight, and just because she is Azalea's friend doesn't mean I won't punish her for putting my Queen at risk.

Gannon growls, snapping at her and pressing his teeth to her neck in warning, causing her to whimper.

"Enough! He didn't make her submit. Stop and look!" Gannon snarls at her, pulling his teeth away and pointing to where I lifted Azalea's shirt. Her wound is already healing, though my hand is filled with her blood. I huff. If she was anyone else apart from Abbie, I would have been furious and hit her for biting me the way she just did, but I know these girls would die for each other. I shake my head while Gannon apologizes on Abbie's behalf. Turning my attention back to my mate, I lean down while lifting her higher and run my tongue over her wound when I spot Abbie standing in front of me, having escaped Gannon.

"See? He isn't hurting her," Gannon whispers, coming up behind her, and she worries her lip between her teeth. However, she doesn't look much better off herself. Abbie is rather pale and sickly-looking. She lets out a breath.

"You couldn't have warned her first instead of just going all caveman and biting into her,"

"Warn her like you did me when you bit me?" I ask. Her face heats, her cheeks turning a light shade of pink.

"I thought, never mind. Fucking Neanderthal men, anyone would think you were raised by cavemen," she says before her eyes go behind me. I turn to see what she is looking at, to find it is Kade's dead body lying on the grass behind me. Abbie swallows before shaking her head when her eyes turn glassy.

"Can we go home now?" she asks, looking at Gannon.

"My King, we have three cars here. They are on the top road." Damian says, coming over to me with Dustin tossed limply over his shoulder. I glare at him before trekking through the forest and up the vast mountain. Stumbling across my car, I click my tongue. They are lucky to be alive; how Dustin managed to pull himself out of that wreckage is beyond me.

When I reach the top, I am struggling to control myself. I feel rabid as her scent grows more potent, and even Damian glances at me nervously as I clutch my mate closer, soaking up her scent and trying to let it calm my urges. However, once we get to the cars and start heading back home, we are halfway there when I smell her scent shift with the ferocity of a tidal wave. As my mark heals her, it also completely burns out the drug in her system. My canines slip from my gums, and my pupils dilate.

"The windows," I growl at Damian and Gannon, knowing if I move right now, I will lose control completely. They quickly do as I ask while Abbie watches me worriedly. Her eyes are wide as she stares at Azalea, who is limp in my arms. She moves on her seat to reach out to touch her. And the noise that leaves me is feral as Gannon jerks her back to sit beside him.

"She is safe, but she is in heat; you need to stay still; you can't touch her when she is like that when he is near," Gannon whispers to her.

"But..."

"No, Abbie, I know you're worried, but right now, the King isn't safe to be around. Don't provoke him while she is in that state," he adds, and I watch as Abbie sniffs the air slightly before wrinkling her nose. It takes a few hours until we finally pull into the horseshoe driveway. Gannon pulls Abbie out of the car with him, only to find Liam had opened the door.

"The boys?" Gannon asks.

"Clarice has them. They are both tucked away in their beds, safe," Liam answers. I want to ask, but right now, I am at war with myself and figure it can wait until I am in more control.

"Kyson, where do you want me to put Dustin?" Damian asks, clearing his throat. Dustin is in one of the other cars, and I know he is awake; I can feel his pack tether is alert when Liam looks in at me.

"My King, I'm not making excuses for him; he did the wrong thing, but..." begins Liam.

I glare at him, who presses his lips in a line. He is protective of Dustin, but I have my limits with my men. At the same time, I trust very few with my mate, or my kingdom for that matter.

Looking down at Azalea, I press my face into her neck and breathe in her scent, and I hear Damian tell Liam he'll handle me and to go.

"You know it wouldn't have been a deliberate act of putting her in harm's way," Damian says, though I can tell he wants to beat some sense into him.

"Just think of Azalea's reaction before you act, my King. You know she won't be happy if you hurt him."

"He needs to be punished," I tell him, and Damian nods.

"He does, but maybe sleep on it tonight and clear your head before deciding what that punishment should be," Damian says. "Dungeons? Or am I sending him to his room?"

"Fuck!" I mutter under my breath.

"His room. I will deal with him tomorrow," I answer, not happy, but he is right. Azalea and Dustin are close.

"Okay," Damian says, holding the door open for me, only I don't get out. I am frozen. If I move right now. I am going to bend her over and fuck her despite her being asleep. My cock is painfully hard beneath her, and my muscles tense as I begin to sweat.

"My King?" Damian asks, and I glare out the door.

"I can't move," I say through gritted teeth.

"Right, I um. I can take her," Damian says nervously, but I have suffered through both his and Gannon's scents, switching back and forth the entire way home as they reacted with each wave as it came. I don't think I could bear to smell his arousal on her skin. I swallow, knowing I have to ask for the help of the one man I want to kill right now.

"Please ask Dustin to come to take her," I tell him.

"You want Dustin to take her back to her room?" I nod once.

Waiting a few moments, Dustin steps into the limo warily. I clench my jaw, but his scent doesn't change as he approaches. He doesn't say anything and waits for me to nod to him before taking her. Dustin scoops her out of my arms, hugging her to his chest. Dustin stepped out of the limo while I waited, still fighting the urge to bury my dick in her tight confines. After about half an hour, I have calmed down enough to get out of the car without wanting to hunt my mate like she is prey.

However, once the cool night air brushes against me, the fresh air fills my lungs. I feel dizzy, and my surroundings spin. Taking a step toward the castle doors, my vision blurs, and I feel delirious. It becomes harder to breathe, and with another step, I lose all feeling as an icy cold feeling slivers over my heat-ravaged body, and my heart thumps erratically in my chest. The ground rushes toward my face, yet I don't feel a thing as I hit it, although I hear the air being expelled from my lungs on impact before my vision goes black.

CHAPTER
THIRTY-SEVEN

AZALEA

My nose tickles as his scent invades my senses. My entire body is overheating, and I'm not sure if the heat is radiating from him or me. His skin is blisteringly hot, while my blood feels like it is boiling and bubbling in my veins. Lifting my head, I find Kyson asleep beneath me. His heady scent makes my mouth water, and everywhere his skin touches, it tingles and buzzes like a live wire is running beneath my skin. My thighs are drenched, and I groan, knowing I am in heat again. But why is Kyson so hot? I wonder. I am about to climb off him and run for the bathroom to take a cold shower when a voice makes me jump.

"Remain where you are. You can't move even if you wanted to," Damian's voice makes me look over my shoulder. A growl escapes me; logically, I know it is Beta Damian, yet my body reacts to the intruder in my den. A den I don't remember building in my sleep. The thin sheet covering me falls slightly, and Damian averts his gaze to the far wall and clears his throat, making me look down to find myself naked. Why am I naked? And who undressed me? My eyes widen, and I scramble to tug the sheet back to cover myself, only to feel Kyson move under me. No, he doesn't move. I am handcuffed to him, my wrist cuffed to his. My movement makes Kyson purr in his sleep while I try to figure out what has happened.

I stare at the handcuff before glancing at Damian. "Why am I handcuffed? Did you undress me?" I ask him, and Damian sits back in his wooden chair, which I know is from the small office behind the door on the far wall. He folds his arms across his broad chest.

"Yes, I had no choice. You are in heat! I need to talk to you, and you will listen to me, my Queen," Damian states, and I can tell he is not going to leave until I hear what he has to say. I roll my eyes and Damian growls.

"Un-cuff me," I demand, but he presses his lips in a line.

"No!" he says, earning a growl from me. I want to check on Dustin and Abbie. Although I'm not sure if that would be possible because with Kyson's skin touching mine, I am barely holding it together, wanting nothing more than to roll my hips against him and claim him.

"Listen to me. I have been with the King for as long as I can remember, and he can be a stubborn idiot at times. However, you are also just as stubborn. You put yourself in unnecessary danger and put your life at risk, and that of Dustin," Damian starts.

I go to protest, but he cuts me off.

"You put my King at risk. Your mate!" he states angrily. I swallow, looking down at Kyson, feeling guilty I tug the blanket higher, I go to move off of Kyson when he speaks again.

"Remain where you are. Kyson's life depends on it. You move, and he can die, and I did not carry him here and undress you for him to drop dead on me now!" Damian snaps, and I freeze.

"What?" I gasp, wondering what he is talking about.

"Kyson asked me not to say anything, but I will not watch him die when you can save him. Both of you are too stubborn to see your flaws or each other's side. Now you will listen to me," he snaps.

I can see his frustration clearly by the tight clench of his jaw and how white his knuckles are as the skin stretches over them when he grips the armrest of the wooden chair. Damian is usually calm. Although, right now, he looks murderous, and I am not sure if he wants to murder me or the King, maybe both? So I figure it probably best to listen and not piss off the Lycan, who looks like he could snap in half like a twig.

"I'm listening."

"About time, my Queen. Now, let's get one thing straight. Everything I do and don't do is for yours and the King's safety, just like me handcuffing you to him is for his safety."

I sigh, wondering what he is getting at.

"You never grew up among Lycans. You are poorly educated by no fault of your own and very young, so please do not take offense, but there are things you now need to be made aware of so you can understand the meaning of all of this!" He says.

Was this what it was like to be scolded by a teacher? Because I imagined so.

"When Kyson had your heat stopped, it didn't stop for him. Lycan men suffer the same as women during the heat. Now, why did Kyson stop your heat, Azalea?" Damian asks.

"So I wouldn't die."

Damian nods, leaning forward in his chair and bracing his arms on his knees.

"It is the same for Lycan men. You denying him isn't just killing you; it is killing the King. Male Lycan's heat cannot be stopped like a woman's. Just because yours has doesn't mean it did for him, which is why he is like that," Damian says, nodding toward Kyson beneath me.

I peer down at him. His skin is scorching, and I feel his heart is racing in his chest. I can feel it thumping beneath my palm, resting in the center of his chest. "Right now, your skin contact is the only thing keeping him from boiling alive, so you will remain in those cuffs until he is better."

"But that means I would have to mate him. You just said his heat won't stop, even if mine does."

"Exactly," Damian says, his eyes flickering onyx as he swallows before crossing his legs.

"What?" I murmur, horrified.

"I am not asking you to have sex with him, Azalea, but I am not letting you out of those cuffs until you have at least marked him, which will buy him a few more days. His life depends on it, so you need to put your issues aside and save your mate."

I glance down at Kyson.

"I have watched King' and Queens fall from war. I will not watch them fall from something that can be avoided, all because of a lack of communication, because both of you are too stubborn to admit when you're wrong."

I open my mouth to speak, but he gets up.

"No, you will do this. You need to realize that being Queen comes with responsibilities, responsibilities you do not understand, but your King does. You will die without him and him you. Before you find another excuse, Abbie is fine, Dustin is fine, but your mate is not. He messed up by not believing you about Abbie, but he cannot make up for that mistake if he is dead." Damian steps closer.

"So it is time for my Queen to grow up and take responsibility for her own mistakes. You are both at fault for this, and now you need to fix it before another kingdom falls. Only this time, it would fall because of stubbornness and ego. And that is not worth dying for," Damian says, storming off toward the door.

"Wait!" I shriek, scrambling to turn to face him without either exposing myself or climbing off Kyson. I only manage to tangle myself in the sheet. However, Damian stops and turns back to face me.

My face heats, and Damian purses his lips impatiently. "You don't expect me to, um... he is asleep! And I don't know what to do!"

Damian sighs and glances around, his eyes stopping on the bookcase. "You and Kyson have had sex," he states, and my face heats at his words.

"No... I." My face heats.

207

"Well, um... you..." he stutters for a second. I don't know who is more mortified at his question me or him at the idea of him giving me a sex talk. Thankfully he doesn't give me the birds and the bees talk, our current chat is awkward enough.

Damian sighs. "Don't ignore your instincts. Your body knows what to do. It's a basic instinct. Listen to them. And think of it as sleeping beauty, you know that story?" he asks, and I nod. Kyson had read that and a few other princess books, one that even had a frog in it.

"Good, think of him as sleeping beastly then, but mark him instead of kissing him, though you can do that too. Just make sure you mark him first. It will help him heal enough to complete the other part."

"So I only have to mark him, and he will wake up?"

"Maybe not right away, eventually, once his temperature goes down and the effects abate," he tells me, and I sigh, looking down at Kyson. My anger toward him is not worth his life; Damian is right about that. I hear the door click shut and lock as he leaves.

Readjusting myself, I sit up, untangling the sheet, my legs straddling his waist, yet his arm is dead weight and bloody heavy as I move. Using my free hand, I turn his face to the side before feeling my mark on my neck, wondering if it matters where I mark him. Yet I had two marks from him and could feel they overlapped each other, so I figured anywhere between the neck and shoulder must be OK. My gums tingle just at the mere thought of marking him.

His bare chest is inviting, and I want to run my tongue over it. *Mark him first,* I try to remind myself, shaking my head. I kind of wish Damian was still here. It is easier to keep my thoughts straight and fight the urges rolling over me.

Leaning down, his chest brushes against mine, making my skin electrified, and I moan at the feeling as it races toward the apex of my legs. I sniff his neck, his scent making my mouth water, and I feel my canines elongate when I run my tongue over his marking spot. My canines buzz as they graze his flesh and prick his skin. The moment his blood touches my tongue, I sink them into his neck. I intended to be gentle; however, my body has a mind of its own as I feel them slide through muscle and tissue before bottoming out when I bite him like a damn animal.

I briefly think I did it wrong when I am smashed with his aura and essence. I feel it roll over every inch of me, filling every atom and making every nerve come alive. My pupils dilate and expand, blowing wider and clearer. The feeling of him is bleeding into me, his life force moving through me and connecting to mine. It makes me gasp and choke on his blood as it fills my mouth.

My entire body buzzes and warms as our bond is forged and sealed. A sense of wholeness envelopes me. I pull my teeth from his neck, running my tongue over his mark, and he shivers but does not wake. With a sigh, I lay down on him, burying my face in his neck and inhaling his scent. *Please wake up.*

THIRTY-EIGHT

KYSON

My body shut down. However, I can hear everything going on around me clearly. Everything! Damian's frantic screams for help are loud, yet my body feels foreign to me, numb. I can no longer feel the cool breeze or the hands grabbing and moving me. All feeling is completely gone. Although my mind is alert. I only know I am being moved because I can hear what is happening around me. It is like my body suddenly died, and I am just a conscious mind living inside an empty shell.

"Fuck! He's burning up!" I hear Liam gasp somewhere off the side of me.

"I will get the Doctor," Clarice says somewhere off in the distance.

"No! Just open the doors. He needs Azalea. It's her heat!" Damian says.

"Liam, grab the other side of him," Damian orders.

I can hear them climbing the stairs, their feet moving on the corridor floors, and the creak and groan of the doors being ripped open.

"Dustin already brought Ivy up here?" Damian asks someone before I hear Trey's voice.

"Yes. Gannon just escorted him back to his room," Trey answers.

"Open the door," Damian tells him. I can smell Ivy's scent. It's odd... I have a sense of her, yet not my own body.

"Out, Trey; you aren't needed in here now."

"Yes, Beta," Trey answers, and I hear the door click shut.

"Help me get him on the bed and strip him down," Damian says, talking to Liam.

"Now what?" Liam asks.

I feel nothing, and can only listen as they try to figure out what to do.

"Um, ah, he is gonna kill me! I need to strip her down, too, but if she wakes, I know she will look for Abbie," Damian curses.

"I have some Justin's handcuffs," Liam says.

"Some... what?" Damian asks, and I am wondering the same thing.

"Justin's handcuffs. Just in case you need 'em. Here, I keep a pair on me at all times, you know, just in case I need to handcuff someone."

"I don't even want to know what you get up to."

"Indeed, you don't, Beta. Now, I am a team player. If needed, I will perform," Liam says.

"Perform what? Give me those handcuffs," Damian says.

"I can swing both ways. If it saves the King, I can close my eyes and stick one in him," Liam says.

If I could move, I would have strangled him for saying that. I'll have to remember.

"That won't be necessary, Liam. Go see Clarice."

"Yeah, rightio, Beta. The offer still stands. If it's just a good fuck he needs, I don't mind breaking him in."

"Out, Liam!" Damian.

"I'm going. No need to get your panties in a wad. Wanna check on the boys, anyway."

"Huh? What boys?"

"Some stowaways. All good, Uncle Liam is on kiddie duty until Clarice gets off."

Fuck! Why did I let him on as my personal guard? The man could fall in a barrel of titties and come out sucking his thumb, that is for sure.

I hear Liam leave before hearing Damian move around to the other side of the bed, followed by the clink of metal. Vaguely, I feel him place the handcuff on my wrist before hearing him attach it to Azalea's.

"Shit! I should have told Dustin to stay," I hear Damian mutter to himself.

"Azalea?" Damian says, and I can hear him tapping her, trying to rouse her awake. "Shit! Azalea, I am going to undress you, okay?"

My growl echoes in my head but doesn't appear to be heard by anyone but me. I can't help it; I don't want anyone to see her in a state of undress, especially while vulnerable during her heat, not that Damian would ever do anything to harm her or upset her. I can trust him to be a gentleman.

"My King, if you can hear me, you will have to get over it. I will try to undress her with my eyes closed," he mutters before I hear him tearing her clothes off. Talking through each step as if he's asking for permission that neither of us could give him.

Yet, it puts me at ease, and the first spark of feeling I get is when he draped her on my chest. Her skin helps slightly, but I am still paralyzed and unable to move or feel anything else. The sound of sheets moving around us signals that he's covering her nudity.

I hear a knock at the door, followed by Trey's voice.

"I don't mind watching over them if you want to get some rest, Beta," he says, earning a growl from Damian.

"I am not going anywhere while they are vulnerable. You aren't needed here. I will call you back when you are, so get out!" Damian tells him.

Silence fills the room, and Damian doesn't seem to leave. I can hear him turning pages in the book he's reading. After what feels like hours later, I slowly get feeling back, yet I can not move, not even open my eyes, no matter how much I try. After a while longer, Azalea stirs, and I listen to Damian berate her and me, in a sense. Although he is talking to her, I listen, knowing he is right, and I feel terrible that she is on the receiving end of his anger over our stupidity, mostly mine. I should have listened to her, and now I have to make it up to her.

When Damian leaves the room, I listen to her talk to herself. Her voice brings me comfort, her touch puts me at ease, and then she marks me. It smashes through every barrier and grips my soul. Her fear for me slams into me as the bond is forged, and I have never felt such immense relief when she does. She is officially mine, and I am hers. Our bond is now forged for life. Or so I hope.

Azalea doesn't move from me. She occasionally whispers to me and bites me as her heat drives her to the edge of her sanity, and instinct comes over her. I lose count of the number of times she asks me to wake up. I listen to her sing her Kingdom anthem and listen to her harsh breathing as she struggles with her heat.

I want to comfort her and let her know I am okay. Want to ease her suffering, not that I am sure she will let me. Time seems to slow, and painfully so. She is in agony as she squirms above me, her claws raking down my skin as she rubs her face against my chest.

I can hear the sheets tearing as she fights the urge to mate me. She doesn't want me unconscious, yet pain ravages her, and my heart breaks, knowing I can do nothing to help her right now. Her tears wet my chest as she writhes in pain. It is torturous, pure agony, as I listen to her beg me to wake up. She wants my calling and keeps pressing her ear to the center of my chest like she can somehow hear it and let it calm her if she listens hard enough.

Her claws rake down my sides, her teeth biting me wherever she can. Nesting and trying to ease her pain, anything to distract herself from the pain of her heat. Still, as my temperature dissipates, hers rises dramatically when eventually feeling returns in my fingertips, my movement slowly returning. Azalea is crying in pain, and out of reflex, I go to touch her to calm her, and my fingers are suddenly tangled in her hair. She freezes, and I blink up at the ceiling, my surroundings coming back to me to find her face all red and blotchy from her crying and her heat as she peers down at me.

"Shh," I whisper, turning my head to kiss her forehead. She rocks her hips against me, dropping her head back to my chest, her ear flat against the center. My calling slips out, and she bathes and soaks in it, her body calming instantly as I run my fingers through her hair. Her breathing evens out when she suddenly starts purring, gently rocking her hips against me and coating my hardened cock in her arousal.

I groan, closing my eyes at the feel of her wet pussy sliding up and down my shaft. I want to bury my cock inside her and feel her walls spasm around me while she moans. My cock twitches at the thought, and she moans softly. Gripping her hips, I forget about the handcuff, but she doesn't complain as I grip her awkwardly and pull her higher.

"I am not touching you until you say it, love," I murmur into her hair.

"Please! Make it stop!" she groans, trying to move lower. Her teeth sink into my chest, and her claws scratch my shoulders, so I roll, flipping her onto her back and kissing her. Azalea responds instantly, kissing me hungrily and wrapping her legs around my waist.

CHAPTER
THIRTY-NINE

AZALEA

He has been out for hours. The waiting becomes pure agony, and my mind keeps wandering if it is too late. I wonder if I have killed my mate. Why didn't he tell me he could die? Did he seriously think I would let him die? Yes, we have obvious issues, but none are worth dying for, so why would he risk his life? He should have told me when I was in heat the first time I wouldn't have let him die despite being angry with him.

My skin is super sensitive, and I try shifting to get out of the handcuffs. The limited movement makes the pain worse when all I want to do is curl up in a ball, but the handcuff restricts that effort. When I shifted, my wrist grew thicker, and damn, did it hurt when the metal dug into my flesh and sliced through my skin, cutting off my circulation. So, instead, I am forced to just lie in the same position.

As the hours drag on, I feel myself turning rabid, the heat boiling inside me, growing stronger. My claws slip from my fingertips and slice into Kyson repeatedly as I battle with the pain and searing heat that makes me feel like I am boiling from the inside out, his scent no longer soothing but excruciating as the urge to mate ravages me.

Would he think I am mauling him if he wakes up? The thought makes me whimper, my heart racing faster as worry gnaws and claws at my insides. My stomach clenches painfully, and my body pulses to its own beat. Death would be kinder at this point. The pain is horrendous as I rock my hips against him, seeking any form of relief. Sweat beads and glistens on my skin, my hair drenched in it as my temperature skyrockets. The pain is so unbearable that I beg to be put out of my misery as I cry out and writhe.

I stare at my tears and bite marks coating his chest, when I suddenly feel his hand in my hair. I freeze, wondering if I imagined it and that the pain has driven me to madness. Only when his fingers caress across my scalp, moving through my hair, do I realize I hadn't imagined it all.

Pushing off his chest, I look down at him to discover his eyes open and staring up at me.

"Shh," he whispers, tilting his face up to kiss my forehead. A sigh of relief leaves me. He was awake. Never have I felt such immense relief before in my life. My heartbeat quickens, knowing I haven't killed him.

My hips rock against him, and then I crash against his chest, pressing my ear flat against the center, wanting the soothing essence of his calling. Kyson delivers instantly, and I was worried he wouldn't. I was worried that he would be mad and let me suffer. His calling slips out, and I soak it in, my body calming instantly as it rumbles through his chest and vibrates against me, soothing my soul and the bond that is running haywire.

Kyson runs his fingers through my hair. My breathing slows before I embarrassingly start purring, imitating his calling while moving my hips against him. Gone is any sort of dignity I have left. I no longer care as long as he gives me what my body desires, what I crave, and what our bond demands. His hard length slips between my drenched folds, my arousal coating his cock and saturating my thighs.

A moan escapes me when I hear him groan, and his hard length brushes my clit. Kyson grips my hips, forcing my hand awkwardly behind me as he moves me higher and away from his pelvis, making me cry out at the loss of friction that reduces the throbbing pain burning between my thighs.

"I am not touching you until you say it, love," he murmurs into my hair. His hot breath moves across my neck and makes me shiver. I try to move lower, but his grip grows tighter, holding me still. Was he really going to make me say it? Yet, with the intense pain destroying me, I would beg if he requested.

"Please! Make it stop!" I groan, trying to move lower. My teeth sink into his chest. The saltiness of his skin is intoxicating, and I run my tongue across my bite marks, his blood washing over my tongue, only arousing me further. Even as my claws scratch his shoulders and I bite into his flesh, his grunt turns to a purr.

Kyson moves; his arm wraps around my waist, and he rolls, flipping me onto my back. His lips instantly mold around mine, his enticing scent making me moan as my lips part, and I kiss him back hungrily. Desire coursing through every inch of me, I wrap my legs around his waist and drag him closer to me.

The handcuff on our wrists clicks as he forces my leg wrapped around his waist up higher before grinding his hips against me gently. I gasp, my lips pulling from his as his hard length slides between my wet folds and hits my clit. My hips lift as I crave the friction he offers when he growls, annoyed at the handcuff making things difficult. My hand falls to his hip, my nails digging into him.

"Did he leave the key somewhere?" Kyson asks, but I don't answer, nor do I care about a damn key. Lifting my head, my teeth sink into his chest as I bite him.

Kyson purrs, his hand going to my hair and holding my face against him. My other hand was trapped at our side. Kyson fists my hair, forcing my head back, only to recapture my lips with his. His tongue delves between my lips, tasting every inch of my mouth, and I roll my hips against him. Kyson rocks his hips against me, his fingers lacing with mine while the other is still tightly gripping my hair as he devours my lips.

I moan into his mouth, my thighs drenched when he sucks on my bottom lip, nibbling on it. His lips travel lower and down my neck to my mark. He sucks on it, making my eyes roll into the back of my head and my toes curl as tingles flood my entire body, causing me to tingle all over. My temperature reduces as the bond comes alive.

Kyson's hot, fiery mouth and tongue continue their descent before his lips wrap around my nipple. He bites down it, making me hiss before soothing it with his tongue, only to turn his attention to the other, teasing it with his hot mouth until it hardens so much it is almost painful.

Moving down my body, he kisses the side of my ribs, going lower with each kiss, sucking and nibbling on my skin, making me squirm every time his lips and stubble graze a ticklish spot. He kisses my hip bone.

His teeth graze over it and scrape down my flesh as he moves between my legs, forcing my legs from around his waist as he settles between my thighs, his handcuffed hand placed flat on my stomach, his fingers still laced through mine while his other hand grips my thigh, pulling my leg further apart. His warm breath sweeps over my pussy before his mouth is covering it in its entirety. He growls, running his tongue across my wet lower lips.

His flat tongue slides across my glistening wet folds before his tongue parts my slit, and he sucks my clit into his mouth. His tongue swirls around the throbbing bundle of nerves, making me cry out and writhe.

As Kyson's gaze meets mine, a surge of electricity courses through my body. His velvety tongue caresses my throbbing nub, igniting a fire within me that threatens to consume everything in its path. With expert precision, he envelops my sensitive bud and sucks forcefully, causing a symphony of sensations to explode throughout my being. My every nerve is alight with pleasure, my breath hitching in anticipation.

The dance of his tongue around my clit is like a hypnotic whirl-wind, each twirl and tease pushing me closer to the edge of bliss. I find myself lost in the sensation, my entire existence narrowed down to the exquisite torment he inflicts upon me. I surrender to the waves of pleasure crashing over me, my body trembling with desire.

My skin flushes as the heat burns and rushes through me. My stomach tightens, and my legs tremble as I cry out. Waves of plea-sure ripple through me as I come on his tongue. My inner walls pulsate and clench as I moan. His tongue slows its rhythm, letting me ride out the intense, rippling effect washing through me.

Kyson purrs, lapping at my juices before kissing my clit, making me jolt before moving up my body and pressing himself between my legs. I roll my hips against him, wanting him inside me. Wanting the heat to abate and feel his length inside me.

Coming back up to my face, Kyson kisses me hard, forcing me to taste myself on his tongue, his tongue invading my mouth. My fingers move through his hair, tugging him closer.

He moves his hand between our bodies as he positions himself at my entrance. I feel him press the tip in, and I move my hips against him when he pushes in a little.

My lips tear away from his, and my eyes water as I choke and clench them shut. My entire body tenses and locks up, and I grip his arm. He stills before pulling out slightly. "It's going to sting," he whispers, his lips kissing my jaw.

I writhe beneath him, trying to get away from him. I know he's big, but I don't expect it to burn this badly with how wet I am.

"Breathe, Love. It will only hurt for a few seconds," he says, kissing my lips and peppering my face in kisses. Kyson floods me with his calling, forcing my muscles to relax.

My entire body submits to it, and I let out the breath I have been holding in, my body relaxing, and I open my eyes, tears slipping down my face. Kyson kisses me, pushing back inside me slightly. His calling washes over me, drowning me in it as he pushes inside my tight confines until his hips are flush against me. I feel full, and I squirm, trying to get used to the odd sensation.

Kyson stills, letting me get used to the feeling of him stretching me before slowly pulling out and thrusting back in gently, working his massive cock inside me, his lips moving to my mark, and he sucks on it. A moan leaves my lips at the sensation as tingles rush to my clit, and I move my hips against him, my juices coating his cock, and he stills, letting me move against him instead while I get used to the feeling of him inside me.

Kyson growls softly. Arousal floods through me when he pulls out, and he thrusts in, meeting my movements, his length slipping in me deeper, stretching me around him, a breathy moan escapes my lips at the friction building when he kisses me harder.

His tongue fights mine for dominance, and he presses his weight down on me, sheathing himself inside me, making me gasp. He moves slowly, his cock slipping in and out, gradually building up friction, his cock rubbing my walls, causing them to clench around his hardened length.

My hand tugs his hip, wanting him to move faster, when Kyson's hand goes under my back, pulling me with him as he rolls, so I am now on top, straddling his lap as he moves and leans against the headboard.

His hands run up my sides, the handcuffed one forcing my hand where he goes. Kyson grips my hips, and he leans forward, sucking my breast, a breathy moan leaving my lips, feeling his mouth on my body. He rolls my hips against him, guiding me up and down his length.

I grip his shoulder, rolling my hips to the movement before his grip loosens, and he lets me set the pace. I move my hips and find my rhythm. Feeling myself building up, my walls clenching his length, and my eyes close at the building feeling in my lower belly spreading a warmth through me.

"That's it, Love," Kyson purrs before gripping my hips and slamming me down on him, moving my hips faster. I moan, my nails digging into his shoulder as I feel myself climbing higher, reaching my peak.

The only sounds are my airy moans filling the room and the wet sounds of our bodies connecting. Kyson reaches up, grabbing a handful of my hair and tugging my head back, his lips trailing down my neck and over my shoulder, his other hand squeezing my ass as I grip his wrist awkwardly, my hand bent from the handcuff as I move up and down his hard shaft. His cock fills me, and I feel my stomach tighten and my skin flush, and I cry out at the overwhelming feeling inside me.

He lets go of my hair, palming my breast while sucking on the other one, his tongue flicking over my nipple. I pick up my pace before feeling the hot wave of my climax rush over me, making my walls clench around his cock before I feel his teeth sink into my flesh, prolonging the feeling, and my pussy pulsates around him, making me moan loudly.

My body turns slack in his arms as he pulls his teeth from my skin, and I drop my face to his neck. The overwhelming urge makes my gums tingle before I feel my canines protrude and sink them into his skin.

Kyson growls, his hands gripping my hips as he rocks them against him, chasing his release before groaning just as I pull my teeth from his skin. My tongue rolls over my marking when I feel him still, and his cock twitches and expands inside me, making me gasp at the strange stretching feeling. I jump as his warmth bathes my insides, and Kyson's arms wrap around me and crush me against his chest.

"You can't move, relax," he whispers next to my ear, flooding me with his calling as I fight the urge to climb off him, his cock swelling inside me, stretching me further.

"Sorry, I didn't intend to knot you, not yet anyway," he whispers, his tongue flicking the shell of my ear.

"What?" I murmur.

"Something Lycans do, I forgot to warn you. I'm sorry," he whispers, sucking my earlobe into his mouth and nibbling on it. I nod my head, too relaxed to care. I didn't want to move anyway, so I melted against him. My breathing is harsh as I suddenly find myself now fused to him. His calling lulls me into a dreamy state, and I feel his fingers trailing up my spine as he moves down the bed to lie down.

My eyelids feel heavy as I listen to his heartbeat beneath my ear. His fingertips grip my chin, tilting my face up toward his. He leans down, his lips brushing mine gently. "I love you," he whispers against my lips before chuckling as I fight exhaustion. My body cools down rapidly, the heat leaving, and in its place, exhaustion courses through me.

"Sleep, my Queen," he says, kissing the side of my mouth as my eyes feel closed, and I am sucked under by the darkness of sleep.

CHAPTER
FORTY

ABBIE

Chaos reigns as we step back into the castle. I walk through the grand doors, and suddenly, Damian's urgent cries for assistance fill the air, summoning Gannon to rush with Dustin toward the King's quarters. Together, they gently carry Azalea, still in a deep slumber. The name feels strange on my lips now - Ivy. It's been our shared secret identity for as long as I can remember. I empathize with her need to shed the label Della, or rather Marissa, bestowed upon her.

Standing in the corridor, I stand uncertain, unsure of what to do with myself as Damian and another man carry the King to his quarters. The King mumbles, his words a jumble of incomprehensible sounds. My heart yearns to seek out Azalea, but the timing isn't right. Lost in my thoughts, I remain rooted in place, observing the chaotic frenzy of people scurrying about frantically.

Do I just return to my old tasks now that I'm here? Should I seek out Gannon or perhaps Clarice? Gannon gave me some of his blood so the worst of my injuries are healed so I don't want to burden him by harassing him. Uncertain of what to do next, I wander aimlessly until I inadvertently reach my previous quarters. Tentatively, I rap on the door in case Beta Damian has enlisted a new personal servant. Yet, met with silence, I cautiously push the door ajar and glance inside only to find the entire guard quarter downstairs also empty; I wonder if I should clean here first since the guard quarters were also tasked to me. The hour grows late, and I decide to see Clarice in the morning about where she plans to assign me and decide I should just stay out of everyone's way and go to bed.

Stepping into the room that used to be mine, I find the bed bare, so I walk down the hall to the closet and retrieve some blankets and pillows. The task is made more difficult by my wounds. The stitches are pulled so tight that some are cutting through my skin like cheese wire.

Blood covers almost every inch of me. It has congealed in my hair and under my fingernails. I swiftly make the bed but realize I can't sleep in this condition. I head to the laundry room, scanning for clean clothes. Spotting some servant uniforms, pajamas, and a pair of socks on the shelf, I snatch them up before grabbing a towel and searching through the first aid kit for antibacterial soap. As I limp towards the servants' bathrooms, my bones ache, every step a painful reminder of the ordeal I've been through.

Stepping inside, I find it empty. One side of the bathroom held stalls for showering while a half wall divided up the middle to the toilets and basins; long mirrors ran the entire length of the center wall on both sides.

As I pass it to head into one of the shower stalls, I glance at the state I am in. My normal auburn hair is matted, and twigs and leaves are tangled in the knots. My clothes are torn, and I can still smell his scent all over me. Gannon's, too, but Kade's is still there. My heart pangs at the thought of him.

The way he lay dead in the dirt. My mate, though cruel, was mine or supposed to be. Looking at what is left of me as I peel off my clothes, I feel disgusted.

My skin marred from years in the orphanage is already horrifying to look at, though my scars were never deep or as jagged as Azaleas. I always felt terrible for how she hated her appearance and the lashes that marred her.

She had taken so many whippings reserved for me, and I had done the same for her. Looking at them, I used to think it was a reminder of what we endured and survived. Though marks were left at the hands of Kade, I noticed something so much worse.

I never survived at all. Instead, I moved from one hell to another. Looking at my ravaged flesh, I am not so sure anyone could look at me again and be anything but disgusted by the sight of me. There are multiple marks on my neck from him that have turned my flesh black like it is rotting away my skin, the skin raised jagged, same as the scars etched into my heart. The hollow void feels like it will never be filled again, bottomless. I press my lips together to stop crying out when I peel my shirt off, dumping it on the floor.

I hiss as I force my pants down my legs. The blood saturates my pants, sticking to my skin and making me feel like I'm being skinned alive. Tears blur my vision, and I bite back the sob as my stitches open and blood cascades down my leg in a stream. I try to step out of my pants when hands fall on my hips, making me jump and hiss as the stitches along my arms and ribs tug from the movement.

"I was looking for you," Gannon murmurs. He kneels, peeling them off, and I grip his shoulder, stepping out of them. He kisses my hip bone, which protrudes beneath my skin. The blood rushes to my cheeks, knowing I am now standing naked in front of the man.

"Why are you in the servant bathroom?" he asks, standing back up. Keeping my back to him, I cover my breasts. Not that there is much point with the giant mirrors. I know he can see every vile inch of me if he glances at them.

"I didn't know where else to go. You disappeared, and I didn't want to bother Clarice to find out where I would be stationed. So I went back to my old station," I tell him.

"You should have just gone to our room," Gannon whispers.

"I am Beta Damian's servant. I don't think he has another. No one was in the room when I went in there," I tell him.

I grab my soap, placing it on the niche before hissing as I start the shower. Gannon growls behind me while I examine my arm, which is black and blue, where Kade mauled me, the stitches pinching my skin, holding it together. The water sprays out, bursting from the shower head in a wide spray, making my injuries burn and sting.

"Can you shut the door?" I ask him, not wanting to turn around. I hear the door close and sigh, stepping under the water, only to cringe away. My head throbs as I wet my hair before turning around. I rub my eyes to rid them of the water. When I open them, Gannon is standing in front of me.

The door is closed behind him, but he is inside the stall. I quickly try to cover my breasts, though I have no idea why. When I asked him to close the door, I didn't mean for him to come into the shower with me.

Gannon's eyes run the length of me, then quickly dart away. My stomach sinks. This is why I didn't want to turn around. I know what he will see, and my mutilated skin is anything but pretty. I look disgusting, my skin carved up and the pieces forced back together like broken puzzle pieces. Turning to face the back wall, a lump forms in my throat.

"Can you get out, please," I whisper, though I know he will hear me with his heightened hearing.

Embarrassment washes over every inch of me, and I suddenly want to scrub myself raw, as if I can clean away the vile marks that lace my skin. As if I can scrub away the memory that comes with them.

"Am I scaring you? I won't hurt you, Abbie," Gannon murmurs next to my ear before his chest presses against my back. He reaches past me, grabbing the soap out of the niche in the wall.

"I saw the way you looked at me, Gannon. Just go; I don't want your pity," I tell him. He growls, the sound vibrating against my back.

"The way I looked at you?" he asks, sweeping my hair over my shoulder. He dips his face into my neck. His nose runs up the side of my jaw.

"You don't have to pretend like it's all okay, Abbie. I know how much this must hurt," he whispers, and I can feel his warm breath tickling my skin. "But please let me take care of you."

I try to pull away from him, but his arms wrap tightly around me, trapping me against his body.

"I don't need anyone's pity or sympathy," I snap at him, anger flaring up inside of me. "Especially not yours."

Gannon's grip loosens slightly, and he takes a step back so that we can face each other.

"Abbie, look at me," he says softly, placing a hand on each side of my face and forcing me to meet his gaze. "I don't feel pity for you. What happened to you is terrible and unfair, and it breaks my heart to see what that animal did to you."

I swallow before answering, my voice coming out shakier than intended.

"I know I look disgusting, so please, leave."

Gannon growls and I become startlingly aware that he is indeed naked behind me. I can feel every ridge of muscle and bump press against my back and ass.

"I only looked away because I could tell you were uncomfortable with me staring, Abbie, not because I didn't like what I could see," he purrs, his voice laced with an undeniable warmth and sincerity.

"But he ruined me. I'm broken," I tell him, my voice cracking as I summon the courage to speak those words aloud without crying. The weight of the realization settles heavily on my shoulders, and I can't help but feel like a shattered doll, its porcelain form broken and cracked, held together by fragile glue, marred and made ugly, never to be whole again.

Gannon's gaze softens, his eyes filled with empathy. "We are all a little broken, Abbie," he says gently, reaching for my arm that shields my chest and the stitching that traces across my skin. His lips brush against my shoulder, and a shiver courses through me at his tender touch.

"Don't hide from me. You never have to hide from me, Abbie," Gannon whispers, his voice a soothing balm against the scars that mark my body. His grip tightens around my wrist, his thumb caressing the back of my hand in a comforting rhythm. With a sigh, I release my arm, allowing his hand holding the soap to glide over my torn-up flesh. The scent of Gannon envelops me, mingling with the steam that fills the small space, creating a bubble around us.

As Gannon's hands move across my body, washing away the physical remnants of my past, a sense of relaxation washes over me. My shoulders drop, and I lean back against him, surrendering to his care, unable to stay strong any longer. The sheer size of his presence could easily overwhelm me, his strength capable of breaking me in half. Yet, at this moment, he is gentle—a tender giant whose fingers massage my scalp, removing the congealed blood and gunk with a tenderness that belies his size.

"I wish I could heal you," he murmurs, turning me around to rinse the soap from my hair. My eyes roam over him, taking in a sight I've never witnessed before. Gannon, usually adorned in at least a tank top, now stands before me shirtless. The scars that stretch across his skin catch my attention, tracing a story of battles fought and wounds endured. They litter his body all the way to his hips. Mesmerized, my gaze fixates on the thick scars that brand his chest —it is as if someone had tried to rip his heart from his chest. The lines are harsh and pronounced, the texture of his skin rough beneath my fingertips as I trace them gently.

Gannon's hand moves, fingers slipping beneath my chin to tilt my face up, ensuring our eyes meet. "Don't hide yours, and I won't hide mine," he whispers, his thumb brushing over my bottom lip.

"These from the wars?" I ask, a little shocked. I always thought Lycans healed quickly.

"No, self-inflicted," Gannon says, looking down at his torso.

"You did that to yourself?" I ask, horrified. He tilts his head to the side, examining my face.

"Why?" I blurt.

"The same reason you gave yourself that scar on your neck, I tried to end it," Gannon says, his hand moving to the side of my face. His fingertips trail down the scar behind my ear. My hand moves over his, and I touch the scar and swallow. The memory of how I got it and Azalea hers will forever haunt me. That day, I wish I could remove it from my memory entirely. If only the rope held and didn't snap.

"You tried to...end your life?" I ask, barely able to get the words out. The thought of gentle, caring Gannon wanting to die is too much for me to grasp.

Gannon nods, his expression pained as he looks down at our intertwined hands. "I was in a dark place," he admits softly. "I know what it's like to look in the mirror and not like the person staring back at you," He leans down, pressing his head against mine. "Just as I know the feeling of not wanting to wake up anymore. Looking for anything to erase the agony you are in."

For a moment, we stand there in silence, lost in our own thoughts and memories. Then, Gannon's hand moves from my face to cup my cheek gently, his thumb brushing over the scar again behind my ear.

"I'm glad you're still here," he says, looking into my eyes with such intensity that it takes my breath away.

"I'm glad you are too," I reply honestly.

With a small smile, Gannon leans down and presses his lips to mine in a tender kiss. It's not passionate or heated; instead, it's filled with a sense of comfort and understanding. Gannon knows what it's like to carry heavy burdens and pain; he knows what it's like to feel broken inside.

"More than my life," Gannon murmurs. "That is what you and Azalea say?" he whispers. I swallow and nod.

"More than my life, Abbie, you are worth so much more than mine. You hold on, and I will for you, I have for you."

"Azalea told you?" I ask him, suddenly feeling dirty.

"No, the King did. Azalea wouldn't betray you. She explained how you both shared similar scars and the meaning behind the words you speak with each other. Not what the butcher did, but I got the picture. Doyle confessed when I found him."

"You met him?" I ask, feeling bile rise in the back of my throat at the mention.

"Yes, and we killed him for what he did. Mrs. Daley, too, he will never come after you again. I will never let anyone hurt you again."

"You killed him?" I ask. I am surprised at how little I feel about that information. He had confessed to murdering someone, but I feel nothing.

"He hurt you, so I made him hurt too," Gannon tells me, and I nod, biting my lip. What do you say to someone who confesses to killing for you? I should be worried he would, yet I felt nothing. Not sadness, not relief, just nothing.

"I wish I could heal you," he repeats, and my eyes dart to him, his eyes roaming over my torn flesh before moving to the marks on my neck.

"Kade never deserved you. I hate that his marks lay on your beautiful neck." I touch them, and they feel bruised. The movement makes me wince.

"You will let me remove his mark from you one day; I can be patient, Abbie," Gannon says, and my brows furrow at his words.

"You can remove them?"

Gannon chuckles darkly. "Yes, when I mark you and when you agree to let me be yours," he says, and I step back. I wasn't sure I wanted anyone to have that sort of control over me again, not after what Kade did.

"Shh, not now. When you're ready. I will wait. For now, having you back is enough for me," he says, stepping closer. His arm goes behind me, and the water cuts off.

"What if I am never ready?" I ask, wondering if he would walk away.

I wasn't sure if I could be with anyone, though I used to want to be with Gannon. I still do; I just wasn't sure how that would be possible now. So much has changed. I have changed, and I know it isn't for the better.

"I'm immortal, Abbie. I have all the time in the world to wait for you," he says before turning and grabbing the towel hanging on the hook. He wraps it around me, pulling me closer. His lips press to my forehead.

"You're worth waiting for," he murmurs, and I sigh, closing my eyes and just enjoying his closeness.

FORTY-ONE

KYSON

Azalea falls asleep quickly, and I run my fingers up and down her spine, enjoying her closeness and her scent. Relief floods me; she is officially mine, and I am hers. An overwhelming feeling washes over me, and I have never felt so complete before as I do now. Yet worry gnaws at me. I knotted her. Lost in the moment, I forgot to pull her off.

Azalea is most fertile while in heat, and the fact I knotted her just upped the chances of me getting her pregnant. Worry eats at me, not because it happened, but because it was clear to me that Azalea had no idea what I was talking about when I told her. Her confusion at my words makes me worry more. Would she hate me if I got her pregnant so soon? My troubled thoughts claw at my insides and give me a headache.

Time slips me by as I become trapped in my thoughts. When I finally feel the swelling at the base of my cock goes down, I am able to slip free of her body. I groan when I notice the damn handcuff still attached to my wrist. Opening the mindlink, I feel for Damian, hoping he has the key.

HIS LOVED LYCAN LUNA

Yet I can feel he is asleep, though Liam isn't, his mindlink buzzing like a live wire in my head. I push on his tether, and he lets me in.

'Finished already, my King, that was fast. Need me to show you how it's done,' Liam taunts.

'Liam!'

'Sorry, my King. Offer still stands.'

'Like the offer to give me a good fuck?' I ask. A stupid smile slips onto my face as I think of the brute.

'If that is what my duty requires, I am up for the task,' he laughs.

'That will not be necessary, but I appreciate the offer,' I chuckle.

'You should get laid more often. You seem to be in a cheery mood now you got rid of the blue balls,' he mocks, and I look down at Azalea and sniff her hair. She reeks of my scent, making me purr with contentment.

'No need to purr at me, my King. I'm pretty sure your calling doesn't work on me, but hey, I can pretend if that is what you are into,' Liam snickers.

'Sorry, Azalea distracted me,' I admit.

'Sure. Now, what can I do for you? I assume you want something, or did you just drop into my thoughts for a friendly chat?' Liam asks.

'Well, I was trying to get a hold of Damian about this customary piece of jewelry I appear to have attached to me,' I tell him.

'Oh, my Justins! Do you like those? I have a hot pink fluffy set, too.'

'I would like them off and was wondering if you had a spare key since Damian is asleep.'

'I do, and Damian is definitely asleep. I am looking at him.'

'Hmm, so who is on guard?' I ask.

'Just little ole me, I noticed Damian needed a grandpa nap and Trey. Hmm, don't like the fella, reminds me of ferret,' Liam growls.

'A ferret?' I ask.

'Yep, cute and fluffy, and then it bites. I had a ferret once, only it bit me, then I wrung its neck, twisted it all the way around, those fuckers' bite hard,' he rambles.

'I remember. The key, Liam.'

'Oh right, should I slide it under the door, or open and toss it. I could try my ninja skills, creep on in slowly, and take you from behind.'

'Liam!'

'Right, I am getting ahead of myself. Should I knock?' he asks, and I roll my eyes.

'Now, why would you knock?' I ask him.

'Well, don't want to be rude, now, do I,' he says when I hear him knock twice. I tug the blanket up and cover Azalea.

"Come in," I laugh. This man is batshit crazy, certifiably insane. He pops his head in and wiggles his eyebrows before covering his eyes with his hands and peering out the gaps between his fingers.

"I see nothing," he says, stumbling over his feet.

"Well, well, well, what have we here?" he asks, dropping his hand and sauntering over to me. His calculated movements remind me of a cat. I roll my eyes at him and wave him forward for the key.

He holds it out to me, then pulls his hand back at the last second. I raise an eyebrow at him.

"Liam, have you been drinking while on the job?" I ask, sniffing the air.

"Just a smidge, my King, want some. I won't tell if you don't," he says, sending me a wink.

"Not a good thing to tell the boss," I scold. He is testing my patience.

"But you've always been more than just my boss, more a brother. I may be many things, but a liar I is not. So if you don't want to know the answer, my King, don't ask," he says, his eyes glistening mischievously.

"Can I have the key, Liam?" I ask. He sighs and quits his mucking around, offering me the key. I take it from him and undo the cuff before rubbing my wrist.

"You seem troubled, my King," Liam says, tilting his head to the side. I look at him. He is drunk, but even I know he could handle himself in this state. He passed the guard trial while obliterated, literally woke up when the starting gun went off, having dozed off at the line, and still placed 5th last year. The guard trials are always a haunting memory for him and for all of us. It's around that time that the anniversaries are.

I bite the inside of my lip and look down at Azalea.

"Ah, I see. You knotted her, didn't you?" he asks, and I nod, stroking her hair. Liam wanders off into the bathroom, and I hear the bathtub turn on as he rummages around in there.

"Get her cleaned up. Never know, might be able to wash it from her."

"Wash pregnancy from her?" I scoff.

"Hmm, I do have another suggestion, but I would like my limbs to remain attached, especially the right hand. I am rather fond of it," Liam says. He leans forward, cupping his mouth with his hands. "I wank with that one," he whispers, and I groan. That is far too much information.

I roll my eyes, and he snickers, the scent of vodka reaching my nose, and I look at him, waiting for him to answer.

"Morning-after pill," he whispers. My brows furrow, and he shrugs. "I mean no offense by that, but if you are worried, should I retrieve you one?" he says.

"Liam?"

"We can keep it on the down-low. No one has to know. I know it is a taboo thing with Royals, but if you think about it, Royals are taboo anyhow, right? Few of you left," he rambles.

"Just ask Doc to keep it to himself; he knows I just don't want it to get out, especially with Clarice. She would be far too excited, and the place would be baby-proofed tomorrow; I also don't want Azalea to feel pressured," I tell him.

Liam nods, rushing out to do my bidding while I get up. I carry a sleeping Azalea into the bathroom, climb in the hot bath, sit her on my lap, and wash her. She moves around, waking, but my calling forces her back under as I wash her the best I can. I heard Liam slip into the room again before shutting the door. When I am sure he is gone, I sit on the edge of the bath and dry her before setting her in the bed and tugging the blanket up.

I noticed the pill sitting on the table with a bottle of water. Climbing back in bed, she instinctively moves closer before crawling on top of me, pressing her body to my chest, and she grabs my hand, placing it over her. I chuckle, running my fingers up her spine.

"I feel cold," she yawns, snuggling against me.

"Because your heat has subsided," I tell her, and she shivers, nodding her head sleepily.

"Do you want kids?"

She is already asleep when I ask this, and I know she would stay in this dreary state for hours. I brush her hair with my fingers for a while before letting myself drift off. I would have to ask her when she wakes. It's not my body and therefore, not my decision. However, I had to tell her there was a chance she could get pregnant.

FORTY-TWO

KYSON

Waking the following day, I tuck Azalea's makeshift den around her. She had built it in her sleep, growling at me when I moved out of it. I always secretly loved seeing female Lycan nests. As dangerous as a nesting Lycan can be, I like the possessive nature behind it. I love how they never lose that primal instinct over time and after changes in tradition.

It is built in their DNA, just like our calling is in us men. Azalea burrows underneath the blanket she had shredded, feathers covering every inch of the bed as she disappears beneath it. Grabbing some shorts, I walk to the door to see Damian standing guard, wide awake and looking alert.

"My King," he nods.

"Watch her for me," I ask him, and he nods to me. I head for the stairs before stopping.

"Don't enter. Azalea is."

"Nesting. I heard her shredding the bed earlier. Also heard you try to save your pillow from her. It woke me," Damian laughs, and my lips tug in the corners.

"When I return, you can go off duty. I won't be leaving her side," I tell him, and I turn for the stairs again when Damian speaks.

"Dustin, my King?" I stop, a growl slipping out of me as I turn to face him.

"He wants to return his post," Damian continues.

"Trey has it handled?" I say, but I am now a little uneasy about Trey.

"About that. I have removed him from her guard." My brows furrow, and I turn to him.

"Very well," I answer.

"You agree?" he asks, shocked. Yet, ever since Liam said something last night, it has bothered me.

"Dustin doesn't trust him, and despite what he did, I know he wouldn't have done it to put her in harm's way. Liam said something last night, too, so keep a close eye on him," I tell Damian.

"Certainly, and Dustin?"

"He can return to his post, but."

"I will tell him to keep his distance. You are doing the right thing, my King," Damian says.

"He's her friend," I answer.

"And yours, my King. He is yours, too," Damian says. I nod, walking downstairs toward the kitchen. I am starving, and I don't want to bother Clarice, so I figure I will make my and Azalea's breakfast. Or is it lunch? I had completely lost track of time. Only when I enter the kitchen, I stop and sniff the air. Rogues.

I stare at the two boys sitting on the bench with a bowl between them. They are licking an eggbeater each, and both of them freeze when I step into the kitchen. Clarice is nowhere to be found, and neither are any of the chefs, so I assume it is between shifts.

"Hello?" I tell them, walking into the room and glancing around. How did they get in here, and where did they come from? They both stare at me like stunned rabbits. The oldest of the two tucked the younger boy closer like he could protect him from me. I watch them for a second. The youngest looks like he was only three or four years old. I can tell by their faintly similar scents that they must be siblings. .

"What are your names?" I ask. The oldest boy answers, while the youngest cowers away from me. I check my aura, making sure it hadn't slipped out, but I gave them no reason to fear me. I look them over, noticing how skinny they are and the bruises that line their arms. Where did they come from?

"I'm Logan. My brother's name is Oliver," the oldest boy answers. He goes to jump off the bench, but I shake my head, and he remains where he is.

The little boy looks up at me as I approach him. I can tell they are scared, their little hearts beating rapidly like a hummingbird's wings in a gust of wind.

"What are you making?" I ask them, looking in their bowl. It looks like a cake mixture.

The youngest boy scoops some out with his finger, holding it out to me. His brother nudges him nervously, but I thought it was cute to offer.

"Want some," he whispers, and I smile, grabbing his little hand and licking his finger.

"And that is Clarice's famous mud cake. You two must be special if Clarice is making cake," I tell them before scooping some batter out with my finger and eating it. They giggle, the sound warming, considering how frail they both look.

The youngest boy, Oliver, turns on the bench and grabs a wooden spoon, offering it to me. I take it, watching as they both use a teaspoon and their egg beaters to scrape the sides, and I join them. I want to ask questions but don't want to scare them. When the back door to the laundry swings open, the boys jump off the bench and hide behind me as Clarice walks in with a washing basket.

"Now, you boys didn't eat all my batter, did you?" she asks, turning around and spotting me with the wooden spoon in my hand. I quickly hide it behind my back. Her mouth falls open, and she glances around for the two boys currently hiding behind me. Oliver sticks his head out, and relief floods her features before her face turns stern, and she places her basket on the bench and folds her arms across her chest.

"Boys, why are you hiding behind the King?" she scolds before spotting her empty mixture bowl. She clicks her tongue.

"Did you eat my mixture?" she asks, and I glance down at them. Her lips tug in the corners, and the boys step out from behind me. Logan, the cheeky little thing, points at me.

"He helped," Logan snitches.

"Is that so, my King?" Clarice asks.

"I was merely helping by making sure it didn't go to waste," I tell her, and she chuckles, turning her attention to the boys.

"Well, you best get me more ingredients, boys. I can't make a cake without mixture," she tells them, and they scurry off toward the pantry. Logan stops at the door to the enormous pantry and looks back at me.

"Are you really the King?" he asks.

"I am," I tell him, and his eyes widen before he rushes inside after his brother.

"You are teaching them bad manners," Clarice scolds me.

"To be fair, they had eaten your batter before I came in and helped," I tell her, and she laughs.

"So, are you going to make me ask, or are you going to tell me where they came from?"

"Gannon and Liam dropped them to me here; now I know I have a full schedule, but they are no-fuss. I can still do my tasks. And I will keep them in line...." Clarice gushes, and I touch her shoulder, stopping her.

"You can keep them, Clarice," I tell her, knowing her too well. She loved kids, and I would never turn away a child. Clarice lets out a breath.

"Thank you, Kyson," she murmurs. "They really are good little boys, timid but sweet." Her eyes sparkle as they rush back out with flour and cocoa in their arms.

"Will you help?" Oliver asks, and Clarice goes to excuse me, but I shake my head.

"Of course," I tell him, scooping up the boy. He is almost weightless, and I look at Clarice, who ruffles his curly locks and smiles sadly.

"Where?" I ask her.

"Where do you think?" she asks, and I nod. Looking at Logan, I notice a few lash marks on his shoulder where his shirt slipped down a bit.

"Gannon took care of it," Clarice answers.

"Yes, I know he would have, but someone needs to take care of that Alpha," I tell her, and she nods once.

"I will see to it," I tell her while turning my attention to the angelic little boy in my arms. Someone definitely needed to take care of that Alpha.

"And I will have you moved into one of the bigger guest quarters to accommodate the boys, too," I tell her.

"Thank you, Kyson," she says, smiling at the boys who were excitedly waiting for her to make more batter.

CHAPTER
FORTY-THREE

A
ZALEA

Every muscle aches when I wake up the following day. Kyson is nowhere to be seen, and his side of the bed is cold. Sticking my head out from under the blanket, I groan when I see the mess I made. I knew I made it because I had not seen Kyson make a den once since being here. He must get sick of having to replace all the bed linens and his clothes. Yet, as I stick my head out, I want to curl back inside my den.

As tempting as that is, I know I can't stay in bed all day or what was left of the day, so I force myself out of bed. Only when I do, my legs give out from under me, pain ricochets up my spine and twists throughout every muscle. Bad enough, we had to go through the heat, but to suffer afterward seemed beyond cruel. Hobbling over to the door, I stuck my head out, keeping my naked body behind the door. I find Damian standing there in front of my door. I was hoping to see Dustin, but right now, I couldn't care less as long as he could help.

"My Queen," he says with a swift nod before turning his attention to me. He looks through the gap in the door behind me.

"Is everything alright?" he asks.

"Have you seen Kyson?"

"He is in the kitchen. I can go get him if you like?" I shake my head. If he is in the kitchen, surely he will be back sometime soon.

"No, it's fine, but can you ask Doc for some painkillers?"

"Ah, I see. Certainly," he says, touching my forehead. His hand feels cold against my skin. "You're still a little warm," he says, his brows pinching together before sniffing the air.

"Yet you're not in heat, must be after-effects. I will go see what I can find. It will probably ease off when Kyson returns, just the bond fretting, so not to worry," he says, and I shut the door.

I half wish I could just be a regular werewolf. They didn't seem to fret or have these bizarre compulsions. Growing up knowing one thing only to find out you're something else entirely really made things confusing. How can I fret for someone I just saw? It makes no sense to me. I make my way to the bathroom. My legs tremble as I stand outside the water spray while waiting for the water to heat. I step under the water as soon as it does, hoping the added heat would loosen my aching bones and wash the tension away.

Hearing a knock on the door roughly 5 minutes later, Damian announces himself, and I sing out from the bathroom to let him know it's okay to come in. He stops next to the bathroom door with his back to me.

"I set some pills on the bedside table. There is already a water bottle there," he tells me.

"Thank you," I tell him, rinsing the soap suds out of my hair.

"Anything else, my Queen?"

"Azalea! Did the King say anything about Dustin?" I ask nervously before rubbing my eyes and looking at his back just outside the door.

"Yes, Dustin will return to his post today," Damian answers.

"So he is okay?"

"Yes, Kyson hasn't punished him yet, but I am sure you can convince him otherwise," Damian says. Hopefully, I could convince Kyson not to punish him. He shouldn't be punished just because he came with me. Either way, I intended to leave. If he wants to be angry with anyone, he should be mad at me, not him.

"And Abbie?"

"With Gannon. She is a little sore, but she is okay. I have given him the week off to spend with Abbie until she readjusts to being here."

I nod, forgetting he had his back to me.

"Anything else, my Queen?"

"Yes, stop calling me my Queen," I tell him, and he laughs.

"Very well, Azalea."

"Thank you. You can go unless you want to chat," I laugh.

"Somehow, I don't think the King would approve of me standing here chatting with you while you shower."

"Wouldn't make much difference. You already saw me naked, but you are probably right. Best to not push the King's buttons."

"I will be outside if you need me," he says before walking off. I hear the door click shut, and after a few minutes, I climb out, wrap myself in a towel, and walk into the bedroom to the closet to find some clothes. Setting them on the bed, I dry myself when I notice the pills on the bedside table.

Grabbing the water bottle, I twist the cap off. I drink half the bottle, not realizing how dry my throat is, only stopping when I remember I need water to swallow the pills. Grabbing the two foil packets, I try to read what they said, but the words are too long and I figure they are both some form of painkiller. I pop the first two out and swallow them down before snapping the foil on the other gray pill. It smells funny, and I try to remember where I have smelled that scent before.

Shaking my head, I tip the bottle to my lips when the door opens. Dropping the empty foil packet back onto the bedside table, I go to put the tablet in my mouth when the wind is suddenly knocked out of me as I land on the bed.

Kyson grabs my hand and lands on top of me on the bed. "Geez, Kyson," I snap at him as he pries my fingers apart.

"What's got into you?" I demand. Kyson takes the pill out of my hand before letting out a breath.

"Ah, thank the Moon Goddess," he sighs. I stare up at him, wondering what the Moon Goddess had to do with any of this. Thank her for making me sore because I would rather curse her out.

Kyson sits up, and I notice Damian standing in the doorway, looking petrified, when Kyson looks over his shoulder at him.

"She didn't take it," Kyson tells him, and Damian visibly relaxes.

"Sorry, I didn't know," he says to Kyson. Well, that makes two of us because I still didn't know what was going on right now.

"It is my fault. I shouldn't have left it there. You can go," Kyson tells him, and Damian shuts the door. Kyson turns back to look down at me before holding up the pill.

"This is not a painkiller," he says, climbing off me. I blink up at him, waiting for him to explain, and he leans down, pecking my lips.

Kyson lets me sit up before dropping the pill in my hand. "That is the morning-after pill. Do you know what that means?" he asks. I shake my head. Kyson scrubs a hand down his face.

"I didn't mean to, but I knotted you," he says. I remember him saying that last night. It is why I couldn't move afterward.

"You take that it will kill off an unwanted pregnancy, but it has to be taken within 72 hours if you're human. Since you're Lycan, you have roughly half that time to take it, but the choice is yours."

"Wait, you impregnated me?" I ask, horrified, while looking at the pill in my hand.

"I'm not sure, but you are more fertile during heat, and since I knotted you, the chances are even higher, so if you don't want to be pregnant, you can take that to stop it," Kyson says before looking at the pill in my hand.

"Do you want me to take it?" I ask him, staring at the pill.

"What I want doesn't matter; it is your body. The choice is yours," Kyson tells me when I hear arguing outside the door. Kyson looks over his shoulder at the door. He growls but climbs off the bed and walks over to the tray Damian had placed on the dresser. He grabs it, walking back to me.

"Here, I made you something to eat. I will be back in a second. Just need to sort out something," Kyson says, and I can feel he is angry about something as he glares at the door before storming outside.

I stare down at the tray, which has different meat, eggs, and toast. Staring at the pill in my hand. I sigh, not knowing what to do.

Do I want kids? More to the question, though, does the King? I'm assuming he wants to continue his royal bloodline; I also suppose mine. However, I'm not so sure. I never gave babies much thought. I honestly never saw myself having a future, let alone one where I could have children. But if I took it, wouldn't that be going against the Moon Goddess? At the same time, Kyson wouldn't have given it to me if he believed that, would he?

CHAPTER
FORTY-FOUR

K YSON

    I want to explain more, but when Damian calls through the link that a fight had broken out down the corridor between Trey and Dustin, I have no choice but to sort it out. Leaving the room, I see Dustin punch Trey, knocking him down the stairs, only to chase after him. Damian is trying to separate them when Trey tackles Dustin as he rushes down the steps. Damian grabs the back of Trey's shirt and rips him off Dustin just as Dustin goes to attack him again. My hand wraps around his arm, jerking him back.

"What the fuck is going on here?" I snarl while Trey shrugs off Damian's hand.

"Answer me?" I command.

"I don't want him near the Queen. He can't be trusted," Dustin snarls.

"And you can, asshole. You ran off with her and put the Queen in danger," Trey spits back at him.

"Yes, it's also your fault. Azalea wouldn't have even known where to go if you didn't show her on her phone!" Dustin growls, taking a step toward him, but my hand falls on his shoulder.

"Is this true?" I ask Trey, who turns his attention to me. He sighed, scratching the back of his neck.

"Yes, my King. But I did not know she would go off after Abbie," Trey admits.

"And you would let Dustin take full responsibility for what happened?" Damian demands.

"I didn't run off with her. I would have dragged her back to the room had I known," Trey defends himself. Damian shakes his head, looking at me.

"You have two seconds to explain yourselves, now," I say.

"Dustin hates me because he blames me for the trials and keeps sabotaging me every chance. Damian pulled me from her guard because of him," Trey says before glaring at Dustin.

"Damian didn't pull you from the guard; I did. There are too many rumors about both of you right now."

"Yet you stationed him?" Trey scoffs.

"Yes, because he is one of my head guards, and Azalea trusts him even if right now I don't," I growl, looking at Dustin. I want to beat him senseless, yet Abbie would probably be dead or, worse still, stuck there if they hadn't gone.

"She was determined to go. Better I went with her than go by herself, my King. You know I would never put her in harm's way. You know I wouldn't risk her like that unless I had no choice!" Dustin says, and I growl.

"You had a choice. You could have brought the Queen back to her room!" Trey yelled.

"Because that worked. Azalea snuck out on you, and you didn't even know she was gone," Dustin retorts and Trey looks away. Damian rubs his temples and shakes his head.

"You are giving me a headache," Damian growls.

"May I be of some assistance?" Liam says, making all of us jump. He is sitting on the windowsill above the stairs. We all look up, not one of us noticing he is even there. My brows pinch, wondering how the heck he even got up there. He jumps down and lands next to Damian on his feet.

"How did you get up there?" Damian asks.

"Ninja skills. I'm as quiet as a mouse and quick and agile as a snake," he chuckles, and I try not to laugh, and I see Dustin trying not to smile at his words. Trey, however, holds a sour expression.

"And why were you up there?" Damian asks.

"My ears were burning, my senses telling me there was information to eavesdrop upon," he says.

"Are you drunk?" Damian asks. Liam shakes his head, straightening up.

"The question you mean, Beta. Are you sober... that would be a never," Liam giggles. I roll my eyes.

I wave him forward, and he straightens himself like some prim and proper gentleman, though he is a gentleman, either way, sober or drunk. When I think of it, I think his question is correct. I have yet to see him sober since Claire. It makes me briefly wonder if he could function without the liquor, although I know I have a drinking problem, so I can't really judge.

"What are you proposing?" I ask.

"Well, you still have to go away, my King, to investigate the killings, and I would rather stay behind. I am sick of looking at dead little ones; Uncle Liam is not made for the kiddie horrors, so I volunteer to watch the Queen, with Dustin, of course," Liam says, motioning toward Dustin and sending him a wink. Dustin shakes his head with a laugh.

"You want Trey to take your place on my guard?" I ask.

"But I was the Queen's guard,..."

I hold my hand up, shutting off Trey's protests when Liam looks at me, his eyes glazing over before his voice is in my head.

"You already know how I feel about the ferret. Dustin is clear about his feelings. What better way to catch a rat than having him by your side, my King? Azalea is safe with me; I don't care if he is from Landeena. He is hiding something. His switch from hating her to almost stalking her is too sudden, but if I remember correctly, Trey is not under the guard pact!" Liam says, making my brows furrow.

I glance at Damian, trying to remember when I set the pact, but Liam is right. It was after the fall of King Garret and Queen Tatiana and just before the death of my sister. Trey got here just after her end and earned his way up the ranks.

'What is it?' Damian mindlinks.

'Ask Clarice if Trey was there when Azalea's food was tampered with,' I ask him, and he nods, walking off down the stairs.

Turning my attention to Trey and Dustin, I see they're still glaring at each other.

"Trey, you're swapping with Liam. Liam will be on guard with you, Dustin," I tell him, and Dustin nods, heading up the stairs to my room.

"He is a fucking drunk!" Trey accuses, glaring at Liam. I blink, only to find Trey shoved against the wall, Liam's hand around his throat, and a knife under his chin.

"Watch it, boy, or I will be wearing your skin as a suit. So I'd watch your tongue, talk about me like that again, and I will remove it for you, one of the King's guards or not. I will show you what a drunk can do and what a pretty suit you would make," Liam warns, tapping the side of Trey's face with his knife. Trey swallows and nods quickly.

Liam growls before shoving off him and walking up the steps to his post, while Trey presses his lips in a line, looking away.

"5 am. We leave in the morning. Be ready," I tell Trey before turning on my heel.

"Yes, my King," I hear him answer before walking off. When I reach the top level, Dustin nods at me. I press my lips in a line, turning to face him.

"You are not off the hook. Unfortunately, my punishment for you."

"I think putting up with me would be punishment enough, don't you think, my King," Liam chuckles. I cluck my tongue, turning back to Dustin.

"It is yet to be decided. Don't fuck up again."

"I won't, my King," Dustin says, and I nod to them, pushing the door open and going to find my mate. Azalea is sitting on the floor by the fireplace, playing with her tablet and an open book.

"Did you eat?" I ask her, and she nods, pointing to the empty tray on the dresser without looking up from the tablet she was typing away on. I sigh, walking over and grabbing it. Opening the door, I go to hand it to Liam when I notice the pill still sitting on the tray. My heart races a little faster, seeing it sitting beside her empty plate.

"Azalea?" I ask, looking over my shoulder at her. She looks up from where she is sitting on the floor to stare at me.

"Did you mean to leave that on the tray?" I ask her. She scratches her neck, and I can feel her worry through the bond, and she grows nervous. She is scared of answering but does.

"You said it was my choice. I don't want to take it," she says, biting her lip, her eyes on the tray in my hand.

"Liam!" I tell him, and he takes the tray, shutting the door. A giddy feeling rushes through me, knowing she wants kids.

"You know what that means, right?" I ask, walking over to her.

"That I could get pregnant," Azalea answers and shrugs. "But I also might not be pregnant, so we'll see."

I stop beside her, and she looks up at me.

"Are you angry?" she asks. I shake my head, sit beside her, and pull her on my lap. I am the complete opposite, but I was worried about how she would take it. Although now, I hold relief.

"No, I didn't want you to take it, but it wasn't my choice," I tell her, kissing her cheek and wrapping my arms around her waist. I bury my face in her neck, inhaling her scent, and she squirms away from my ticklish stubble.

"What are we reading tonight?" I ask her, kissing my mark on her neck. Azalea shivers, and she holds up the book.

"*Treasure Island*, you seem to like this one," I tell her, and she leans back against me while I take the book and open it.

"I have to leave tomorrow, but Dustin will be here with Liam," I tell her, finding the spot she was up to.

"Can't I come?" she asks.

"I thought you wanted to see Abbie. Maybe next time," I tell her. Azalea sighs, but as soon as I mention Abbie, I know I am right in that assumption. Opening the book, I read, stopping now and then to let her try. Her reading has gotten better, and she can identify a few new words by the time I stop.

CHAPTER
FORTY-FIVE

KYSON

The next few days passed by quickly. We are no closer to finding anything about the rogue children, but another woman was found, and we divert our route to investigate. Like Blaire, we found she was rogue. Only this one was different. She was found wearing scrubs and appeared to be a nurse, rather than the usual sex worker, making it difficult to find any pattern to the killings. Getting ready to leave again, I felt like I had spent hardly any time here lately. I missed Azalea terribly when I was away, usually crawling into bed late at night while she was sleeping, only to leave early in the mornings.

"Azzy!" I whisper, shaking her shoulder, and she groans, rolling onto her back.

"No, let me sleep. I will do it later," she whines, and I growl, scooping her naked body up off the bed. The same argument every morning as I hauled her to the bathroom and drop her on the toilet. She huffs and glares at me with tired eyes.

"I don't understand why you have me testing every morning. It's too early to tell," Azalea growls but holds her hand out for the preg-

253

nancy test. I unwrap it, passing it to her, and she glares at me until I turn around.

"Because Lycan pregnancies are only 12 weeks compared to normal pregnancies or werewolf pregnancies; if you are, we should be able to tell any day," I tell her, and she mumbles incoherently.

"You know I can't just pee on demand, right?" she says, and I roll my eyes, turning the tap on, hoping the water facilitates the need to pee; it worked yesterday. I tap my foot impatiently, waiting with my hand out for the test. Only when she passes it to me does she giggle as she drops the test in my hand. It takes me a few seconds to figure out why she is laughing as she dashes off into the bedroom.

She didn't put the cap on, and the part she peed on is now in the palm of my hand. I blink at my hand, holding her pee, and drop it on the counter, quickly washing my hand.

"Azalea!"

"That's what you get for waking me," she laughs, and I growl.

I can still hear her giggling as I wait for the test to show. I growl; inconclusive, nothing appears; this time, the test is faulty. Shit, I rifle under the sink for another and stick my head out the bathroom door to look for her to find her inside her den, still laughing to herself.

"You little brat! It was faulty. You need to do another," I tell her.

"No can do. I no longer need to pee," she says as I stalk out of the bathroom. I try unraveling her den, earning a feral growl from her. She swipes at me as I ruin her den, trying to get to her. She frantically tries to put it back together, making me worry. This is precisely why I want her to do the test; her instincts are out of control, and it has only been three days.

She assured me she feels the same, yet her instincts tell me otherwise. *I will call Doc to do a blood test*, I think to myself as I help her rearrange her nest, feeling bad, I upset her before I had to leave. Leaning over to kiss her, she growls at me, her eyes on my shirt, and I roll my eyes, peeling it off, knowing she wants it for her nest.

My poor bed has been reduced to torn sheets, clothes, and duck feathers as she rips the damn pillows every night. She reaches for it, but I pull it back before she can grab it, wanting a kiss. She growls but leans forward, knowing what I want. Just before her lips brush mine, she snatches my shirt from my hand and turns back, rearranging her nest.

"Brat!" I scold, leaning across the bed and grabbing her hips, dragging her toward me. I nuzzle her neck and purr, letting the calling slip out. Azalea relaxes before turning her face toward mine. Her lips part as I kiss her, and my tongue slips between her plump lips, my tongue tasting every inch of her mouth, savoring her taste. With a sigh, I let her go, knowing the others will be waiting for me.

"I will be home as soon as possible," I tell her, watching her crawl into her den. I stop by my office on the way down to the car to grab a fresh shirt, which is the last one I have left clean in the room. Thankfully, I have a cupboard full in the office. Slipping one on, I step out of my office while buttoning it up.

Walking out to the car, I find Gannon standing beside it. "I thought you had the week off?" I tell him as he opens the door. I duck my head, stepping inside.

"I do, but I wanted to speak to you before you left," Gannon tells me, peering in the car at me. Trey clears his throat behind him, and Gannon steps aside to allow him to climb in the back with me. I am wary of him, especially since finding out he had, in fact, been around and handled Azalea's meals. Yet, when I commanded him and questioned him, it was clear he was not the one that poisoned her food, so we were still no closer to finding the culprit at the same time.

After spending the last few days with him, I too am getting strange vibes. Or maybe it's the rumors about him messing with my perception. Regardless, until the person responsible is caught, I only trust her with very few people, and Trey isn't one of them right now.

I turn my attention to Gannon, who looks at me. "What do you need?" I asked him.

"I want to take Abbie away for a few days, but I wanted to clear it with you first."

"Of course. Where are you taking her?"

"Don't know yet, somewhere, but I will be back before my week off is over."

"Take your time, Gannon. I can manage without you. Besides, when was the last time you had time off anyway?" I ask, knowing it has been years. Like Damian and Dustin, the man never took days off.

"Thank you."

"Just make sure Azalea sees Abbie before she goes."

Gannon nods just as Damian climbs in the car also. I open the mindlink ,observing Gannon stop as he goes to shut the door. He looks at me questioningly, but I don't want to ask out loud with Trey in the car. Not that he's paying attention; he seems too busy playing on his phone.

'Have Doc come to take blood from Azalea for me before you leave,' I tell him and nod.

'Still no luck with the tests?' he asks, and I shake my head.

'Will do anything else?'

'Yes, enjoy your time off,' I tell him, and he smirks, shutting the door.

CHAPTER
FORTY-SIX

A ZALEA

Walking out of my room, Liam greets me by looping his arm through mine in a gesture that feels both familiar and comforting. "And what adventure do we embark on today, my Queen?" he asks with a playful glint in his eyes. I scan the area, searching for Dustin.

"Dustin went to fetch your breakfast," Liam informs me as we start descending the steps.

"I'm not hungry. I simply wish to see Abbie," I reply with a slight furrow of my brow, heading towards Gannon's room. Abbie has remained secluded in the room since our return, prompting Gannon's desire to take her somewhere. Before she departs, I need to make sure she's healing alright.

Kyson told me she was leaving through the mindlink. It always freaked me out when he used it. I'm not used to having someone in my head, let alone being a part of something. Abbie was rogue again, and I hated that, but she refused to let Gannon mark her. Every time I asked Kyson to make her part of the pack, he said she refused and he couldn't unless he changed her.

257

I understand why. It's not just about her feeling unworthy of deserving good things. If Gannon fails to help her, she won't remain Lycan, and I can't fathom a world without Abbie by my side. Shortly after the King's departure, Gannon had visited to inform me that he plans on whisking her away, and they'd depart after lunch.

Walking through the winding corridors that led to the back of the castle, I rap my knuckles against the door, hoping for a response. But silence greets me instead. I glance up at Liam, and with a determined grip on the door handle, he pushes it open cautiously, peeking inside.

"I'll wait here. Gannon isn't around," Liam informs me, his gaze averted as if avoiding something uncomfortable. I nod in acknowledgment before making my way into the dimly lit darkroom. The heavy curtains are drawn shut, blocking out any trace of light and making it challenging for my eyes to adjust. In my attempt to navigate the room, I accidentally stub my toe on a coffee table, a surge of annoyance coursing through me. Cursing under my breath, I press forward towards the bathroom door.

"Abbie? It's me," I call out softly, hoping for a response. None comes. However, it sounds as if she is crying behind that door, and suddenly, I understand why Liam hesitated to enter. Taking in my surroundings, I push the door open wider and close it behind me. As I turn towards the darkened bathroom, I notice that the mirrors have been concealed by large sheets of black paper, rendering the space even darker than the main room. The air is thick with the saltiness of her tears mingling with billowing steam.

An instant wave of perspiration breaks out across my skin; it feels like a stifling sauna in here. Strained murmurs emanate from within the enormous glass shower stall, its surface fogged up by steam.

"Abbie?" I whispered, my hand reaching out to open the shower screen. And there she was, huddled at the bottom of the shower, scrubbing herself with a ferocity that seems it will be painful while she presses into the corner.

Her skin is flushed and raw from the scalding water. It is evident that she isn't okay. Everyone knows it, but seeing her like this shatters my heart. Abruptly, she halts her movements as if only just realizing my presence. Slowly, she lifts her head and stares blankly ahead.

Clutched tightly in her hand was a scourer, the kind one would use to clean heavily stained pots, not delicate skin.

"I can still feel his hands, Az. Still taste his vileness in my mouth," she whispers, her vacant gaze fixed on some distant point. A tear slips down her cheek, mingling with the cascading water before disappearing down the drain. Her quivering lip reveals the pain etched deep within her. Without hesitation, I step into the scalding hot shower, my clothes immediately becoming soaked.

I move towards her, near the far wall, and sit down beside her. Some parts of her skin are bleeding, evidence of how harshly she had scrubbed herself. The scars that litter her body are raw and angry, although thankfully, they have healed and are now nothing more than raised reminders.

"Sometimes, it's alright to remember the darkness, Abbie. Just don't linger there for too long. Don't let it trap you or give him control that he no longer has over you," I told her gently, my grip tightening around her hand that held the scourer.

"I don't want control. I want to forget, to hate him without loving him. How can you still love someone even after they do something like that? I should have listened to Gannon. I should have stayed," Abbie whispers.

"That wasn't love, Abbie. It was the mate bond, a twisted version of what you thought love should be," I explained.

"I was naive, foolish," she scolded herself bitterly.

"No, you wanted something more than what we have been given, and that's not your fault," I tell her. I sit with her, letting the boiling water scald my legs.

Thankfully, she only had her legs under the water, the rest of her pressed against the wall.

"I can't live like this, Az. I don't want to anymore. I don't want to be the broken doll."

This isn't the Abbie I know. This is who remained after everything had been taken from her. She seems as helpless now as she did when we first entered that orphanage. Back then, we were just children, unaware of the true horrors of the world, accepting whatever fate was dealt to us because we didn't know any better.

Now that we are older, our eyes have opened to the harsh realities, the monsters that lurk in the shadows, and the lies that shaped our childhood. What we once considered normal has become distorted; what we thought was normal no longer is, and we are still uncertain of this new normal.

We have grown accustomed to pain because pain is familiar, comfortable in our own misery because it has become routine. Brokenness has become our norm. But how do you fix something that has become so deeply ingrained?

How do you break free from a cycle where pain is perceived as normal? Pain is not normal yet, all we know, or I did know until I met Kyson. Abbie hasn't met her new normal; she is still suffering in the version we grew up with. Kade has compounded that feeling exponentially. And I could see that she is tired - tired of the old normal. Though she wore her resilience like armor, now it lay exposed, revealing her desire to shed its weight.

"You're not broken," I whisper despite the fact she looks it.

"I am. I don't even know who I am anymore," she murmurs, her gaze distant and emotionless.

"You're my best friend, my sister. You are more than my life," I tell her, squeezing her hand.

"No, we are you! We are rogue. We are whatever they let us be and nothing more," she says.

"Only if you allow yourself to be. You are not defined by what he did to you, Abbie. You are not a reflection of the butcher's actions, and we are not limited by the beliefs Mrs. Daley instilled in us," I counter.

"You aren't. You are a princess and soon-to-be Queen. You are Azalea Ivy Landeena. I am rogue, I am nothing, and now everyone knows what they did, everyone knows the dirty things I wished I could forget; I am sick of them looking at me with pity, sick of them looking at me with disgust, sick of being what he made me!"

Abbie buries her face in her hands, tears streaming down her cheeks. Her shoulders shake with each anguished breath, and I can't even begin to fathom the depth of her pain. But one thing is certain —she will make it through this. She has to because a world without her presence is no world worth being in.

"Then be Abbie," I tell her, putting my head on her shoulder.

"But I don't know who she is," Abbie murmurs, her voice emotionless.

"What they did to you is not you, but a reflection of them. That is who they were. Were Abbie. They are dead, and you are still breathing. They don't get another chance, but you do, so take it; don't let them chain you down in the memory of what they did. They don't deserve it. Live because you can and want to," I tell her, and she shakes her head and pulls her knees to her chest.

Abbie puts her head in her hands and cries. Her shoulders shake, and I can't begin to imagine what she is going through, but she *will* get through this. She has to.

"You sound like Gannon, but even he looks at me the same as everyone else, even you do; I know you can't help it, but-" she chokes out, her entire body shaking.

"I don't look at you with pity, Abbie. I see beyond the pain and the scars. I see the strength and resilience that define who you truly are. You are so much more than what they have done to you. You are the girl for whom I would risk my life, the one who has stood by my side when all hope seemed lost. And now, right here in this moment, I need you to make a choice. Are you going to jump? Because if you do, I will jump with you?"

Abbie's voice trembles as she responds, her words carrying the weight of her self-doubt. "But I am nothing compared to you. I am just a werewolf while you are a Queen."

Her belief in her own insignificance pains me deeply. "You are everything to me, Abbie. My title means nothing if I don't have you by my side, and you will be my Beta, so don't tell me you are nothing because the only reason I am still here for any of this is because of you."

Abbie chuckles and shakes her head but lifts it, placing it against the wall. "I am a werewolf. You are Lycan, I can't be your Beta, and I wouldn't know the first thing about being a Beta."

"Do you think I know how to be a Queen?" I laugh softly, sitting up higher to meet her gaze.

"I can't even read, but we have people here that will help us. I have Kyson. You have Gannon and me."

"But what if Gannon leaves me when he realizes I can't give him what he wants?" Abbie's voice trembles with fear.

"He wants to change you and mark you, Abbie. He isn't going anywhere. And even if he does, I will always be here for you," I tell her.

"You would change me?" she asks.

"Wouldn't think twice about it, but we may have to ask how, though because I am not that good at being Lycan yet," I chuckle.

A chuckle escapes Abbie's lips, mirroring my own. But her smile fades all too quickly, replaced by a somber expression. "Who would have thought that freedom could be worse than the chains that once bound us?"

"Freedom isn't something that is given, Abbie. It's a mindset. Only we can free ourselves."

"Do you feel free?" she asks, and I sigh.

"I don't know, but I know we aren't the orphan rogues anymore. I don't know who I am either, but I am determined to find out, and I prefer we find out together," I tell her, and she swallows.

"More than my life," she whispers.

"More than my life," I reply, the weight of those words sinking deep into my soul.

"More than my life," Gannon's deep voice interrupts our conversation, catching us off guard. Neither of us heard him enter the room. As he leans against the sink basin, his presence commands attention.

"Gannon?" Abbie sighs, shaking her head beside me.

"How long have you been there?" I ask, surprised by his sudden appearance.

"Long enough," he answers curtly. "Now hop out. We are leaving."

Abbie remains unmoved, her body curled up against the wall as if trying to hide from him. Gannon's eyes briefly meet mine before he rubs his tired face, a reflection of the blacked-out mirror behind him. I glance back at Abbie, taking in the scars that mark her skin.

"I told you I am not going," Abbie says, staring vacantly ahead.

"You are. You can't stay in here, love. So please," Gannon begs, crouching down in front of us when he opens the door. I look to Abbie, who makes herself smaller as if she is trying to hide her body away from him.

But I refuse to let her feel ashamed of her body. Her scars may not be easily hidden like mine, but they are a testament to her strength and survival. She must know that.

"Can you please get out?" Abbie whispers, her voice barely audible.

Gannon's eyes flit to me for a second before he scrubs a hand down his face, and I see the blacked-out mirror behind him, glancing back at Abbie and looking at her scarred skin. We nearly look the same. We have the same markings. No doubt, hers are causing her more pain because while the cuts will heal, the marks on her heart... I wasn't so sure.

Nonetheless, I can tell she is ashamed of her body, and what has become of it, and if that is what is preventing her from leaving the room, she needs to know she has nothing to be ashamed of. Her scars can't be hidden by clothes like mine can be, but that doesn't mean she should feel ashamed of them.

"Can you get out, please?" she whispers, her knees close to her chest.

"I have already seen you naked, Abbie," Gannon responds matter-of-factly. Her face flushes crimson, her lips quivering.

"I can't go out there," she confesses, her voice filled with anguish. I take note of the scars that trail down her neck and shoulders, as well as the cuts on her face that have left white lines once healed. To me, she is still beautiful. I remember the shame I felt when the King asked me to undress in front of him and how Abbie pleaded on my behalf. Gannon sighs, frustration etched across his features, but he never directs it at Abbie.

"It's just skin, Abbie," I whisper gently. But for her, those scars hold memories and pain that I cannot fully comprehend.

"He mutilated me. It's one thing for everyone here to know, but it's another for the whole world to see," she croaks.

Trying to feel for the mindlink, I push on it, hoping I can open it myself, yet when I struggle, Kyson opens it for me. I really can't get used to him being in my head. The bond is one thing, but the mind is something else. Kyson makes it look easy, but it's not. .

'Why do you feel embarrassed?' Kyson's voice resonates through the mindlink.

'Abbie hates her body,' I relay to him.

'And that embarrasses you?' he questions, his words causing my face to flush with shame. 'Hmm, I don't like this feeling. Where are you?'.

'In the shower with Abbie,' I respond.

'I see,' he acknowledges.

'Not like that. I have clothes on, but....'

'But what?'

'I want to take them off,' I admit, my cheeks burning even hotter. Being naked in front of Abbie doesn't faze me. We have seen each other unclothed countless times before.

'*You're both girls, and I don't see a problem with that.*'

My face heated even more. I am not afraid to be naked in front of Abbie.

'*Spit it out, Azalea. Your hesitation is making me uneasy. What is it?*' Kyson demands, an edge to his voice.

'*Imagine if I were to walk outside in the castle completely naked,*' I blurt out, surprising myself with the audacity of my statement.

'*Definitely not,*' Kyson growls. His words anger me and fuel my next answer

'*I wasn't asking permission,*' I tell him, though I was kind of hoping he would give it because I didn't exactly want this to cause an argument.

'*Then why are you telling me?*' he snaps back.

'*So you don't find out from the staff,*' I explain.

'*Azalea!*' he snaps.

'*Will be naked, walking the corridors naked,*' I answer.

'*Like hell you are!*'

I cut him off, only for the mindlink to open up again, and he forced his way back into my head.

'*Somebody shut off the damn cameras,*' Kyson snarls through the mindlink, broadcasting his message to all the castle staff. Their voices flood my mind, overwhelming me with their presence.

'*Do we have cameras?*' I ask, bewildered by this revelation.

'*Yes, they were installed two days ago. And you are absolutely not doing this,*' Kyson declares adamantly.

'*But I am,*' I insist, my determination unwavering.

'*Why are we shutting off the cameras?*' Gannon's voice interjects suddenly through the mindlink. The multitude of voices in my head begins to give me a headache, and I struggle to regain control. I struggle, trying to shut them off, only for Kyson to force his way back into my head.

'*Do not let Azalea leave the bathroom,*' Kyson growls at him.

'*Pardon, my King,*' Gannon answers. Abbie touches my arm as she stands, making me jump and pulling me back to focus on the room.

I watch her grab a towel and wrap it around herself, and I stand, stepping out of the shower. My face is already heating. I start shredding my clothes, dropping them in a wet heap as Abbie sticks her head out the door. Kyson is yelling at me through the mindlink and the guards, and I try my best to ignore him.

"I will get you some spare clothes," Abbie says.

"Don't bother," I tell her, and she glances at me but quickly rushes into the room. Kyson is still talking through the mindlink and arguing with the guards about leaving Gannon's quarters. While Liam asks a barrage of never ending and inappropriate questions, I find it hard to keep tabs on how many people's voices were suddenly flitting through my head.

I grab a towel and dry myself, and Abbie runs back into the room with a cami and shorts, trying to pass them to me while she starts pulling on a turtle neck and long pants.

"Here," she whispers, but I shake my head. "Az?"

I move to step past her when she stops in front of me.

"Gannon is out there," she says, gripping my arm when he suddenly opens the door, standing completely naked. I have no idea where to look, so I stare up at the roof, and so does he. Awkward.

'Hang on, we're doing this in style,' Liam says through the mindlink and I look at Gannon, who sends me a wink.

'I swear, Azalea, when I get home,' Kyson starts.

'Well, that sounds like a challenge, my King,' I tell him.

'Put some clothes on, and Liam, stay away from my mate,' he snaps.

'What? No, I am streaking with her, got my best apron for this, and if Gannon is strutting his stuff, so is me; sometimes you gotta air out the old skinsuit,' Liam says.

'I said clear the halls,' the King commands.

'Everyone remains at their posts!' I command back, a little shocked at how easily I did.

The King growls. *'Azalea!'*

'My King?' Clarice says through the mindlink.

I can hear Abbie asking what is going on, but I grab her hand

almost blindly as everyone's faces flit through my head along with
their voices.

'I can't do this with you in my damn head,' I tell Kyson.

'Good because you aren't doing it,' he growls.

'What is going on?' Clarice asks.

'Azalea is about to streak through the damn halls,' Kyson tells her.

I focus on the mindlink, trying to get him out of my head. When I
manage it, I am still standing in the bathroom, though I can see
Gannon now. I make sure to keep my eyes above the waist. I do not
want to see more than I need to. However, I am shocked to find his
flesh torn apart more than ours.

"Are we doing this?" he asks, looking at me.

"Doing what?" Abbie squeaks, looking between us.

"Oh good, I am not late," Liam says, busting into the bathroom
with only a floral apron on.

"Oh la la, my Queen, lovely birthday suit," he said, not even
being subtle as he looked at me. I swallow under his leering gaze.

'Eyes off my mate Liam.'

'Hitting above your belt there, my King,' Liam chuckles, earning a
growl through the mindlink Kyson keeps forcing open. Liam reaches
past Gannon, grabs my wrist, jerks me to him, and loops his arm
through mine while Abbie stands stunned. She grabs my arm as
Liam tugs me toward the door.

"What are you doing?"

"We are showing you. You aren't the only one a little broken,"
Gannon says, offering his arm to her.

"Man, the King doesn't shut up. Bit Bossy if you ask me. How do
you put up with him," Liam says. As Kyson keeps trying to order his
men out, when I realize something, his commands on Liam and
Gannon are not working. That realization hits me, and at the same
time, it hits Kyson, and I know something is amiss.

'Azalea?' he asks.

'I love you, but I am doing this for Abbie,' I tell him, and he
growls.

'Them Cameras better be fucking off?' he calls through the open mindlink.

'Already off,' I hear Dustin call back.

"Well, now this is definitely an adventure, so I guess we are off," Liam says, opening the door and bowing. Abbie giggles behind me, and I glance over my shoulder to see Gannon put his hands over her eyes when Liam shakes his ass at her. I try not to laugh and close my eyes, willing myself to step out the doors and not run back to the bathroom.

'You are in so much trouble when I get home,' Kyson snaps at me.

Anger courses through me, and Abbie gasps. I open my eyes at the sound and gasp myself. All the guards are still stationed at their posts, their clothes at their feet in a heap, their eyes straight ahead, and hands over their privates. I look at Abbie, who is fully clothed, gripping Gannon's arm tightly, looking like she wants to run back into the room.

"Ready, my Queen?" Liam laughs, looping his arm back through mine.

I nod my breathing heavily and look straight ahead before I start walking. I head for the King's quarters, and I can hear Abbie crying behind me as she follows Gannon. Every staff member lined the halls naked, eyes straight ahead, thankfully. My chest warms, knowing they did this for her. Kyson growls through the bond angrily, and I can almost see the angry look on his face.

As we walk through the halls, I feel a strange weight lift from not only Abbie but also me as her crying stops. Each person we pass bow or nods, and she looped her arm through mine. She rests her head on my shoulder as we climb the last set of stairs to find Clarice and Dustin standing up top, also naked.

"I knew you were a fine lady, Clarice, but damn," Liam says, giving a whistle.

"Liam, you are not too big for me to spank or wash your mouth out with soap," she scolds.

"Lucky me, which knee would you like me over?" he laughs, and she folds her arms across her chest, and her eyes narrow at the man.

"My Queen," she says and nods. Dustin walks over and opens the door for me.

"Abbie?" I whisper.

"You didn't have to do this," she tells me, yet the tension in her body has left; she looks more relaxed.

"Yes, I did. You needed to see," she looks out at all the naked guards and staff.

"Did you have to make them do it too?"

"No one made them do it, Love," Gannon whispers, and everyone in the hall bows or tips their heads to her, and her cheeks flush pink.

"So, can I take you somewhere now and put some pants on? It is a little chilly?" Gannon asks, and I give her a nudge.

"Go, no one cares what you look like," I tell her, and tears brim in her eyes as she hugs me.

"More than my life," she whispers.

"More than my life," I tell her.

"More than my life," all the guards and staff murmur in unison, making my heart skip a beat.

I look at Dustin, who nods, keeping his eyes on mine. I wait for Abbie to disappear around the corner near the stairs before racing to the cupboard for clothes. Clarice steps into the room as I pull on some pajamas, and I let out a breath.

"You're a Good friend," Clarice says, wrapping a sheet around herself.

"I can't believe everyone did it for her," I chuckle. Clarice also laughs.

"Yes, but also you, you are our Queen. Where you go, we follow even if it is doing something as silly as being naked," she says when Kyson's voice booms through the link.

'For god's sake, please tell me she has clothes on now,' he growls.

'I have clothes on,' I tell him, and he growls and goes to say something, but I cut him off. *'I will deal with you when you get home,'* I say.

'With me? You better bloody run when I get home,' he snarls.

'Good, I will do it naked,' I tell him, and he growls, but I shove him out of my head.

"He is a little angry," I sigh, turning to Clarice.

"Don't worry, my Queen, you have an entire castle to back you," she says, and my brows furrow, remembering how I was able to override the commands of Kyson.

"How?" I ask her.

"How what?" Clarice asks.

"They all listened, Kyson commanded them, and they listened to me instead."

"Ah, now that is something you need to ask your King about, my Queen," she chuckles before walking out. I sigh and sit on the bed. Now, I have to deal with my King when he comes home.

The day passes by quickly. A doctor comes by to take blood. I work on my reading with Liam and Dustin. At first, I am a little embarrassed by my earlier spectacle, but as I walk the halls, it is like it never happened; everyone is completely normal despite all of us being naked this morning.

After dinner, I go to bed, yet I can feel Kyson's burning anger dissipate; he almost seems giddy and excited to get home. I find this odd, and wonder what made his mood switch so fast. His anger is still there, but it had dissipated unusually fast, knowing Kyson.

Crawling into the comforting embrace of my den, I meticulously rearrange the edges of my makeshift bedding, twisting and turning them in a futile attempt to find a fragment of comfort. My weary eyes flicker open at the sound of the door creaking open, alerting me to Kyson's arrival.

I sit up, waiting for his wrath, having decided I am too tired to argue with him, so I will just listen to his ranting if it means I can sleep.

Kyson's entrance is accompanied by an unusual silence. He strides towards me with purpose, his jacket slipping effortlessly from his broad shoulders and landing nonchalantly at the foot of the bed. His piercing gaze bore into mine, devoid of its usual fiery intensity, as he methodically unfastens his cufflinks and places them delicately on the bedside table. He starts unbuttoning his shirt, one by one, and I stare at his sculpted chest. A heady wave of his intoxicating scent envelops the room, triggering an involuntary purr to escape my lips. Kyson's smirk deepens as he witnesses my internal struggle against the urge to surrender myself to him completely.

"You are in trouble," he declares, his voice laced with a mixture of authority and restraint. My heart skips a beat, anticipating the reprimand hanging in the air like an unspoken threat.

"But I think I can forgive you," he adds.

"You think, or you have?" I ask, forcing myself to remain where I am. I want to bite him, taste his skin and inhale his scent like a damn animal. It infuriates me, yet my mouth waters all the same way. Kyson raises an eyebrow at me before taking his shirt off and offering it to me; I reach out for it, wondering what he is playing at. He lets me take it before walking off into the bathroom.

The sound of running water fills the silence, amplifying the weight of his unspoken thoughts. "Kyson?" I call out, my voice tinged with a mixture of confusion and concern.

"My Queen," he says in return, making me purse my lips at his weird behavior. When he finishes showering, he comes out and tugs the duvet back I am huddled under.

"You didn't eat all your dinner," he growls, reaching for me.

As his touch graced my skin, a delightful tingle courses through me, his warmth seeping into my very core as he cradles me against him.

"I wasn't hungry," I tell him, nipping at his chest; he lets me brush his fingers through my hair as the calling slips out of him.

"I thought you were angry?" I ask.

"I am," he answers, and I sit up, straddling his waist.

"You don't seem angry?" I tell him.

"Clarice said you didn't eat your lunch either?" Kyson growls, his fingers tangling in my hair; he tugs me back down and pulls my head back before brushing his lips against mine gently.

"What does it matter whether I eat or not? Did you discover anything about the murdered rogues?" I inquire, my eyes rolling in exasperation as I attempt to push away from his chest. However, Kyson's firm hold prevents any escape, drawing me back into his embrace. His lips feather across mine with a tenderness that belies the lingering anger between us.

"Because, my love," he purrs, his voice laced with a mix of possessiveness and concern. "You're eating for two." And with those words, his tongue invades my mouth.

About the Author

Join my Facebook group to connect with me
https://www.facebook.com/jessicahall91

Enjoy all of my series
https://www.amazon.com/Jessica-Hall/e/B09TSM8RZ7

FB: Jessica Hall Author Page
Website: jessicahallauthor.com
Insta: Jessica.hall.author
Goodreads: Jessica_Hall

ALSO BY JESSICA HALL

Authors I Recommend

Jane Knight

Want books with an immersive story that sucks you in until you're left wanting more? Queen of spice, Jane Knight has got you covered with her mix of paranormal and contemporary romance stories. She's a master of heat, but not all of her characters are nice. They're dark and controlling and not afraid to take their mates over their knees for a good spanking that will leave you just as shaken as the leading ladies. Or if you'd prefer the daddy-do type, she writes those too just so they can tell you that you are a good girl before growling in you ear. Her writing is dark and erotic. Her reverse-harems will leave you craving more and the kinks will have you wondering if you'll call the safe word or keep going for that happily every after.]

Follow her on facebook.com/janeknightwrites

Check out her books on https://www.amazon.com/stores/Jane-Knight/author/B08B1M8WD8

Moonlight Muse

Looking for a storyline that will have you on the edge of your seat? The spice levels are high with a plot that will keep you flipping to the next page and ready for more. You won't be disappointed with Moonlight Muse.

Her women as sassy and her men are possessive alpha-holes with high tensions and tons of steam. She'll draw you into her taboo tales, breaking your heart before giving you the happily ever after.

Follow her on facebook.com/author.moonlight.muse

Check out her books on https://www.amazon.com/stores/Moonlight-Muse/author/B0B1CKZFHQ

Made in the USA
Monee, IL
02 August 2024

63151383R00164